Praise for Katerina Diamond

'Diamond is the master of gripping literature'
Evening Standard

'A terrific story, originally told. All hail the new queen of crime!'
Heat

'A web of a plot that twists and turns and keeps the reader on the edge of their seat. This formidable debut is a page-turner, but don't read it before bed if you're easily spooked!'
Sun

'A page-turner with a keep-you-guessing plot'
Sunday Times Crime Club

'Diamond neatly handles a string of interlocking strands'
Daily Mail

'This gem of a crime novel is packed with twists until the last page'
Closer

'A deliciously dark read, Katerina Diamond keeps her readers guessing throughout as she leads us on a very secretive, VERY twisted journey . . . everything I was expecting from a well-written, pacy thriller'
Lisa Hall, author of *Between You And Me*

KATERINA DIAMOND burst onto the crime scene with her debut novel, *The Teacher*, which became a *Sunday Times* bestseller and a number 1 Kindle bestseller. It was longlisted for the CWA John Creasey Debut Dagger Award and the Hotel Chocolat Award for 'darkest moment'. Her second novel, *The Secret*, became a #1 Kindle bestseller too and received widespread acclaim. Her third novel, *The Angel*, published in 2017 and again hit the bestseller lists. *The Promise* published in 2018 and went in at #7 on *The Sunday Times* list. Katerina has lived in various glamorous locations such as Weston-Super-Mare, Thessaloniki, Larnaca, Exeter, Derby and Forest Gate. She now resides in East Kent with her husband and children. She was born on Friday 13th.

By the same author:

Truth or Die

Katerina Diamond

avon.

This novel is entirely a work of fiction.
The names, characters and incidents portrayed in it are
the work of the author's imagination. Any resemblance to
actual persons, living or dead, events or localities is
entirely coincidental.

AVON

A division of HarperCollins*Publishers*
1 London Bridge Street,
London SE1 9GF

www.harpercollins.co.uk

A Paperback Original 2019

2

Copyright © Katerina Diamond 2019

Katerina Diamond asserts the moral right to
be identified as the author of this work

A catalogue record for this book is
available from the British Library

ISBN-13: 978-0-00-828292-9

Typeset in Sabon LT Std by Palimpsest Book Production Ltd,
Falkirk, Stirlingshire

Printed and bound in Great Britain by CPI Group (UK) Ltd,
Croydon CR0 4YY

To Audrey,
Over the last 13 years, I've come to think
of you as someone who lives in my house.
Love Mum

Chapter One

Six months ago

'Is this thing on?' Toby said into the camera on his phone. 'OK, watch this. It's going to be incredible.'

The camera was placed on the ground, resting against Toby's empty can of cider and pointing up at Exeter Cathedral. The angle meant the whole cathedral was in shot. Toby switched on the GoPro on his head as well and ran towards the front of the building. He wasn't sure how many people would be watching the live stream at this time in the morning, but he had to assume that there was a possibility the police could turn up at any point, so he needed to hurry. The front of the medieval building had enough nooks and holes for him to place his feet and fingers in, to grip and pull on, to climb. This would be the biggest achievement for Toby; he had climbed many buildings in the town, but this was surely the jewel in the crown. It wasn't the tallest building by a long shot, but it was so iconic, there was no way he wouldn't score some major points with it – it might even go viral. Heavily decorated with carved and moulded stonework, he wasn't sure why he hadn't thought of this before.

Toby had been doing parkour for five years, since he was fourteen years old. In the last year his game had really improved though. This was barely a challenge now that he looked at it. The west screen, the front of the cathedral, was covered in half-sized statues of knights, angels, kings, apostles and other small figures nestled in the niches. At school they had learned that these small animated figures were once painted in brightly coloured medieval paint, long since eroded and washed away. Lots of knobbles and bobbles to wrap his fingers around. Even the safety net wouldn't be much of an obstacle as it had a little give in it.

Toby started to climb. He grabbed a hold of one of the angels on the first row of niches. They were holding up the other characters. A vision of heaven that Toby was putting his feet all over. Even where there were no sculptures to use as footholds, the walls weren't smooth but rugged, and the stone bricks were chipped or broken at the corners, often providing enough space for the front inch of his trainer or for his fingers to hold onto. His nerves weren't too bad because he had had a couple of drinks on the way here, just enough to take the edge off without dulling his instincts.

Toby had hardly broken a sweat by the time he reached the end of the first part of the challenge and grabbed hold of the crenelated wall at the top of the figures. He slipped through the gap in the wall and turned around, making sure the GoPro on his chest was pointing forwards. He leaned over and waved at his own phone. He didn't want to waste any more time and so he turned back around and looked up at the rose window.

The rose window itself was the easiest part to climb; it was practically a ladder once you got past the long slim windows into the actual rose. He got to the top of the structure in no time. He made sure to look down, so that he could get a shot of the ornate window directly beneath him with the camera strapped to his head. He wondered how many viewers he had now. No sirens yet.

At the top of the window he had a couple of tricky manoeuvres to do before he could get over the second ledge onto the small balcony. Once they had been executed, he grabbed the thin ledge and pulled himself up, and then hoisted himself over the wall. One last push before he could get onto the roof. He could go to the side and climb up that way, but it wasn't as interesting for his followers and so he continued on his path straight upwards. He was feeling a little tired – probably the cider; next time one can would be enough. He didn't know why he had been so nervous in the first place; this was a doddle.

He climbed up the final window and grabbed hold of the feet of the statue standing at the top of it. He didn't know who it was of, probably St Peter. Neither history nor religious studies were his subjects at school, so he hadn't paid attention on the various school trips they had made to the building over the years.

He got his hand around the spike at the centre of the top of the roof and pulled himself up. He didn't give himself time to rest; he wanted his followers to see the view and so he spun around and looked out over the city. His phone was a tiny blip on the ground from where he was standing, but he waved nonetheless. He would splice the footage together later and put it to music. This was going to look awesome; he couldn't wait to watch it back.

He looked behind him at the lopsided crossed roof and then to the North Tower. He had to go up there; it was the highest point after all. The roof was battered and difficult to navigate, the central beam covered in an ornate metal design, presumably specifically to stop these kinds of shenanigans. From the centre of the roof he couldn't see his phone any more, but he wasn't particularly worried about anyone stealing it. He made his way across the central beam towards the North Tower and started to climb.

Halfway to the parapet, his leg started to cramp. He tried to get to the top faster, but the pain in his leg deepened. He shook it to lessen the pain but it just got sharper. His thigh was spasming now and he had to decide whether to go up or down. The top was closer and at least if he made it there then there was a flat surface to stand on. He pulled himself up, wincing with the pain, his leg pulling him down. He should have just stayed at the top of the western screen. It's not like the camera could see him any more, anyway.

Toby reached for the thin ledge and his hand slipped. All too quickly and without him knowing in which order his body was failing him, he started to fall. His shin hit the triangular spine of the roof with the full weight of his body behind it. The spikes tore through the fabric and the flesh straight through to the bone. He cried out. Still no sirens to be heard. He continued to fall and bounce from stone and slate for what felt like an eternity, his skin grazing and bruising with each thud. This was the last one though, the last fall. Was there any way to survive a fall from this height?

He hit the ground, his head cracking against the pavement. He was facing west and he could see his phone on the grass pointing up at the rose window. It wasn't even capturing this moment. He was dying and no one would even see it.

Chapter Two

DS Adrian Miles looked at the pink envelope on his desk. He glanced around the room and his partner, DS Imogen, Grey shrugged.

'Don't look at me!'

'Is this a joke?'

'Someone obviously loves you,' Imogen said, although it sounded like more of an accusation than anything else.

He opened the card to see a picture of two bears cuddling, and inside, just a question mark.

'This isn't funny. Who left this here?'

'It could be anyone in this place, Adrian, I've seen the way the new recruits look at you. If only they knew.'

'What's that supposed to mean?' he said with more indignance than the question probably deserved.

'Maybe it's the duty doctor. What's her name? Dr Hadley? She was in earlier.'

'We went for one drink, that's all. We decided not

to go out again. I doubt it's from her,' he said, not convinced and more than a little uncomfortable getting this information from Imogen. He had been on a date with one of the doctors who worked invariably at the station. She had been their point of call on a couple of cases in the past and she had asked him out for a drink last week. He'd said yes – and in another life he might have been more interested. But the truth was that his friendship with Imogen was getting complicated, and so it felt really odd to be on a date with another woman.

'Face it, Miley, you're wanted.' She winked.

Adrian looked at Imogen, who then nodded over to Denise Ferguson, the duty sergeant.

'Didn't you say you'd help her out with booking tonight?'

'Oh, shit.' He remembered promising something like that. He guessed being stuck behind the front desk processing drunks on a Saturday night was better than being subjected to dating shows on TV, by yourself, because you live alone.

Valentine's Day was not typically the quietest of nights in the station. Even if you ignored all the drunken roadside domestic disputes and the minor pub brawls because someone looked at someone else's woman the wrong way, nationally it was still a night that saw a statistically significant increase in crime. Petty criminals taking advantage of the fact that most couples were out enjoying a romantic meal or a nice walk meant that break-ins and car theft were higher on this night than most others. Fingers crossed tonight would be a slow one.

'I'm not in until Tuesday now. I've got a couple of personal days,' Imogen said.

Adrian wasn't sure what she was getting at. Was she inviting him over? Over the last few weeks they had made a regular habit of staying over at each other's houses, more as a comfort than anything else. Both happy to be alone, but still not totally OK with being lonely. They would sleep in the same bed together; it had become comforting, if a little strange. Almost platonic, but not quite. There was a definite undertone to what they were doing, but it had been a little over six months since the woman Adrian was seeing, the woman he was falling for, had been taken from him violently. It had been even less time since Imogen had ended her intense relationship with an ex-con. Neither of them particularly relished the idea of dating anyone right now, but still, they were growing closer. Despite that, Imogen hadn't yet spoken to Adrian about her mother's death, and her funeral was on Monday – Adrian kept wondering whether she wanted him to go with her.

'Have you met the new DI yet?' he asked, changing the subject. If she wanted him there she would ask. He hoped.

'No, who is it?'

'Someone who's transferred in.'

'Not from Plymouth, I hope,' Imogen said quickly, shuddering at the thought of her old job.

'No, someone from the DCI's old area. I think they wanted an outsider, someone who wasn't caught up in any of the local shit,' Adrian reassured her. Imogen herself had transferred from Plymouth under a bit of a black cloud and so he knew she wouldn't appreciate working with any of her former colleagues.

'Yet.'

'Apparently she personally endorsed his transfer. The DCI has worked out all right. Maybe it's a good move.'

'Him? Is he hot?'

'Why are you asking me?'

'You can't objectively say whether a man is attractive? Are you worried that I might think . . .'

'Don't finish that sentence. His face is very symmetrical, which suggests he is probably quite good-looking.' Adrian smiled at her.

'Wow. I'd hate to hear how you describe me.' She gathered up her things to go.

'I don't think I have ever described you.' He paused for a moment, not wanting her to disappear completely until Tuesday without at least giving her an option to invite him to the funeral; he didn't just want to assume. There weren't many people that Adrian felt completely at ease with, but Imogen was one of them. 'If you're not busy you can have lunch at mine tomorrow,' he said, as much for himself as for her. Valentine's Day, a painful reminder of your situation, whatever that situation was.

'Text me when your shift ends,' she said as she walked out.

Adrian had found himself noticing more and more how difficult he found things when Imogen wasn't there; it was as if something was missing, or there was something he was forgetting, like he had left the oven on.

There was always a part of his mind that was aware when she wasn't around, and it wasn't happy about that at all. He pushed the feeling aside and went to help Denise.

All in all, the night passed without much beyond the usual; in fact it was unusually quiet for Valentine's Day. He sat mostly in silence, occasionally grunting a response when someone called his name, or when someone was brought in. Still, Adrian was grateful that he wasn't at a loose end this evening. He couldn't handle the endless whirring of his brain; he needed a break from thinking about himself and his situation. He had never been a strong believer in depression, but it was certainly knocking on his door, trying to get a hold of him.

'Thanks for agreeing to this. I wasn't sure if you would have plans,' Denise said to him.

'Nope, no plans.'

There was a pause, awkward, too long to be natural.

'You could come over to mine when we've finished if you want . . . no strings,' Denise said, a cheeky smile on her face, the kind of smile that had worked on him several times in the past.

'Um, wow, thanks, but I think I have a migraine brewing.' Strange that she would proposition him now; maybe it was just the idea of being alone. Valentine's Day seemed to magnify any feelings of loneliness in everyone; Adrian knew because he could feel it, too.

'I thought maybe you wanted to get together, I thought that's why you agreed to do this.'

'Denise, you know I like you a lot, but I'm just not in the right headspace to be in a relationship right now, no strings or otherwise.'

'Oh. Sorry I brought it up. Let's get back to work. No big deal.' Her face was flushed, easy to see against her porcelain skin and bleached bob; the pink shone through like sunburn. She seemed embarrassed at her assumption and shut down completely.

Just then, the station door opened and one of the uniformed officers walked in, dragging a sullen-looking boy behind him, his face white with a tinge of green. The boy looked up and grinned at them both behind the counter, then projectile vomited against the window. Both Adrian and Denise jumped back to avoid the spray, stopped abruptly by the clear wall of glass, all that was between them and a shower of gloopy stomach contents.

Adrian groaned to himself. Why did he volunteer for this?

'Who's this charmer then?' he asked.

'Name's Finn Blackwell,' the constable said, 'student up at the uni, caught him driving the wrong way around a roundabout. We had to breathalyse him and he's well over the limit. We've brought him in to sober up.'

'Whereabouts?'

'Marsh Barton. No one around, but you know.'

'Well that was silly, wasn't it, Finn?' Adrian said as Denise scribbled down the information. The glass had become almost clear as the pale brown gelatinous liquid pooled at the bottom of the counter and over the edge onto the floor.

11

'I do apologise,' the boy said with a sarcastic wobble of his head.

'How old are you?'

'I'm nineteen. Twenty in August. You interested, darling?' He winked at Denise, who just rolled her eyes and continued writing.

'Chuck him in number four while we get this cleaned up,' Adrian said.

The constable took Finn Blackwell through to the holding cells.

'I don't know what's going on up at that university,' Denise said.

'What do you mean?'

'Well, last week I had a couple of other incidents up there. A kid was arrested for possession. A couple of disturbances – nothing major, just a little unusual. Then, of course, there was that idiot Toby Hoare, who climbed up the cathedral and fell off.' She still wouldn't look Adrian in the eye.

'Look, Denise, about earlier.'

'Please, don't mention it,' she said. He could tell from her tone that she meant it.

'I'm going to get this cleaned up,' Adrian said. He did regret their previous fling a little; he had used her, and he wasn't proud of it. Just because she'd let him didn't make it any better. He knew he couldn't be that person any more. Adrian needed to be better, he wanted to be better and he couldn't quite put his finger on why.

Chapter Three

Imogen felt comfortable in black; it suited her. It seemed strange to have picked out her dress the day before; she could only imagine what her mother would have said about it. An insult disguised as a compliment: how it would look nicer if it was longer, or shorter, or a different colour. But not the way it was, never the way it was. It was the same with everything; Imogen always thought that one day she would be good enough, would do something right. Not today though, never today.

She tried not to be resentful of her mother on the day of her funeral, but the anger she felt towards her was not something she ever thought would go away. She didn't know why either, not really. Her mother had made a lot of questionable life decisions, but Imogen wasn't unhappy with the person she had grown up to be. It seemed unfair that she should feel this way about the one member of her family who had always been there for her, but there was no changing it, there was always just this low level of anger. She couldn't pinpoint when it had started, either. The mother who raised her probably did the best she could.

Then there was her absent father, reconnected now but a figment of her imagination for most of her life. She didn't have all those petty squabbles or embarrassing moments to refer back to, there was no point of reference, no resentment bubbling under the surface for years and years. He was just not there. She knew how difficult her mother was; if she told her father she didn't want him having a relationship with Imogen, then it explained why he hadn't been around. Irene Grey had a knack for getting her own way. Imogen felt like maybe she should hate her father for not being there. But she didn't; she blamed her mother for it instead.

She smoothed her dress down with the palms of her hands. She didn't even know if anyone would see her in it, apart from her father, Elias. She hadn't invited Adrian to the funeral as she felt that it would add an extra dimension of complication to their already complex relationship. She had invited the friends of her mother's that she knew about and just hoped that word would spread, because her mother's life was a mystery to her. She probably knew her mother as well as her mother knew her, which wasn't that well at all. Even though she had visited her frequently, her mum had always been into something new, some new hobby or collection or charity. Imogen had tuned most of it out. She wished her mother was there now and she would listen, she would take an interest in what she was saying and not just fob her off and look for an excuse to leave.

Imogen imagined Irene telling her that she was putting too much mascara on as she dragged the wand across her eyelashes until they clumped together. Going to a funeral like that was just asking for trouble. Imogen wasn't a crier, unless you counted movies like *Armageddon* and *The Shawshank Redemption*. She had managed to fine-tune her apathy in the real world, but as soon as she was immersed in fiction she seemed to be able to connect to the part of her that had emotion. She was thankful for it. If it wasn't for those experiences, then she might worry about her own humanity; it was reassuring to know that the idea of a meteor hurtling towards the planet and wiping everyone out was distressing to her.

When she felt like she had enough war paint on she pinned her hair back, ready to put on her mother's yellow pillbox hat with black net across the eye. It was in the box of things she had taken from her mother's place. Just one box from her mother's hoard, Imogen hadn't wanted any more than that. There were no great memories among all of Irene Grey's possessions; she seemed to collect and discard items indiscriminately, and so Imogen had arranged for house clearance to go and sort it out after she had taken the few items she had wanted.

Imogen picked up the hat and put it on. A touch of colour – her mother hated black. She picked up her phone, unsure whether to text Adrian; he had offered to come, but it just didn't feel right. There was also the issue of Elias. Being with Elias reminded Imogen of her ex-boyfriend Dean, and she wasn't over him yet. She had met Dean during a case, before she had even met her father. Her relationship with Dean was incompatible with her job; he didn't quite operate on the right side of the law. Her father and Dean were more than friends, they were family. Her father operated several businesses and Dean was the person he sent round when all other forms of communication had broken down. Whenever she was with her dad she was aware that he was in contact with Dean and the idea of Adrian being there at the same time was a conflict Imogen wasn't ready to deal with just yet. She would have to do today alone. It felt wrong to want support anyway; it was her mother's funeral and Adrian barely knew her mother. She put her phone on silent and chucked it inside her bag.

The day seemed to move as though she were on fast forward, occasionally stopping to take it all in, but mental absence seemed preferable to being upset. She found herself standing by the grave, her father opposite her, tears in his eyes, genuine love and affection in his disposition. She could feel the emotions creep to the surface as she thought of her parents, apart for all those years, knowing the other would come if they would only ask. How did they wait so long? If they had really loved each other wouldn't they have just been together? She couldn't imagine being told you couldn't be with someone else and actually listening. How could he stand to be apart from the woman he loved? How could he stand to be apart from her, his daughter? A part of her would always resent him for that.

She brushed her eye with the back of her hand, trying to make it look less like she was wiping away a tear. Why did she care if people saw her crying? Why wasn't she allowed to cry?

They lowered the coffin into the ground and the people gathered around for a few seconds, registering the moment until it was over and then dispersing. Back to life.

Imogen suddenly felt overwhelmed. Was that it? Was her mother really gone? It just didn't make sense. Irene Grey had been Imogen's entire family for so long; she was the only thing Imogen could depend on being there no matter what, always where Imogen left her. It felt so wrong to leave her here.

'Imogen,' Elias said, snapping her out of her thoughts. 'Come on. Let me buy you a drink.'

'I don't really feel like it right now, to be honest with you,' she said. She had managed to avoid spending any meaningful time alone with Elias since she had found out who he was. Somehow, talking to him today felt like a betrayal. Her mother hadn't wanted them to pursue a relationship, and Imogen had to wonder why.

'Let's go and raise a glass to your mother. Please.'

'OK,' she acquiesced; it didn't feel right to just slip back into real life immediately. She would have a gin, then go home and watch black-and-white movies, maybe some Fred and Ginger.

In the pub, the news was running, the same

scaremongering, hate-fuelled drama that she had stopped watching years ago. It was no good for her anxiety.

'It was peaceful when she died,' Elias offered. 'She didn't even feel the aneurism; it took her in her sleep. When I woke up, she was just gone.'

'That must have been awful for you. I still can't believe it,' Imogen said, both upset and relieved that she hadn't been with her mother at the end.

'No. It doesn't feel real. I only just got her back.'

'I'm sorry,' Imogen said. She was genuinely sorry that they had spent all those years apart. Arranged marriages seemed so archaic and she just couldn't get her head around the fact that he hadn't fought for her and her mother, that he had chosen someone else.

'Do you believe in fate?'

'I try not to think about it. I don't know what I think about things like that. I barely believe in coincidences though.'

'I think maybe your mother and I weren't meant to be. The obstacles were too many for it to be an accident.'

'I'm not sure where you're going with this.'

'I think that me and her were never about us. I think we were brought together so that you could exist. I think you are the reason we fell for each other. You are special, important in some way.'

'Isn't everyone?' Imogen said, brushing off the compliment. Is this how he let himself off the hook for not being around?

'Maybe, yes. Your mother loved you very much, even though I know you struggled together, but because of your struggle you are a remarkable person.'

'Is that what you tell yourself? That me growing up without a father is fine because it was character-building?'

'I'm sorry to make light of it. I am sorry I missed all those years with you.'

'I'm not. We did OK,' Imogen said more defensively than she intended.

'We can talk about the past if you want to. We can talk about why I wasn't around.'

'I know – you had to marry a good Greek girl and my mother wasn't one.'

'That's true. I did have to marry someone I didn't want to,' Elias said, a hint of exasperation in his voice.

'So why did you?'

'Arranged marriage is a complicated thing that seems quite alien to people from other cultures. We were in financial trouble and my father had promised. I couldn't dishonour him and so I married into the family.'

'So, your money isn't yours, it's your wife's?'

'No, I worked hard and made sure not to repeat my father's mistakes; my money is my own. Kiki has taken her half and we are now in the process of getting a divorce.'

'And your children? Did you ever love their mother?' Imogen said, still confused as to how he could have left them both.

'Not like I loved your mother,' Elias said, staring into his empty whisky tumbler.

'So, what changed in your marriage?'

'Our parents died, and we didn't feel the same way about divorce as they did. She was in love with someone

19

else, also. Our parents were the only winners in that situation. But we got our boys and we love them very much.'

'All sounds very amicable,' Imogen said, finding it hard to believe that the relationship that stopped her from having a father was that easy to dissolve.

'It is.'

'What do they think about me?' Imogen said. Elias, a man who had been a ghost when she was growing up, suddenly thrust in to her life during a murder investigation barely a year ago. She had always been an only child and so it was hard to think of herself as an older sister to three grown men.

'Your brothers? Surprised, but they want to meet you.'

'They do?' Imogen hadn't even considered meeting his children, but hearing Elias call them her brothers made that seem inevitable and her discomfort returned.

'Yes. We're having a family gathering soon, would you like to come?'

'I don't know. It feels too soon for that. I can't just get a whole new family now that my mother has gone.' Imogen said. Irene was the only parent she had ever known; she had longed for more when she was younger and now that her mother was dead, she felt like it was wrong to replace her immediately.

'At least consider meeting with me properly – we could have dinner on Friday night.'

'I'm sorry. It's too soon. I need more time.'

Imogen stood up and left her half-finished gin on the counter. This was all too strange. First he wanted to get to know her, now he wanted her to meet her brothers. Just the word brother sounded alien to her in this context; she had no reference for it. It didn't mean anything to her, not in the same way as mother did, not in the same way that orphan did. That's how she felt, orphaned, even though her father was sat right opposite her. It didn't matter; she was all alone in the world now. No more Greys.

He stood up and held his hand out for her to shake. She took pity on him, knowing full well that she was the only person he could truly share his grief over her mother's death with. She put her arms around him and felt his tension ease within her embrace. From now on, he would be the only connection she had to her mother, too. She had to consider carefully what to do next. There was a whole other world that she could immerse herself in, but the idea of it scared her. She was only just getting accustomed to the one she was living in now. Imogen needed to decide whether she wanted all her life changes to happen at once, get it over with. Could she handle any more heartbreak?

Chapter Four

'Please state your name for the tape,' Imogen said. She had barely got into work when she was informed about the young girl waiting to be processed and questioned.

'Caitlin Watts,' the girl said, not looking at Imogen but clearly sizing Adrian up.

'And how old are you?'

'I just turned nineteen.'

'You were spotted breaking into the old chapel on Smalling Street, is that correct?' Adrian said.

'Yes, I'm sorry.' She tilted her head down, keeping her eyes on him.

'Was there a reason for that?' Imogen asked.

'Not a good one. I just wanted to see if I could,' Caitlin said, still staring at Adrian.

Imogen noted that there was no nervous disposition with this girl at all; she seemed almost defiant, even a little defensive. What was her game?

'We're trying to get hold of the reverend in charge, who will tell us if anything is damaged or stolen.'

'He's away at the moment, gone to some pilgrim site in Kent.'

'How do you know that?'

'Because I live with him,' Caitlin said with a hint of a smile. 'He's my grandad.'

Imogen tried to gauge whether this was a lie or not; there was something very hard to read about Caitlin, a dishonesty about her. She looked over to Adrian, who shook off his surprise at this revelation very quickly and recomposed himself. Imogen could tell the girl was fixated on getting a reaction out of Adrian; her strange flirtation seemed to be working on him, he was visibly flustered by her.

'Do you have any way of contacting him?' Adrian said.

'Not for a couple of days. He will be back before the weekend, though. He'll tell you that nothing is missing or damaged; I'm not like that.'

'If that were true you wouldn't even be here at all,' Imogen said.

'We'll check out your story – where will you be if we need to contact you?' Adrian said.

'I'll be at my grandfather's house, or at class. One of the two.'

'What are you studying?' Adrian said.

'Psychology at the university. I want to be a shrink, get inside people's heads and stuff.' She smiled at Adrian.

'You're not staying in halls?' Imogen said.

'Not really any point, seeing as I live in the town. It

saves money, which my grandad doesn't have that much of.' She answered Imogen coldly, seemingly annoyed that she was there at all, as though this would be a lot easier if Adrian were the only person in the room. She was an interesting girl – there was a definite vulnerability about her, something she was trying desperately to hide. Imogen could identify.

'Are your parents not in the picture?' Imogen asked.

'No, apparently being parents was boring and not nearly noble enough, so they skipped off into the sunset together. I think they live in South America somewhere. They're missionaries or something.'

That explained her strange behaviour – abandonment issues.

'You don't have any contact with them?' Imogen pressed.

'Not for around ten years now. But you know, I'm privileged apparently, so I don't really deserve their attention. They only have time for Third World children.' She brushed her glossy black hair behind her ears. The hair was the same colour as her perfectly groomed eyebrows, which almost looked painted on, but they were natural, Imogen could tell. Caitlin was making Imogen self-conscious; she watched as the girl's striking blue eyes bore into Adrian and no doubt pulled at his heart strings.

'I'm sorry, that must be hard,' Adrian said.

Imogen shot him a look; it wasn't like him to make personal comments like that. There was something a little mesmerising about Caitlin. She couldn't tell whether it was intentional and manipulative or just the

24

way she was, but Imogen was almost certain it was the former. Imogen was the one with a record for falling for suspects; it was the reason she'd lost the opportunity to get the DI job, because the DCI had found out about her relationship with Dean, which although not entirely illegal was most definitely frowned upon. The truth was that Imogen was a little relieved about not getting the position; she wasn't sure she could handle the extra responsibility as well as everything else she had going on, on top of losing her mum.

That fleeting thought of her mother sent a chill through her; she couldn't call her, she couldn't go and visit.

Imogen shook off the impromptu melancholy and stood up.

'We'll check out your story. If your grandfather is happy not to press charges, you'll be able to leave,' Imogen said.

'The uniformed officer will take you to the cell for a little while; it won't be long though,' Adrian said gently, taking the edge off Imogen's words.

'Thank you, Detective Miles.' Caitlin smiled and blinked slowly, her thick black lashes closing then opening to reveal those eyes, almost in slow motion. There was an aura of 'trouble' around her, something Imogen couldn't quite put her finger on.

'Interview suspended at three fifteen,' Imogen said and turned off the recorder.

Caitlin Watts folded her arms and winced a little.

'Is something the matter?' Imogen said.

'I cut my arm on the window while I was trying to get through it, no big deal.'

'Let me see?'

The girl pulled her cardigan off her shoulder, locking eyes with Adrian while she did it. There was a gash in the top of her arm, about ten centimetres long, certainly not nothing.

Imogen held her breath and counted to three before speaking again.

'You need some medical attention. I'll get hold of the doctor on call to come and see you. I think that's going to need stitches.'

Imogen opened the door to see PC Ben Jarvis standing there waiting for instruction. Ben was new to the district and already he had made no secret of his interest in Imogen.

'I need you to take the suspect to holding, then get the duty doctor to check her out,' Imogen informed him.

'Whatever you need,' he said, smiling in a way that made her a little uncomfortable.

He brushed past Imogen – she felt like he was making sure that some part of his body was in contact with some part of hers – before leading Caitlin Watts out of the room.

Imogen sat on the edge of the table and looked down at Adrian, who was watching the girl leave, not pulling his eyes away until she wasn't there to look at any more. She thought it was funny how his perception of the situation in that room was so different to hers; she had been preoccupied with Jarvis, he had been preoccupied with Caitlin. He hadn't even noticed her awkward inter-action with the PC. She folded her arms, and her movement made him turn and see her looking at him, his face reddening, as though he had been caught doing something he shouldn't.

'What?' he asked.

'She's pretty,' Imogen said.

'No. That's not what I was thinking.' He tried to hide his smile.

'Then what? You seemed to find it hard to look away.'

'Don't you think there's something odd about her?'

'I think there's something odd about you,' Imogen said.

'Pot. Kettle.'

'Do you think she's telling the truth?'

'Not even slightly,' Adrian said. 'I mean, the stuff about her grandad? She's definitely lying, God knows what about. You know those people who just lie about everything? I think she's one of those. They just can't help themselves.'

'You think she was trying to steal something?'

'No idea. I don't think we've seen the last of her, though,' Adrian said, still staring at the door long after Caitlin had been taken through it.

'I'm sure you're devastated about that.' Imogen raised her eyebrows.

'I'm not the one who's into suspects,' he said.

'Touché,' Imogen said, unsure whether to take offence or not. But she was uncomfortable having Dean and Adrian in the same headspace these days. She noted a hint of something whenever the subject came up between them, which was thankfully a rare occurrence. Was

27

Adrian jealous? It certainly felt like it sometimes. Maybe she was paranoid, maybe it was wishful thinking. Why did everything have to be so complicated?

'You didn't tell me how your mum's funeral went,' Adrian said, cutting into her thoughts.

'It went. It was tough. Glad it's over.'

'Was your father there?'

'Still can't get used to calling him that, but yes, Elias was there,' she said, pulling the door open; she wasn't in the mood for talking about herself right now. If she opened up to Adrian, she might start crying and never stop. She wasn't sure she was ready for Adrian to see her like that just yet; she wanted him to think of her as strong.

As they left the interview room, they saw Denise walking towards them in the hall. There seemed to be some discomfort between her and Adrian, as they avoided eye contact. Workplace relationships rarely worked out, unless you were lucky enough to find 'the one' – an ideal Imogen wasn't entirely sure she believed in. Most of the time, though, all that was left after the intimacy was resentment and embarrassment. Imogen promised herself she would never put herself in that situation again, which of course meant it was absolutely inevitable.

Chapter Five

Adrian lay in Imogen's bed. His house had felt haunted since he lost Lucy, the girl he had fallen for, the girl he'd barely had enough time to get to know, the girl who had been killed to teach him a lesson. It seemed as though that haunted feeling was following him around though; maybe it wasn't the house at all. Maybe it was him.

Behind him, the door opened. Imogen walked into the room and slid under the covers. White T-shirt and bare legs. He turned and stretched his arm out for her to rest her head on. Neither one of them liked being alone and so this filled a need, and they could trust each other with it.

Adrian was having one of those rare moments of simplicity. He wondered why they felt like they needed to keep this a secret, not just from the rest of the world, their friends and families – but from each other, from themselves. It was as though there was something wrong with this platonic intimacy, as though it were weird because they weren't ripping each other's clothes off. It almost made him feel dirty in a way that sex wouldn't, more complicated, less understandable. Why would anyone want this? They never spoke about it; it was a silent agreement between the two of them. They had yet to acknowledge it even happened outside of this house. This was a moment, in context, that didn't exist anywhere else. They drifted off together and in the morning one of them would go before the other awoke.

Adrian's phone rang at six thirty a.m., a whole hour before his alarm was due to wake him. He looked at the screen, it was Denise. The bed was empty.

'Denise? Why are you calling me?' Adrian said quietly before realising that Imogen wasn't next to him and so he didn't need to keep his voice down.

'Good morning, sunshine.'

'Get on with it,' he snapped.

'There's been a murder up at the university.'

'What?'

'The call just came in. I thought you might want to get up there. I tried to call you before the new DI got up there, but DCI Kapoor called him and asked him to deal with it.'

'So, he's already there?'

'Yeah, him and DS Grey.'

'What?' he said, managing to soften it a moment before it came out of his mouth.

'She said she tried to call you, but you didn't answer.'

'I'm on my way.' He hung up and jumped out of Imogen's bed.

Adrian pulled his jeans on and roughly pulled back the sheets, noticing the full mug of coffee on the side table. He picked it up and it was still warm; she hadn't long left. This was her apology. He drank it and left it on the bedside table.

At the university it didn't take him long to find them, and as he walked through the halls of the humanities department, he could hear Imogen speaking before he saw her. He turned the corner to see her standing next to DI Matt Walsh, the newbie in CID. He must have been approaching fifty years old, with white-grey hair, but somehow still quite youthful in appearance. He wore jeans and a blazer, and his hair was thick and floppy, reminiscent of the nineties somewhat.

As if sensing his presence, they both turned to look at him in unison. He noticed Imogen's eyes dart away for a second before resuming her composure.

DI Walsh held his hand out immediately. 'Detective Miles, good to see you again.'

'Detective Walsh. Please, call me Adrian.'

'Likewise, call me Matt though, not Adrian.'

Adrian half-smiled. 'What's happened?'

'Professor of Philosophy found dead in his office.'

'Dead how?' Adrian asked, annoyed that he was out of the loop and the information was being drip-fed to him.

'Murdered. Looks like he got his head bashed in with a large glass paperweight,' Matt Walsh said.

31

'This feels like an episode of *Columbo* already,' Adrian said.

'The techs are just in taking photos and logging evidence, but go ahead.'

Adrian walked into the office, where three crime scene technicians were doing their business. He stayed in the corner and looked around the room. Being there in person was different to seeing photographs; in Adrian's experience, memories of scenes could be powerful, things could get burned into the mind. Photographs just didn't give you the same perspective. He had heard of cases in the military where they had to get in and out of a scene without touching it, so they would use special cameras to capture the scene, then use giant 3D printers to recreate it perfectly, just so they could get the perspective and walk through the scene as many times as they needed.

The professor's face was hardly a face at all; caved in from the force and weight of the instrument used to kill him, the attack seemed almost frenzied. There were signs of a struggle, with books and papers strewn across the floor. Blood was spattered all up the walls, across the desk, everywhere, and the resin ball lay on the ground near the body. A blue flower was trapped inside, striking against the red of the blood. Someone must have been very angry to commit this level of violence, there was something crazed about it. No effort to tidy up or hide anything either. Adrian couldn't imagine it was opportunistic in motive at least.

'Any fingerprints?' he asked the crime scene technicians.

'Hundreds. But it looks like our perp wore gloves, so I doubt we're going to find any,' the technician closest to him said.

'Any ideas at all?'

'I'd say with the force used that you're definitely looking for a male. And the stamina suggests someone young. They mashed his head. It's going to be nigh on impossible to recreate the skull; it's in tiny pieces and totally smushed in with brain matter.'

'Vivid, thanks,' Adrian said.

Adrian left the room; he'd seen and heard enough for now. Imogen and Matt Walsh were in the corridor, chatting about his previous placement.

'Did you know DI Walsh used to work with DCI Kapoor?' Imogen said.

'I had heard that, yes,' Adrian said, almost certain he had discussed it with Imogen before.

'They used to be partners.'

'Interesting,' Adrian said, playing along with whatever Imogen was doing.

'She's one of the good ones. You guys got lucky getting her. I was happy to hear a placement opened up here so that I could apply,' Matt said.

'It's not weird, working under your former partner?' Imogen asked.

Adrian knew she was talking about them – one of them was bound to get promoted one day and he didn't know how that would work, if it even could work.

'It's pretty great knowing someone you can trust has your back, actually.'

'Sounds like you've been burned before,' she continued.

'Haven't we all?'

'Were you two ever . . . together?' Adrian asked.

Imogen shot him a look.

DI Matt Walsh let out a raucous laugh, completely inappropriate given the situation. It reverberated so much in the room that everyone turned to look at him. There was a momentary pause before normal crime scene hubbub returned.

'Nice to know she hasn't changed,' Matt said.

'What do you mean?' asked Adrian.

'She doesn't exactly talk about herself much, does she?'

'True,' Imogen acknowledged.

'Well, she's not exactly into guys.'

'Oh.' Adrian was surprised.

'I didn't find out 'til three years in, so you've got the jump on me,' Matt said.

'What do you think of this crime, then?' Imogen asked, clearly uncomfortable with talking about the DCI's personal business.

'Messy and inexperienced.'

'A student?' Adrian said.

'Maybe. Have a chat with some of the faculty in this block, see if they know anything. I'll go and speak to the dean.'

He walked away. Adrian liked him already, which was a relief.

Adrian and Imogen made their way upstairs and knocked on the door to the psychology professor Gillian Mitchell's office, but there was no response. The hallways started to fill with students getting to their morning lectures. There was a lot of mumbling; news of the murder had obviously got around. They knocked again.

'Can I help you?' A voice came from behind them.

They turned to see a blonde-haired woman, standing tall and lean in a brown linen suit. Her hair was almost iridescent in colour.

'Are you Gillian Mitchell?' Adrian asked.

'Are you here about Hugh?' the woman said.

'Can we talk in your office?' Imogen asked her.

'Actually, I'd rather not. I'm waiting for someone to come up and sort out the giant spider I have locked in there. I may never go back in there again. What is it you want to know?' She smiled.

'Did you know Professor Norris well?' Imogen said.

'In passing. We weren't friends or anything. He was a bit too chatty for my liking. Sometimes less is more. You find that with philosophers, though; they always want a bloody conversation.'

'Not psychologists?' Adrian mused.

'I'm more of an observer.'

'Did he have any enemies?' Adrian said.

'Absolutely not, he was a nice man.'

'Any problem students?' Imogen asked.

'Here? Not really. Now and then we get one, but no one springs to mind.'

'Did you teach any of the same students?' Adrian followed up.

'Sometimes we would guest on each other's topics, try to show a different perspective, and we run the debating society in this block too. It's got a big mix of students, mainly philosophy though; they love a debate.'

35

'I see, and who was close to Professor Norris?' Imogen asked.

'Doctor,' Gillian said.

'Excuse me?' Imogen said.

'Technically he was a doctor, he had a doctorate, so he was a doctor, that's his official title.' She smiled, a hint of annoyance at having to explain it crossing her features. It seemed that Gillian might have a bit of a hang-up about her colleague's status.

'Was anyone close to *Doctor* Norris?' Adrian said. Something about this woman was annoying him. Even though she was being pleasant, he found she had a bubbling hostility. It may just have been because they were police officers, or maybe it was something else entirely.

'He always ate alone, seemed pleasant enough, but I never really saw him with anyone in particular. Sorry I can't help you more.'

Adrian looked down at his notepad, then flicked back to a previous page, searching for a particular name. 'What about Helen Lassiter? She's got an office in this building, hasn't she?'

'I'm afraid she's not in today. She's away with some students on a trip. I'm not sure when she's back off the top of my head.'

Adrian felt a hand on his shoulder. He turned to see Caitlin standing next to him.

'Detective Miles.' She smiled at him. 'Are you here to arrest me again?'

'You weren't actually arrested, Miss . . .' Adrian said, struggling to remember her name.

'Watts, Caitlin Watts,' Caitlin replied.

He noticed how she left her mouth open when she'd finished speaking, moving her tongue gently against her top lip. She was flirting with him. He looked away quickly.

'Excuse me a moment,' Gillian Mitchell said, 'I just saw one of the maintenance men disappear around the corner and I really do need to get rid of this damn spider; I have notes in there I need later this morning. If that's all?'

'Don't leave town,' Imogen said as the woman hurried off, unclear if Gillian Mitchell had heard her or not.

'You're here about the murder?' Caitlin said to Adrian, her head tilted back, the long line of her neck exposed, leading right into the V-neck of her clingy black sweater.

'Do you know anything about it?' Adrian asked.

'Not really, except that there was lots of blood. I heard it was pretty intense.' She smoothed her hair down, drawing his eyes to her chest. He could feel Imogen's eyes rolling even though he couldn't see her face.

'We'd better be going then.' Adrian pulled his card out of his pocket and handed it to her. 'If you hear anything or think of anything else, then let me know.'

Caitlin took it and walked away, turning back once to look at Adrian.

Imogen and Adrian made their way out of the building and back to Adrian's car.

'How did you get here this morning?' Adrian asked,

being careful not to mention the fact that they had left from the same place.

'Matt swung past my place and picked me up.'

'Oh. OK,' Adrian said, uncomfortable with the fact that this annoyed him.

Chapter Six

Imogen was still trying to figure out DI Walsh. He was charming, and he genuinely seemed nice, but there was something false about him. It was the disguise of someone pretending to be happy, or at least OK. She wanted to get to know him better. From what she knew about DCI Mira Kapoor, she didn't trust easily and for her to bring him in from another division meant that he was probably on the up and up. Imogen tried to remember a time when she wasn't so distrusting; it had been a while.

She watched Walsh and Kapoor through the interior window; they were talking, DCI Kapoor had her hand on Matt Walsh's shoulder, consoling him about something. She wished she knew how to lip-read, even though that was a massive invasion of privacy. She just couldn't get the measure of him and she wasn't sure why it was bothering her so much.

Adrian reappeared after going outside for a cigarette.

She had given up and it was clearly annoying him. He was the one who gave up first, and she was the one who talked him back into it. The truth was, though, that she hadn't felt much like smoking since her mother died; her own mortality was suddenly playing on her mind. Her life seemed to be forcing her to make some big changes at the moment, why not at least have one or two of her own choosing?

'Anything?' he asked.

'What do you think they are talking about?' She nodded towards DCI Kapoor's office.

'Not you,' Adrian said. 'Why do you care?'

'I can't figure him out, that's all.'

'What makes you think there's something to figure out?'

'We're detectives, that's our job.'

'He's a nice guy, let him be. If there's anything we need to know, then we'll find out.'

'Are you tired or something?'

'I'm supposed to be going to see Tom tonight, but he's cancelled on me. I'm a bit pissed off, that's all. I had hoped things would change now that piece of shit stepfather of his is gone but if anything, I am seeing him less,' Adrian said.

'He's a full-on teenager now, you need to let him have his space,' Imogen said, wishing there was a way she could help, but she knew better than to get involved in Adrian's complicated relationship with the mother of his son.

'I had space and ended up having a baby at sixteen years old; I want something better for my son.'

'Don't let him hear you say that.'

'That's not what I mean, and you know it. What are you doing tonight?'

'Nothing,' Imogen said, her eyes shifting to the floor. 'Home alone, again. Elias has asked me to meet my brothers, but I don't think I can do it.'

'Not surprised. I can't even imagine finding out I have siblings. Although it wouldn't surprise me; my father put it about a bit.'

'Talking of putting it about . . . look who it is!' Imogen said.

Adrian looked up and saw Denise Ferguson standing with Caitlin Watts.

'I can't believe you just said that about a teenage witness.' Adrian shook his head in fake disapproval.

'I was talking about you,' Imogen said.

'Jealous?' He winked at her.

Denise walked Caitlin over to the desk. Adrian sat on the edge of the table and directed her to his seat. Imogen noted the girl's submissive vibe with Adrian, head tilted back, looking up at him with her animated eyes. Denise raised her eyebrows at the scene; Imogen was glad that she wasn't the only one who noticed.

'We only saw you a few hours ago. What is it?' Adrian said.

'You asked me if I knew anything about Doctor Norris.'

'Oh, you do?'

'I remembered after you left. A while back he was going out with one of his students. A girl. I don't know who though.'

41

Caitlin was painting herself as some kind of damsel; Imogen would have to remind Adrian how they met her. She hadn't been the victim of a crime. Imogen had met girls like her before, girls who flirted in a bizarrely subservient way, to play to the man's sense of machismo. The whole idea of it disgusted Imogen.

'How long ago was this relationship?' Adrian asked.

'A couple of months. Everyone suspected everyone at the time.'

'Did anyone suspect you?' Imogen asked, but Caitlin didn't look at her. She wanted to laugh – it was so obvious what the girl was doing.

'Although I do like older men, he wasn't really my type.' She licked her lips coyly, biting gently on the bottom one, and looked up slowly at Adrian again.

'Jesus!' Imogen said under her breath.

Adrian shot her a look and she realised she'd spoken aloud.

'What else can you tell me about him?' asked Adrian.

'A few months ago, one of his students killed themselves.'

Now this was a fact they could check; the rest just felt like an excuse to get closer to Adrian – a mystery relationship, a rumour that couldn't be proven or disproven.

'Could it have been the one he was having an affair with?'

'No, it was a boy. His name was Owen Sager; there's a weird little memorial bench to him in town.'

'Weird how?'

'Well, you just associate memorial benches with old

42

people, don't you?' Caitlin glanced at Imogen briefly, a tone in her voice that was slightly derisive.

'How did he die?' Adrian asked.

'Hung himself in his parents' garage.'

'You seem to know a lot about him, were you close?'

'No, they wrote about him in the college paper, a big bit on depression and how we should seek help if we're feeling suicidal. He's become the poster boy for exam stress. Which is stupid because he started in September. He was barely here three months before he hung himself – sorry, I mean hanged himself. I always get that mixed up. I brought the article for you.' She pulled out a printed sheet of paper and handed it to Adrian.

He looked it over and put it on the desk. 'Is there anything else?'

'Not that I can think of right now. If I do, I'll come and speak to you again.'

'You do that,' Imogen said.

'I have something really embarrassing to ask you,' Caitlin said to Adrian, continuing to ignore Imogen's existence.

'Shoot.'

'I lost my bus pass and I need to get back home. I don't suppose you could lend me money for a taxi?'

It took all of Imogen's strength to stop herself from rolling her eyes.

'I can get someone to drop you home if you want?'

Imogen folded her arms and looked at Adrian.

'Could you do it? I'm a little weirded out by this murder. It's probably someone I know, and it was so violent. Who does that to another person?'

43

And just like that, she was crying.

To Imogen's amazement, Adrian picked his coat off the back of his chair. Whatever this girl was doing, it was working. She was a stunning-looking girl; the kind of girl Imogen might have stared at for long periods of time in school and wondered if maybe she wasn't heterosexual after all. Her jet-black hair and big blue eyes, now watery and vulnerable, were a winning combination. Was it really this easy? Was every man just looking for a damsel in distress? A chance to be a hero?

'I'll see you later, Grey.' He ushered Caitlin Watts towards the door and left with her.

Imogen couldn't believe what she had just seen. Adrian had been the one who commented on the trustworthiness of the girl and now here she was, wrapping him around her little finger.

Imogen grabbed the article off Adrian's desk and read through the piece that suggested the boy just couldn't cope with university and had taken his own life. There was a quote from Hugh Norris, the dead professor. He had said Owen had a 'bright and promising future' in philosophy and that he was a 'deep thinker', which had probably added fuel to his depression. Imogen wondered if his depression was documented in his medical records. Seeing as she had lost her partner to the siren call of whatever the hell that was, she needed someone sensible to help her work through this new evidence; Gary Tunney, the district's forensic computer analyst, could help her find out. There had to be a connection between Owen's death and the Hugh Norris murder. Maybe someone thought Norris was responsible for Owen's death. She needed to find out if Owen had bonded with anyone on his course – maybe a friend would be able to shed more light on what actually happened.

She started writing down questions, annoyed that she couldn't just fire them at Adrian because he had already gone. He had been acting strange since he met DI Walsh. Or maybe it was because she had left without waking him up. Things were getting complicated between them and she knew that their current situation was unsustainable. She was going to have to put a stop to their sleepovers if it was going to make things awkward between them.

Chapter Seven

When Imogen got into work, Adrian was already sitting at the desk, reading the questions she had left the night before when he had taken Caitlin home. She could tell that he knew she was there; he was staring extra hard at the paper, as though he were afraid to look up. Was he feeling guilty about something? Had something happened? She had no right to judge him if it had, except maybe for the age difference, but, morally speaking, Imogen didn't have a leg to stand on after her relationship with Dean. She hated not having the moral high ground.

'Well? You disappeared pretty sharpish last night, so I wrote out some stuff for us to look at today.'

'Sorry, I'll get started on this list of things you want checking out. If you want me to?'

'I already sent the list to Gary. If there is anything to find, he will find it. What happened last night?' she said, noticing the scrapes across his knuckles.

'Doesn't matter,' he said, keeping his head down.

'Look at me, please.'

Adrian sighed and looked up. He had a bruised eye and a scratch across his face. His neck was bruised. He'd been fighting.

'I got mugged last night; I was walking back from the pub and I got jumped by someone. I think it was one person, I'm not sure.'

'Who did you go to the pub with?' Imogen knew that he sometimes got into pub fights; he didn't exactly broadcast it, but he didn't usually lie about it. Maybe he was embarrassed because he had sought comfort there instead of with her. Maybe he didn't go to see Imogen because of something else.

'I went alone. I just wanted a drink.'

'Right. You sure you're OK?' She had to admit to feeling a little jealous of the way he had so blatantly tried to avoid looking at Caitlin Watts yesterday. She could almost see him willing himself not to be attracted to her. Maybe it was even making Imogen a little insecure about what was happening between them. They were in a strange and untenable limbo, not friends but not lovers. At some point they would need to decide one way or the other. She couldn't bring herself to admit that she didn't want it to end; she didn't want to go back, but at the same time she didn't want to go forwards. She had managed to get out of one complicated relationship and straight into an even more confusing one. Not to mention the fact that it was completely and utterly against the rules for them to see each other.

'Fine, Grey. Let's just do some work.'

'You don't want to file a report on the mugging?' Imogen said, wondering why Adrian was struggling to keep eye contact with her. What wasn't he telling her?

'Maybe later. What are we doing now?'

'Well, we need to go and speak to Owen Sager's parents. They live local-ish. See if they know why he killed himself. I already told DI Walsh we would head straight there this morning.'

'We'd better get going then.' He stood up.

She winced when she looked at his eye. The white was pooled with red, a subconjunctival haemorrhage. The lid was swollen and the bridge of his nose was also bruised. He had taken quite the thump. She wondered why he did it to himself, why he would go out looking for trouble. It wasn't the first time he had turned up at work with a black eye or a broken rib.

'Tell me the truth. Did you go out looking for a fight?'

'Not this time, no.' He walked out before she could respond.

His eye wasn't the only thing that was bruised, so was his ego.

She grabbed the list of queries she had written about the Norris case and followed him outside. He was already sitting in the car, already smoking a cigarette. She waited outside for him to finish before getting in. Somehow, they had gone from their previous conversation to not speaking and she wasn't even sure why. What had she said that upset him?

She handed him his sunglasses. 'You'd better wear these when we speak to them; you look pretty bad.'

* * *

48

They got to Owen Sager's house and knocked on the door. A woman answered immediately, a haunted look on her face, hollow and empty. She was in pain and you could feel it; she was transmitting her pain to anyone who would take some of it from her, release her from this burden. Imogen had seen it before in parents who had lost their children.

'Mrs Sager?' Imogen said.

'Can I help you?' Mrs Sager replied, an emptiness in her voice.

'We're currently working on a case that may or may not be connected to your son's death. I was wondering if you wouldn't mind answering some questions?' Imogen said.

'What do you mean, connected?' Mrs Sager asked, visibly surprised, pulled from her trancelike melancholy.

'His philosophy professor, Doctor Norris, was murdered yesterday, which we believe was an anniversary of sorts,' Adrian said.

'I found my son exactly three months ago yesterday.' Mrs Sager looked down and Imogen noticed she was holding a small piece of fabric in her hands, like a comforter. Probably something of Owen's.

'I'm so sorry for your loss. There probably is no connection, but it warrants a discussion,' Imogen said.

'What's left to discuss?' Mrs Sager scrunched the fabric in her closed fist.

'Did your son give you any indication as to what he was stressed about?' Adrian asked.

'He seemed happy. I thought he was OK.' Her eyes widened, letting even more emptiness in.

'Nothing changed in the days before his . . .' Adrian tailed off.

'Suicide,' Imogen finished. They had been told in plenty of seminars how important it was not to mince your words around families of grieving victims. Don't use words like passed away, say dead. Make it real.

'Yes, he had begun to act erratically in the weeks before, but I thought it was just all the extra work he was having to do. The police told me that it was probably depression. He may have planned his suicide for some time. He never said there was anything wrong.' She pulled at the edges of the fabric again.

'This is not your fault in any way, Mrs Sager,' Imogen said.

'I wish I could help more. I'm sorry,' she said, her eyes glassy and her voice fragmented.

'You've been a great help,' Adrian offered.

'Did he ever talk about Doctor Norris?' Imogen asked.

'He really liked him, at least he did at first, talked about him all the time.'

'That changed?' Imogen pressed.

'Now that you mention it, it did a little. I guess, as the time went on, the work got harder and Owen lost his shine for Doctor Norris. I just didn't really think about it.'

'Did they fall out?' Adrian asked.

'No, Doctor Norris was nothing but kind to Owen. Owen got in because Doctor Norris endorsed his application to the university even though he didn't quite get the correct grades, and he also sent a letter

50

recommending Owen for a full scholarship. He got turned down, but he did get a twenty per cent reduction in fees. Which was great.'

'So, they had a close relationship, then?' Imogen asked.

'I know it sounds a bit unconventional, but Owen was so worried about starting at the uni, especially with his lower than average score, and Doctor Norris was really kind to him and took him under his wing. Before you say anything, there was nothing seedy going on. He was just a nice man.'

Adrian and Imogen's phones went off simultaneously. Imogen pulled her phone out of her pocket and looked at the screen. A text alert from the DCI. She wanted them at the hospital immediately.

'Thank you, Mrs Sager, we had best be going now,' Imogen said. 'Here's my card, call us if you think of anything.' Imogen put her card in the palm of Mrs Sager's hand and closed both hands around it. 'So sorry for your loss.'

'Thank you, dear.' She attempted to smile and stepped back into the house, closing the door behind her.

Adrian blew his cheeks out, obviously feeling the woman's pain. 'God, I can't even imagine,' he said.

'Let's get to the hospital,' Imogen said, knowing full well that Adrian *could* imagine it – his son had come close to being killed in a previous case and it almost destroyed him.

They got back in the car and made their way across town to meet the DCI. Imogen couldn't help looking at the scrapes on his knuckles and wondering if he was telling the truth about being mugged. It certainly wasn't the first time he had shown up to work with unexplained cuts and bruises. She reminded herself he had no reason to lie. Did he?

Chapter Eight

Adrian couldn't stop thinking about the look on Mrs Sager's face. He remembered back to the time recently when he'd thought his own son was dead, and the visceral memory of the way he'd felt, even for the briefest of times, was enough to make him want to throw up. But to live in that state, to know that you would never see your child again – that would be too much for Adrian. He wasn't sure he would even want to carry on.

The hospital was busy, and by the time they found DI Walsh, visiting hours had begun. DI Matt Walsh stood with his arms folded, staring ahead of him. Adrian couldn't help but look at Imogen's face as they approached him, to see if he could work out what she was thinking. She had seemed preoccupied with finding out more about the new DI and for some reason that annoyed Adrian. He couldn't admit to himself that he was feeling jealous.

'What's going on?' Imogen called out, getting the DI's attention.

'A girl has been brought in. She's in and out of it a bit, but she's been completely brutalised,' DI Walsh said.

'Sexual assault?' Imogen asked.

'It seems highly likely at this point; I'm just waiting for the doctor to come and give me a clearer picture of what happened.'

'Do we know who she is?' Adrian asked.

'Barely. I mean, you wouldn't know it from her face; she has a lot of swelling and several nasty abrasions.' DI Walsh seemed to stop dead in his tracks, obviously noticing the state of Adrian's own appearance. 'What happened to you?'

'I got mugged last night, nothing serious though, I'm fine.'

'You don't look fine. Are you OK?'

'Yeah, seriously. I managed to swing a couple of punches, so he didn't get anything. Really, it's no big deal. I'll file a report on it later on, I was planning on it anyway, but I don't have much information at all.' Adrian wanted to stop talking about it now. 'Tell us about the girl.'

'She managed to tell us her name, but her throat is pretty damaged; looks like he strangled her. My guess is whoever did this is going to be very disappointed when they realise she didn't die. She was beaten so badly, there's no way they intended her to walk away from that.'

'You said she told you her name?' Imogen said.

'Caitlin Watts.'

'What?' Imogen shot Adrian a look again.

54

'You know her?'

'We had her on a B and E the other day; all turned out to be fine though,' Adrian said, his voice catching a little as he spoke. What the hell was going on?

'Did she say if she felt like she was in danger from anyone?' Matt Walsh asked.

'No, not at all. She was in yesterday and she was fine,' Adrian said.

'So, you saw her yesterday?' DI Walsh pressed.

'She knew the professor; she came in to give us more information on the Norris case,' Imogen explained.

'She was the witness who came forward? Do you think this attack could be linked to the murder? Did she give you any indication who she thought might have killed Doctor Norris?' DI Walsh asked.

'No, but she was the one who told us about the kid who committed suicide. Owen Sager,' Imogen said.

'I dropped her off at home at around six and she was fine,' Adrian added.

'You dropped her off at home?' DI Walsh queried, and there was an element of derision in his voice that Adrian didn't like.

'She said she couldn't get home. I was making sure she got back all right,' Adrian said.

Dr Hadley appeared at that moment and Adrian was relieved to have the spotlight off him. He didn't appreciate the way DI Walsh was speaking to him.

'She's awake and she's stable; you can talk to her for a couple of minutes. The damage to her throat at this time means she can only talk in a whisper. She's been through quite an ordeal.'

'Was she raped?' Imogen asked.

'Yes, she has extensive damage to both her vaginal opening and her rectal lining. She also has some cracked ribs, a supraorbital fracture and more bruises than I can count,' the doctor said, clearly very angry.

'Jesus,' Imogen muttered.

'I have done a rape kit and sent it straight to the lab,' Dr Hadley noted.

'Can we go in now?' Adrian asked. Caitlin was a sweet girl, if a little misguided, and the thought of this happening to her, of this happening to anyone, was stomach-turning.

'Sure. But be considerate; please, she's been through a lot.'

They walked into the room and could immediately feel the heaviness in the air. The nurses were working with a solemn concentration, not speaking but still somehow comforting with their presence.

The sight of Caitlin was something to behold: her face was swollen and bandaged, and she was barely recognisable. The one eye that was on display was full of tears as she stared out the window.

Imogen went over to the bedside and sat in Caitlin's eyeline. Caitlin blinked a tear away as Imogen gently placed her hand on top of hers.

'Hey, Caitlin, do you remember me?' Imogen spoke softly.

Adrian felt like an intruder. Even though they were there to get a statement so that they could find the bastard who did this, he couldn't help thinking they should leave the poor girl in peace.

'Hello,' she whispered and closed her eye.

'I know this is difficult, but can you remember any details of the attack?' Imogen asked.

'Yes, I can,' she whispered, her voice rough and crackling with pain.

'I'm sorry, but would you be able to tell us what happened?'

Caitlin blinked slowly and wheezed in a deep breath before speaking.

'He put his hand around my throat and told me he would kill me if I called out,' she said, tears flowing freely from her one uncovered eye. 'I thought I was going to die. He punched me in the side of the head and I just felt the pain in my eye exploding; it was so horrible. I was dizzy. He told me to get on the floor, but I said no, and that's when he punched me in the stomach and made me take my pants off. He got on top of me and I tried to push him away, I even hit him, but he still wouldn't stop. I tried to fight him . . .' Caitlin's whisper disappeared into a breathy cry as she got more and more distraught. She was fighting back the tears.

How could anyone do this to someone else? Adrian never could get his head around this kind of crime.

'Just take your time,' Imogen said.

Caitlin nodded gently before taking another deep breath.

'After he was done, he made me do other stuff, too.'

'How long was he there?' DI Walsh said.

Imogen shot him an angry look, but he ignored her.

'A couple of hours, I don't know.'

'Did you know your attacker? Could you tell us his name?' DI Walsh said.

For the first time since they had entered the room, Caitlin turned towards the men who were standing at the door. She lifted her hand and pointed at Adrian. What was happening?

'He did it.' She burst into tears as she said it.

'Excuse me?' Imogen removed her hand from the girl's immediately as though a bolt of electricity had just shot through her.

'After Detective Miles drove me home last night, he raped me,' Caitlin said.

'*What?*' Adrian finally managed to push a word out of his mouth; he wasn't even sure what word it was. His head was thumping and his ears were ringing. This was up there with his worst nightmares. This couldn't be real. Being accused of rape was one of those unshakable accusations. Once it had happened, everyone would always wonder. Once the seed was planted, there was nowhere to hide. It would be a rumour that would follow Adrian for the rest of his life. He wanted to throw up. 'Caitlin!'

'Could you wait outside the room please, Detective Miles?' DI Walsh said calmly.

'This is not true. Caitlin, why are you doing this?' Adrian said – he knew he shouldn't say anything, but the impulse was too strong.

'Just for a moment, I'll be right out,' Matt pressed.

Adrian looked at Imogen for guidance. She nodded that it was best for him to leave. He walked out of the room and watched intently through the glass of the door as they spoke to Caitlin. Why would she do this?

It wasn't long before Imogen and the DI came out of the room. Imogen kept staring at Adrian, willing him to look at her; he could see her out of the corner of his eye. He kept his eyes down though. If he didn't focus on the floor, he would be sick.

'We have to investigate this,' DI Walsh said.

'I swear I didn't do this. I couldn't!' Adrian said, struggling to breathe.

'That's not for me to decide, I'm afraid. There has to be a proper investigation. Do you at least have an alibi for last night?'

'Not really. I went to the pub, someone might have seen me there. What happens now?'

'We go and tell Mira. She will have to contact the Professional Standards Division and they will send someone to come and figure out who is telling the truth here.'

'You think I did this?' The idea of having PSD looking into his conduct at work made Adrian uncomfortable. He had been investigated for evidence tampering before and even though he was eventually exonerated, the process was degrading. He could just imagine the talk that would be flying around the station. It didn't even bear thinking about.

'I don't know you. I think at this point it doesn't matter what I think.'

'It matters to me,' Adrian said, trying to ignore what he felt DI Walsh was inferring.

'I think you will probably get assigned to desk duty

for as long as it takes to clear your name,' DI Walsh said unapologetically.

'Imogen. You believe me, right? I didn't do this.' He could feel his voice getting higher as he got more agitated.

'I know you didn't,' she said without hesitation, calming the swirling in his head for a second.

'False rape claims are a lot rarer than people think they are,' DI Walsh said. 'There's a lot of physical evidence that she's been assaulted.'

'I'm not saying she wasn't raped, I'm saying it wasn't me,' Adrian said.

'Well, the PSD will clear it up. Now, let's get back to the station.'

'Am I under arrest?'

'That's not my call. DCI Kapoor will make that decision. I think there will be at least some preliminary investigation before that happens. See what the rape kit turns up.'

All Adrian could think about was what had happened to Caitlin; it was horrific and brutal. Maybe the head injury she'd sustained had messed with her memory and she really did think he had done it. He had dropped her off, but then driven straight home before walking to the pub. Something was bothering him about the timing of all of this though. For him to coincidentally get mugged on the same day, covered in scrapes and bruises on the exact same night, what were the chances? Maybe the attack on him wasn't a random mugging, after all. Maybe he was targeted. But why would someone target him? And what did Caitlin have to do with it? Adrian couldn't help feeling paranoid at this point. After what he had been through in the past with Dominic Shaw, his son's stepfather – a man who dedicated his life to messing Adrian's up – he didn't believe in coincidences and the fact that the attack on Caitlin happened the same night as his attack meant that someone had planned this. But why? What was the end game?

DI Walsh walked in front as they exited the hospital and Imogen dropped back a little until she was by Adrian's side.

'What are you thinking?' she said to Adrian in a whisper, clearly not wanting to draw DI Walsh into the conversation.

'I swear I didn't do this.' Adrian felt compelled to say it over and over again.

'I know you didn't,' she reassured him.

'I was telling the truth about last night, too. I got jumped. What if that and this are connected?'

'That seems a little far-fetched.'

'After everything we've seen over the last couple of years you think that's far-fetched?'

'OK, say it is connected. What is it about? Hugh Norris? Owen Sager? Is it because of what she told us at the station yesterday? And why would they target you?'

'Your guess is as good as mine. Do you think she's lying, or do you think she's just remembering it wrong?'

'I don't feel confident to say; it's possible she's got confused, that it was a nasty attack. I say for now we give her the benefit of the doubt. I don't like to think

61

anyone would falsely report a rape. The amount of damage it does is unbelievable. Not just to the accused but to the whole system. So, for now we work on the assumption that she's confused. But that's between you and me.'

'Thank you,' Adrian said.

'What for?'

'For not doubting me.'

'I'd like to think I know you well enough to know you weren't capable of something like that.' She paused. 'What was the name of the pub you went to last night?'

'I went up to The Imperial.'

'You went to the biggest pub in town?'

'Someone might remember me,' Adrian said.

'Well, let's hope so. Did you go into her house?' Imogen said, looking away from him, obviously afraid of the answer.

'Nope, absolutely not. I pulled up outside, she got out and then I drove away. I swear to God that's what happened.'

They arrived back at the cars.

'Adrian, I think you should come back with me,' DI Walsh said.

Adrian didn't know whether DI Walsh believed him or not, but he knew in his situation, he would be inclined to believe the victim. A thought that gave him no great comfort. Either way, this was a shitshow and Adrian was the main attraction.

Chapter Nine

Imogen stood with her arms folded, looking down at DCI Mira Kapoor, who was responding to an email from PSD, the department that were sending someone over to investigate Adrian. She had come in to speak to the DCI on her own, without DI Walsh breathing over her shoulder. She knew he wasn't actively trying to piss anyone off, and that he was right to question what was going on, but he seemed to have made his mind up already. Admittedly, looking at Caitlin Watts in that hospital bed was enough to give anyone pause. It really wouldn't make sense for her to make it up, why would she? Wouldn't she want to see her attacker put away for what he had done to her? Meeting Caitlin before and forming a strong opinion about how manipulative she was was definitely clouding Imogen's judgement. She knew there were plenty of people who would be happy to think of Adrian as someone who would do this. The truth was, of course, that even though there was no doubt in her mind that Adrian was innocent, there was still that voice in the back of her mind, demanding to be heard.

'You can stop looking at me like that, DS Grey. This is procedure, there is nothing I can do. My hands are tied.'

'He didn't do this. No way,' she urged.

'I'm glad you have his back, and while I admire your loyalty, I don't have that luxury.'

'Can I help with the investigation?'

'I think we both know the answer to that.'

'I can't just do nothing. This isn't right,' Imogen said.

'Between us . . . you met the girl before. What did you think of her?'

'Honestly? She was all over Adrian, disturbingly so. Flirting and desperate for his attention.'

'And you don't think he could have taken that the wrong way and maybe—'

'No. Aside from the extreme violence towards her, which I am positive Adrian would have no part in, I just don't think he'd be into it if the person wasn't into it, too. If you know what I mean,' Imogen said, unsure if she was making things better or worse, worrying she was digging Adrian into an even bigger hole.

'Why do you say that about the violence? People can surprise you,' DCI Kapoor said gently, as though she were trying to prepare Imogen for the worst.

'On previous cases, Adrian has been quite affected by violence against women. His father was a violent man, apparently; hit both him and his mother frequently.'

'I didn't know that,' DCI Kapoor said apologetically.

'He doesn't talk about it much, but I just can't imagine him raising a hand to a woman. Let alone this,' Imogen said. Adrian hadn't talked about it much but on the few occasions where he had said something it was clear to her that it was something he felt very strongly about.

'Have you and he ever—'

'No,' Imogen said before she had a chance to finish the sentence.

DCI Kapoor's computer pinged and she clicked on something. She folded her arms and leaned back in her chair, exhaling and scrunching her face up. She was obviously trying to decide what to do.

'PSD are sending over Detective Chief Constable Trevor Sneddon. If you would, please meet him and bring him to my office. He'll be out front in about five minutes. I'll see if he has a problem with you observing the in-house interviews. Observing being the key word. You won't be able to sit in, but you can watch from the control room if he gives you the OK.'

'Thank you,' Imogen said, breathing out a small sigh of relief at not being shut out completely.

'Any idea why Miss Watts might make this up?'

'None whatsoever.'

'OK, thank you, Imogen. Can you send Adrian in?'

Imogen left the DCI's office and sat back down at her desk. Adrian was perched on his chair with his head in his hands – anxious was an understatement. She could see he was lost in his own thoughts.

'The DCI wants to see you now.'

Adrian stood up and barrelled towards DCI Kapoor's office. Imogen hoped he didn't lose his temper. She couldn't stay in here and try to guess what the DCI was saying to Adrian; she needed some air. It had been raining earlier, so she grabbed her coat and went outside to wait for the DCC to show up.

Just being outside made Imogen want a cigarette, but she hadn't had one since about three days after New Year's Eve. One more week and she would have gone two whole months without one.

A car she didn't recognise pulled into the forecourt and a man she wasn't familiar with got out. She wrapped her coat around her and walked towards him, the wind whipping her hair into an unruly mess.

'DCC Sneddon?' she called out.

'Yes, how did you know?' He was tall with sandy blond hair and a stern face, but she liked to imagine he didn't look unreasonable.

'You just look like PSD.'

'I'll pretend that's a compliment.' He held his hand out and she took it; he had a firm shake, confident, that of someone in a position of authority.

'I'm DS Imogen Grey. The DCI has asked me to take you through to see her.'

'Do you know the accused?' he said sombrely.

'I do. He's my partner.'

'I'm guessing you believe him.'

'Correct.'

'OK, let's get this show on the road,' he said in an apologetic voice.

This at least gave her hope that he wasn't just out to nail someone. She hated her job sometimes.

Chapter Ten

Being on this side of the interview table was no fun. Adrian waited patiently for DCC Trevor Sneddon to start asking questions. They had already got the formalities out of the way: date, time, name, rank. Adrian could feel the beginnings of a migraine, or maybe he just really wanted a drink.

'Could you tell me about the first meeting with Caitlin Watts?' DCC Sneddon began.

'She was brought in for breaking into a chapel. Her grandfather was a reverend, though, and so no charges were brought and we let her go,' Adrian said.

'Did she steal anything?' Sneddon asked.

'Apparently not.'

'How did she seem at that time?'

'I don't know. Normal. She was quite friendly,' Adrian said. Did that make him look bad?

'And the next time you saw her?'

'Yesterday morning. She said hello to us near the

scene of the Norris murder. We went to speak to one of his colleagues, who turned out to be her lecturer. Psychology, um . . . her name was Gillian Mitchell. Miss Watts walked past and said hello.'

'And you hadn't arranged to meet Caitlin Watts there?'

'Of course not. It was a murder that we were called out to. How would I know beforehand that it was going to happen?' he said, trying not to get annoyed at the questions. He knew they had to ask them.

'And then the next time?'

'Yesterday again. She came in late afternoon and told us that she thought Hugh Norris was having an affair with a student. She also told us that one of his students committed suicide exactly three months ago. She brought in an article about the suicide and I put it on the desk.'

'Then what happened?'

'She told me she couldn't get home and that she was a bit upset by the murder, so I offered to give her a lift.'

'You offered? Why?'

'Actually no, I offered to get someone else to drop her home, but she asked if I could do it. She said she was nervous because of the violent nature of the murder.'

'And you said?'

'I said, fine. I was leaving anyway.'

'And what happened then?'

'I drove her home, she got out and I drove home.'

'You didn't get out of the car and see her to her door?'

'No, I didn't. I didn't even really watch her go inside. I just left. Then I parked up at home and walked to The Imperial.'

'Were you alone?'

'Yes. I was a bit pissed off because I was supposed to have my son stay over last night, but he made other plans.'

'So, no one can corroborate your story?'

'Sorry, no.'

'OK. Let's talk about you for a moment,' Sneddon said with a heavy sigh, clearly not enjoying this any more than Adrian.

'I thought that was what we were doing.'

'Are you in a relationship?' Sneddon asked.

'Not that it's any of your business, but no.'

'I heard your last relationship ended rather traumatically. Is that correct?'

'Do they ever end well?' Adrian said, trying to make light of it.

'Have you sought any counselling for what happened? It's hard losing someone to an act of violence.'

'I'm dealing with it just fine,' Adrian lied.

'Have you ever dated anyone in the station?'

'I had a casual relationship with Duty Sergeant Denise Ferguson, but that ended a long time ago. I haven't had a relationship at all since Lucy died.'

'Anyone else?'

'Why does this matter?'

'Just answer the question.'

Adrian thought about Imogen for a moment. Should he mention it? It wasn't a relationship, it wasn't even sexual, but somehow it was important. Far too important to talk about here.

'I went out with PC Tessa Burgess briefly and a couple other officers who have since transferred out.'

'Does briefly mean a one-night stand?'

'Yes. But there wasn't any drink involved or anything. It was a consensual situation and it was before she worked in this division.'

'We'll speak to her, but for now, you can see yourself out.'

Adrian left the interrogation room feeling worse than he had done before he went in. Everything he had said made him sound like a complete scumbag.

Imogen was waiting outside. He struggled to even look at her at the moment. It was taking all of his energy not to just throw himself in front of a bus right now.

Chapter Eleven

Imogen had tried to explain her feelings about Caitlin Watts to DCC Sneddon without making her sound like a psychotic vampire. It didn't sit well with her at all, not believing the victim. She felt like she was betraying every rape victim that had ever walked through the door. Imogen tried to imagine what she would feel had she not met Caitlin beforehand and immediately distrusted her. Did that distrust automatically mean she was lying now? For all she knew maybe she was all of those things that Imogen thought about her beforehand. That didn't exclude her from being attacked, that didn't mean she would never tell the truth ever again. Sometimes people lie, sometimes they tell the truth. If it were any other man, she might even have given Caitlin Watts the benefit of the doubt. But this was Adrian.

'You and Detective Miles have worked together for some time now,' DCC Sneddon pressed.

'Yes.'

'Have you ever noticed a particularly sexist or negative attitude towards women at all?'

'For being women? No.'

'He's had some relationships within the station. Did you know about them?'

'I knew about him and Denise. I don't tell him everyone I sleep with either though, to be fair.'

'Denise Ferguson? Did she say anything to you about the relationship?'

'No. I know she wasn't happy when it ended though.'

'Does DS Miles have many impromptu relationships?'

'A few, I think. Or at least he used to. What's that got to do with anything? Sleeping around doesn't make him a sexual predator. Women like sex, too. Not all of us are being manipulated into it when we have a one-night stand.' She hated the constant portrayal of women as easy to 'trick' into sex. As though a woman who wants to sleep around is being taken advantage of each time because she has a low self-esteem. So much stigma around women who liked sex.

'What about you? Have you ever been intimate with DS Miles?'

'Depends what you mean by intimate.' She tried to laugh off his question, but he looked at her curiously, as though he knew she were hiding something. She wasn't about to tell him about her and Adrian's arrangement. It didn't mean anything, and it certainly didn't bear any relevance to this case.

'Have you ever had sexual intercourse or taken part in any sexual acts with DS Miles?'

'No, I haven't.'

Not a lie, not quite the truth either.

'Would you say your partnership is solid? Do you think he keeps secrets from you?'

'No, I don't think he does. I trust him implicitly.'

'OK, thank you, Miss Grey.'

'That's it?'

'That's it for now at least. Unless we hear anything that contradicts your statement.'

'Should I send Denise in?'

'Thank you, yes.' DCC Trevor Sneddon attempted a smile to comfort Imogen, but she left the room without returning it.

She walked straight outside, needing some fresh air. Within a few seconds, Adrian was standing beside her.

'Well?'

'Well what, Adrian? You know I can't talk about it.'

'Fuck that, what did you say?'

'I said what I would have said if you were standing in the room. Don't worry, I'm on your side.'

'Did he ask you about us?'

'He did.'

'And what did you tell him?'

She felt her eyebrows involuntarily raise as he said the words. Neither of them had spoken about this, let alone outside work in the daylight.

'That there was nothing going on between us. There's nothing to tell,' Imogen said.

A weight clearly lifted from him when she said that.

'That's what I thought. I just wanted to check with you. I didn't tell him either.'

'I don't see how it would make any difference to the

73

investigation. Apart from getting us into a whole heap of shit.' She changed the subject. 'Sneddon's speaking to Denise now. I might go and watch. Why don't you speak to Gary and see if he can find any CCTV footage around The Imperial to prove where you were. If she is lying, we can prove it, just remember that.'

'What do you mean *if*?' Adrian snapped.

'Don't be like that, you know what I meant.'

Adrian relaxed. 'Thanks for having my back on this. Not everyone would.'

'I hope if the situation were reversed you would do the same for me.'

'You know I would. Good idea about Gary, I'll see if he can work some of his magic. Is anyone speaking to Caitlin Watts?'

'I think DI Walsh is back over there taking a statement. I'll speak to you later.'

Imogen left Adrian outside. She noticed how uncomfortable she felt around him, and she couldn't help but wonder why. Was it just that they had finally spoken about their strange sleepovers out loud? Or was it something else?

Not wanting to think about that right now, Imogen wanted to hear what Denise had to say, so she went into the adjacent room and watched the live feed.

'How often would you say you and DS Miles had sex?' Sneddon asked Denise.

'Do you have to be so crude? Every few weeks.'

'But there was no relationship?'

'I don't know how to answer that question. We were

both single, consenting adults. Yes, we hooked up for sex. Is that wrong?'

'I'm afraid I'm going to have to ask you if the sex was particularly rough?'

'It was as rough as we both wanted it to be,' Denise huffed.

'That's not an answer. I'm going to need more than that,' DCC Sneddon said.

Imogen felt wrong listening in, but she couldn't tear herself away. Denise was obviously holding something back.

'It was a bit rough. But only because I wanted that. Adrian wasn't like that at first.'

'So, you're saying his aggressive sexual behaviour escalated?'

'No! I'm saying I asked him to be rougher and he was. I told him what I wanted, that's all. He didn't do anything outside of that. He never did anything I was uncomfortable with.'

'Did he ever hit you during sex? Did you ask him to?'

'No. I feel like my words are getting twisted up here. Adrian's a good guy.'

'What about choking? Did he ever strangle you? Either with his hands or anything else?'

'I don't want to answer that question.'

'I think we're probably past that now. You have to answer the question.'

Denise took a deep breath and Imogen found herself closing her eyes, waiting for her to say what everyone now knew she was about to say.

'I asked him to choke me, and so he did, yes.'

'More than once?'

'Yes, more than once.'

'And did you ask him every time? Or did he sometimes just do it?'

Denise exhaled loudly, exasperated. 'I didn't ask him every time, no.'

'Did he ever choke you until you passed out?'

'No, never. It wasn't like that.'

Imogen was growing more and more concerned for Adrian; Denise wasn't doing the greatest job in the interview. Rather than alleviating any concerns they might have about Adrian, she was sure that Denise had just opened a whole other can of worms.

Imogen left the room, unable to listen to any more. Over at the bank of desks, Adrian and Gary were huddled together. She noticed people looking at Adrian and the occasional whisper from some of the newer members of staff. Adrian did have a reputation for being a bit promiscuous, and it was completely justified a couple of years ago, but even in the time that Imogen had known him he had grown up and changed. Anyone who knew him well knew he wasn't capable of this.

'Any luck with the CCTV?' Imogen asked Gary as she reached the two men.

'I'm fast, but I'm not that fast. I'm collecting the feeds and will get straight on it after I grab some dinner from the canteen, I'm starving. I'm just trying to get a clear picture of Adrian's movements so that I know where to look before I start.' Gary smiled nervously.

'Do we know what time she says the attack took place?' Imogen pressed.

'Around ten p.m.,' Gary replied.

'Did you take any money out? Most cashpoints have a camera on them; we could see if there's anything,' Gary asked Adrian.

'I did, at the Lloyds cashpoint by St David's Station. At around nine thirty, I think.'

'I'll see if I can get some footage from the station at that time.'

'What time were you mugged?' Imogen asked.

'Around eleven, I think. I left before last orders,' Adrian said. He looked tired and a little manic. Imogen couldn't imagine how he must be feeling.

'Adrian, why don't you go home and sleep? I'll go through the footage with Gary. I'll stay here all night until we find something, OK?'

'What if you don't find anything, Imogen? What then?'

'We will. I won't stop until we do.'

'I've seen the way people are looking at me today.'

'Of course they're going to look at you, that's to be expected. It doesn't matter because you are going to be exonerated.'

Adrian nodded. 'OK, I'll go home. I just wish I knew why this was happening.'

'I know. We're going to figure it out,' Imogen reassured him.

Adrian grabbed his coat and left, while Imogen settled down to the desk and put the headphones on. She started watching the CCTV footage they had so far, mostly on fast forward as nothing was happening in the majority of it.

Later, Gary sent her a text to tell her that the bank was shut and so they would have to wait until the morning to get the cashpoint information. This was going to be a long night.

Chapter Twelve

Adrian was on his third glass of whisky when he decided to run himself a bath. He needed a way to de-stress that didn't involve him going out, getting drunk and then getting into a fight. As much as that was the only thing he really wanted to do right now.

The thoughts that kept circling his mind were foetid. Why would anyone do this to him? Who had actually hurt that poor girl and why was she accusing him? Nothing made any sense. He lay in the water, wondering if he could drown himself. He had heard it was impossible to do it in a bathtub, that the desire to live was too ingrained, too prevalent to be overridden by sheer will. That no matter how much you might want to die, something inside you would stop that from happening. Still, Adrian slid under the hot water; even for a new perspective it was worth it. He tried to stay under, but even when he knew he could hold out a little longer, his body forced him out.

He grabbed the bottle from the side of the bath and filled his glass again. He could see the bruises starting to form on his ribs, the bruises they had photographed with the UV camera and catalogued at the station. He felt unclean as a result of being treated like a suspect. He thought about all the people he had arrested in the past, especially the ones who maintained their innocence until they were put away. Having to have the inside of his mouth and his penis swabbed was humiliating, especially when it was a colleague who had to do it, a colleague who suspected you of rape, who treated you like a rapist. He drank.

Feeling somewhat soothed after getting out of the bath, on the outside at least, Adrian pulled out some comfortable clothes and decided to settle for the night in front of the TV with what was left of his bottle. He couldn't help but think about what people must be saying about him. The idea of it turned his stomach.

He thought about the attack, whether it was something he was even capable of. He'd had one-night stands that were slightly rough, but nothing that hadn't been invited first. He recalled his relationship with Denise Ferguson and how she liked him to put his hands around her throat. He hadn't agreed at first; he'd made her promise him that she would let him know if he was squeezing too tight. The thought of doing that without her permission, with her struggling to get away, made him feel sick.

He had to distract himself from these thoughts. He needed to replace the image of himself hurting someone like that. He grabbed a box of beer from the fridge for when he ran out of whisky and took it into the front room.

The lounge still smelled of paint from where he had redecorated after his ex and son had sold all of his collectable toys to pay for a deposit on a flat. With every payday since Tom was born Adrian had bought some kind of collectable and over the last sixteen years they had increased in value. After Tom's stepfather died and all his assets were seized, they sold all the toys and cards to put a deposit on a flat and now the house that had been overflowing with boxes was empty. They had spent the weekend painting together to make Adrian's front room nice again and it *was* nice, it just didn't feel much like home. It looked like he had been burgled by some painters and decorators.

He settled in and turned the TV on. There were a couple of shows he had been recommended, by people who probably hated him now, but hey, at least he had time to watch them.

He was awoken by a gentle knock at the door. He answered to see Imogen standing in front of him. She didn't look particularly happy. He walked through to the lounge and she followed.

'What's going on?' he asked.

'You know how it is. I fucking hate looking through CCTV, it's so dull. Can I get a drink?'

'Sure. You didn't find anything then?' He picked up a beer and opened it before handing it to her.

'The bank was closed and so we have to wait 'til morning to get the footage from the cashpoint. Gary

81

phoned the twenty-four-hour helpline, but they said there was nothing they could do from there, that it was an onsite digital recording and there was no way of accessing it remotely.'

'Thanks for trying.'

'Don't be silly,' she said, rolling her eyes.

'You seem angry. What else is going on?' Adrian said.

'This is just bullshit, Adrian. I hate it.'

'How do you think I feel?' Adrian asked.

'I hate everything about it. I hate thinking she's a liar, I hate knowing for sure she *is* a liar. Because what if one day some other poor woman comes in and says she was raped, and I decide that I know for sure that she's lying too? Who the fuck am I to be able to decide that? Without evidence, just a decision I have made.' She took a long swig.

'I don't understand,' Adrian said. He wasn't lying; was Imogen saying that she didn't want to believe him or that she wished Caitlin was telling the truth?

'I thought I would be able to be objective!' Imogen replied, more animated than he had ever seen her before.

'Aren't you being objective?'

'Well no. Not even slightly. The evidence at the moment kind of says you did it. I saw her get into a car with you, Adrian, I saw the way you were with her, the way she was with you. I saw her injuries, I saw *your* injuries. Your alibi is shit! There's no evidence to suggest you didn't do it!'

'But?'

'But I still know you didn't do it.'

'And that's annoying you?' He smiled a little, trying

82

not to anger her further. He had been worried that she might think he had hurt Caitlin. It had been the thing that scared him the most in all of this. It was nice to know at least that Imogen's faith in him was unwavering.

'Wouldn't it annoy you?' she asked.

Before he knew what he was doing, he put his hands on Imogen's face and kissed her hard on the lips. He pulled away and looked her in the eyes. She probably didn't look as surprised as she should have, and she pushed back and kissed him on the lips herself. He put his arms around her then, pulling her in. Imogen dropped the bottle and they stumbled backwards onto the sofa; he heard the beer fizzing as it permeated the carpet, but he didn't care. He could feel her angry heart pounding against his chest. They kissed for several minutes, angry kisses, and as their hearts slowed down, so did the urge to kiss each other – and then it just stopped as quickly as it had started and Imogen clambered to her feet.

'I'm so sorry,' Adrian said, the half-smile still lingering, trying to bust out, completely gobsmacked by what had just happened.

'I should go home,' she said awkwardly.

'Wait, no, stay for a drink,' he said, the smile appearing properly this time.

'I'll see you tomorrow.'

She left and Adrian sat there, wondering what the fuck had just happened.

Chapter Thirteen

Adrian sat at his desk; Gary was on his way up and DI Walsh had called a meeting in one of the sound-proofed rooms to discuss the case. Imogen still hadn't made her way into the office yet; in fact he hadn't heard from her since the other night. He had lain awake most of that night thinking about what had happened, thinking about what might happen in the future. He'd taken the day off work and had tried to put the case out of his mind. Had forcing their relationship to the surface taken it to a whole new level? All he knew was that he didn't hate it and that maybe he wouldn't mind if it happened again.

The door to the side room opened and several detectives came out. DI Walsh motioned to Adrian and Adrian went over to his desk.

'Well?' Adrian asked.

'I found a witness who corroborated your version of events. The results of the rape kit were negative.

Forensically speaking, there are no crossover points, which is strange, considering you were in a car together for some time.'

'What do you mean the rape kit was negative?' Adrian said, confused.

'I mean there were no traces of semen or anyone else's bodily fluids, bar her own.'

'What does that mean?'

'It could mean any number of things; the point is we went over her statement several times and never once did she mention prophylaxis or penetration with a foreign object. Plus, there were no traces of lubricants.'

'So, she's lying?'

'Something happened to that girl. There is no possible way she could have inflicted all of those wounds on herself. The bruises, the breaks – those are real, and we need to treat them as such.'

'How do we find out the truth?' Adrian probed.

'We've spoken to the hospital, but they have said Caitlin is not well enough to be interviewed today. The bruising around her throat has made it almost impossible for her to speak. They think she should be fine by tomorrow morning, at which point I will go and interview her. She doesn't want her grandfather present for the interview, so her psychology professor is coming.'

'What about the CCTV? Or the camera from the bank? Did they corroborate my story?'

DI Walsh sighed and looked down. Adrian could tell that he wasn't a man who liked to be put on the spot. Adrian also didn't really care. He had to know.

'Yes. Whatever happened to Caitlin Watts, it didn't happen the way she said it did. If she is lying about that, then we have to ask ourselves why. What on earth would make a girl falsely accuse a police officer of rape?' Matt Walsh said.

'I have no idea,' said Adrian, wondering why anyone would do that.

'I'm not sure anyone does, but the fact is we need to find out what is going on. I'm sorry if you feel like you've been treated unfairly, but we had to do this by the letter. No room for error.'

'I understand. I'm just glad that the truth is out.'

'Well, actually, we need you to keep it under wraps for now. At least until after we interview Caitlin. We need to hear her side of the story again and look for holes. Or listen to her in case she remembers something else. It's entirely possible that because of the level of trauma involved, her memory has been affected. You won't be officially off the hook until after we either confirm your alibi or secure a confession. Best if you only tell Imogen for now. If the press get wind of it they will think it's a massive cover-up, as usual,' Matt said.

Adrian supposed it was better than nothing. He knew that the officials at least believed him now. He knew they had his back. No doubt rumours would continue to circulate and there would be some insinuation that the witness had been pressurised to change her statement. To cover up the truth. Adrian couldn't worry about that. The evidence was enough for him to keep his job and that was what mattered right now.

At that moment Imogen walked in and sat at the desk. At least now he had something to talk to her about, something other than their kiss.

Adrian waited until he saw Gary approaching before he made his way back to the desk. He didn't have the courage to face her alone. As ever, Gary was holding a thick wad of paper. For someone so tech-savvy, Gary sure did like hard copies of everything.

'What have you been up to?' Adrian asked.

Imogen looked up, her face flushed. She obviously thought that Adrian was addressing her. He kept his focus on Gary.

'I've been looking into Caitlin. There are some strange things going on with her file,' Gary answered.

'Strange, how?' Adrian said.

'Technically speaking, she shouldn't even be on that course. She looks like a charity project.'

'What do you mean?' Imogen said.

'Her grades were nowhere near as great as the ones she should have achieved in order to get onto that psychology degree. I learned that she got a partial scholarship and that her entrance to the university was personally endorsed by her lecturer, Gillian Mitchell.'

'I've never been to university, so you'll have to explain that to me,' Adrian said.

'I'm saying that Gillian Mitchell wanted to make sure Caitlin Watts came to that university, and what's more, she wanted her in her department. The entry requirements for the psych degree are three As and Caitlin got B, C, C,' Gary clarified.

'Didn't Owen Sager's mother say something similar

happened with him and Hugh Norris?' Adrian turned to Imogen.

'She did. I think once we've got to the bottom of what is going on with Caitlin, then Gillian Mitchell should be the next person on our list to interview; she was quite evasive when we spoke to her at the university,' Imogen said.

'Do you think she is part of this?' Gary asked Imogen.

'I only wish I knew what *this* was,' Imogen said.

Chapter Fourteen

Gillian Mitchell had agreed to be present at her student Caitlin Watts' police interview. Caitlin was a first-year student of hers. The only family Caitlin had was her grandfather, the Reverend Nigel Watts. Her parents were still alive but no longer a part of her family and, for obvious reasons, she didn't want her grandfather to have to listen to her witness statement of a violent sexual attack. Gillian made herself look presentable but nothing too overstated. She opted for a matt lipstick instead of her usual metallic shade; she wanted to look respectful, sombre.

Gillian had noticed Caitlin's potential from the first day of the course. Some kids just got it. Having an unconventional and somewhat traumatic background usually went some way towards an understanding of psychology. If you have had to spend your life adjusting to your own world versus the world around you, or what you perceive to be normal, then you just see things differently. Over the years, Gillian had noticed that it was usually the kids from atypical backgrounds who took an interest in psychology anyway. Caitlin was different from the other girls in the year, though. First of all, she had this magnetic power over men – completely unintentional, but it made Gillian almost glad she wasn't a straight man; she would hate to be a slave to sexual attraction.

There was some jealousy there, of course. Gillian had got better looking with age and she knew how to do her hair and make-up in the most flattering ways, but she was no natural beauty. She had small hazel eyes and thin eyelashes, and her nose was slightly off-centre, thanks to a hockey accident when she herself was at university. Her lips were small and modest. She wouldn't say she was obsessed with her looks, but now that she was getting older, noticing the crow's feet, she had considered a face lift or Botox or something to slow down the ageing process. This was her time.

The interview was early morning; Gillian had asked the police officer if he wouldn't mind doing it that way because she would find it hard to get cover for her first lesson. Caitlin agreed and so it was set. Caitlin had already had a preliminary interview, where she outlined the basics of the attack and labelled her accuser. They had tried to interview her again but couldn't get much out of her, so they asked for her to have someone she knew and trusted present. Naturally, she asked for Gillian. They had grown close over the last few weeks.

Gillian now settled in her seat next to Caitlin, whose

face was multicoloured with bruising, reminiscent of the greasy rainbows you would see in oil-slicked puddles, circles of colour radiating out from her eyes. Gillian tried not to be pleased that Caitlin's pretty face had taken a beating. She had never really liked beautiful girls; it was jealousy, pure and simple. Although she had finally figured out her own look and how to turn heads, albeit significantly fewer than someone as beautiful as Caitlin would, she'd realised long ago how much easier life was for attractive people and that made her mad.

'Tell us in your own words what happened,' DI Walsh said, his notebook out.

'I asked for a lift home, from anyone at the station. He offered to take me himself.' Caitlin's face screwed up as she tried to swallow. The doctor was poised to stop the interview if Caitlin appeared to be in too much pain.

'Do you want some water?' Gillian asked, squeezing Caitlin's hand a little harder than necessary. She really needed Caitlin to sell this.

'We got home and he walked me inside. I made us a drink in the kitchen, and he pushed me up against the units and kissed me. I was nice, but I asked him to leave. He grabbed me by the hair and hit my head against the cupboard.' She reached up and touched a gash in her forehead.

Caitlin started to cry and looked at Gillian. Gillian could see what she wanted, she wanted Gillian to stop this so that she didn't have to say the next few words. Gillian dug her nails in as she squeezed Caitlin's hand this time. The tears poured out of her and Gillian pulled her hand away.

'If this is too much . . .' Doctor Hadley said.

'No, it's OK. He hit me and told me that he could do what he wanted because he was a police officer. He pushed me over the table and pulled my pants and tights down. Then he raped me.'

'After he attacked you, what happened?'

'He had his drink and I didn't do anything, I just waited for him to leave. I was too scared to say anything. Then he raped me again. He was there for a while. He already knew my grandfather wasn't coming back that evening, so I guess he was in no hurry. He really hurt me.'

Gillian was pleased with Caitlin's performance. She was really selling it. She just hoped the men in the room were so blinded by their own hero complexes that they wouldn't question her too much. She didn't like the way DI Matt Walsh was looking at Caitlin though. She would have to keep an eye on him; they could deal with him later.

Gillian made all the right noises when Caitlin was explaining the horrific ordeal that she had been through and the DI made a face every so often in Gillian's direction. He was trying to convey how sorry he was, how awful what had happened to Caitlin was, how not all men were rapists. Caitlin kept looking to Gillian for comfort, for a clue of what to say, for a way out. Occasionally Gillian squeezed Caitlin's hand in support, occasionally she squeezed it because Caitlin was pissing her off, and in those instances she made sure she squeezed it hard enough to hurt. Gillian always picked the pretty girls. They needed to be taken down a peg or two.

When the interview was over, Gillian played the distraught and concerned friend, enough for the uniformed police officer to put his arm around her; she could feel his biceps through his shirt. In a couple of weeks maybe, she would seek him out again for comfort. He wasn't wearing a wedding ring and so when she did offer him no-strings sex, he would probably jump at the opportunity. Most men did. She would use him for a couple of weeks and then finally get rid of him when he started to notice her lack of feeling, lack of empathy for others. Gillian had left a string of meaningless relationships behind her and that was fine with her.

She walked back to the car and got in, throwing her bag on the back seat, pleased with how the interview went. When she arrived at the university, it was still in the process of waking up. She loved this time of day. The time before everything started; it was like the sucking in of breath before a large exhale. It was a time of possibility. The night was over and the new day could begin.

Gillian put her key in the door to her office, but it clicked open – it was already unlocked. She was sure she had locked it the night before. Since the murder of Hugh Norris everyone at the university was on high alert, everyone was paranoid, except for Gillian. She knew that bad things were just a fact of life. Hugh's office was directly underneath Gillian's. She hadn't heard or witnessed anything, though; she was elsewhere, she had made sure of it beforehand.

There was something wrong in her office; someone had been here, someone had been looking for something. She wondered if they had found what they were looking for and what that something was.

She couldn't quite understand why she was jumpy this morning. There was something in the air, a taste she wasn't used to, a feeling she hadn't felt for a long time: she was afraid. Not even the police presence had made her particularly nervous, so what was she sensing now? Whatever it was, it was making the hairs on the back of her neck stand on end. There was someone else in the room.

'I know what you did.' The man's voice came from behind her. 'Don't turn around.'

'I don't know what you're talking about. This is ridiculous. Get out of my office.'

'I know all of the things you did, Ms Mitchell. I've been watching you.'

'You should go before you get in trouble,' Gillian said.

She could hear his voice getting nearer until she could almost feel his breath disturbing her hair.

'With who? You? I'm out of your league.'

'You don't know what you're getting into!' she said. She had heard the voice recently, but for the life of her she couldn't place it. It wasn't someone she knew, but it was someone she had spoken to before.

'That's where you're wrong.'

A hand on her shoulder and a punching feeling in her back distracted her momentarily as the strange sensation passed through Gillian's stomach. She looked

94

down and saw the end of a fireside poker; the harpoon-like hook had gone right through her. Blood had started to trickle out. She felt the man behind her grip onto her shoulder and she knew what he was planning to do next. He pulled hard, the speared end of the poker taking parts of her with it. The blood started to glug from her wound, destroying her linen suit, a strange consideration for her to have given the circumstances. But then Gillian had never been quite right in the head. That's what had drawn her to study psychology in the first place – to learn why she was the way she was.

She fell to her knees, hands trying to clamp the gaping hole in her stomach shut. She was aware that it was just as bad at the back and that this was probably the end of her.

'Please . . .' she whimpered, unsure what she was pleading for. In a way, she was intrigued by the situation, which she knew wasn't the right way to feel.

'I can make this last more or less time. It's up to you.'

'All things considered, I think I would like it to be over.' She tried to play it cool, but the truth was, this hurt. She was done, this was the end of her fight, she had no reason to protect anyone else any more.

'Then you have to give me something and it will be over in seconds.'

'What is it you want?'

'A name.'

Chapter Fifteen

Imogen stared down at the body of Gillian Mitchell. She lay with a pattern akin to blood-red wings spread out from her neck and waist, almost like a butterfly. Her stomach was an unholy mess. The rest of the room was untouched; this scene looked nothing like the scene of Hugh Norris's murder. There was a calculated calm to it, a measured approach, confident. They would have to wait for the forensic evidence, but every part of Imogen knew that this was not the same killer. She was also completely convinced that this was no coincidence. Two killers? Both brutal, victims in the same building, the same department? What were the chances? What the hell was going on? She needed to find DCC Trevor Sneddon again and hurry him up. The sooner he wrapped up his investigation into the false rape allegation against her partner, the sooner things could return to normal. She needed Adrian.

'What caused those injuries?' she asked Karen Bell, the forensic tech standing next to her

'Whatever it was, it went straight through her. In and out. There was no way she would survive it,' Karen said.

'Then why cut her throat?'

'Well, maybe it was to shut her up, or even an act of mercy. It would take a bit longer to bleed out with that stomach wound.'

'Mercy? Why?'

'Don't ask me. That's your job.' Karen bent down onto the ground and continued placing markers.

She looked around as much as she could without disturbing the crime scene. DI Walsh was waiting outside on his mobile, talking to DCC Trevor Sneddon. Imogen folded her arms and waited patiently for his phone call to finish. She took the moment to really study Matt Walsh; with all that had been going on, she had forgotten about her initial curiosity. He had a lovely face really, not something she would normally think about someone, but there was something genuinely lovely about his features. He looked trustworthy. How does a person look trustworthy?

It was always hard getting used to a new team member, deciding whether to put your life in their hands. With everything she had been through in the past with former colleagues who'd stabbed her in the back – and sometimes even the front – trust did not come easy.

Matt hung up the phone and turned his attention to Imogen. 'Well, what do you make of that then? Have you ever seen anything like it? I was just talking to her this morning.'

Actually, Imogen thought, she had, and a lot worse besides. But she didn't want to disappoint him with her answer. For some bizarre reason, she wanted to please him. There was no rhyme or reason to it, other than the fact that she genuinely wanted to like Matt Walsh.

'No. It's pretty horrible.'

Matt Walsh's phone beeped and he looked at the screen. 'The DCI needs to see us, immediately.'

DCI Kapoor had three empty coffee mugs in front of her. She looked somewhat harassed and rubbed her eyes before letting out a big sigh. They were all acutely aware of how little headway they had made in the investigation and no one would be feeling more pressure than the DCI. Imogen was glad that the responsibility for this mess of a case wasn't falling to her.

DCI Kapoor turned to them. 'We don't seem to be getting any closer to any kind of motive for these crimes and they appear to be getting worse. What with the allegations against Adrian as well, the press are having an absolute field day.'

'As soon as we can figure out what the connection is, then we should make some headway. If only we could get Caitlin Watts to speak to us again,' Imogen said.

'That's why I called you in. The uniformed officer stationed with her at the hospital called and asked to speak to you.'

'What do you mean?' Imogen said, raising her eyebrow. After everything Caitlin had put Adrian through – not just Adrian but the entire station – Imogen thought if she had to sit in the same room as her she might lose it.

'Apparently, Caitlin has asked for you specifically, Imogen. After they asked her if she knew anything about this, about Gillian Mitchell.'

'What? Why would she ask for me?'

'Go and find out. See if you can push her on the exact nature of her relationship with Gillian Mitchell and anything else she might know about Doctor Norris' murder. It's worth ascertaining if the information she gave us before was even accurate – did he really have an affair with a student?'

'Has she given a statement to DCC Sneddon yet?' Matt asked.

'She wouldn't agree to do it until after she has spoken to Imogen. So you had both better get over there now.'

'Not just DS Grey?' DI Walsh said.

'I don't think I want any of my detectives alone with her, given what we know about her propensity for lying.'

'OK, Ma'am,' Imogen said; the investigation had to take precedent over her personal feelings. The truth would come out eventually, she knew that much, she just had to hope that Adrian's career wouldn't be over before it did.

DCI Kapoor nodded and they both stood up to leave. Imogen didn't particularly ever want to see Caitlin Watts again, but if it meant getting a statement that could exonerate Adrian faster then she would just have to suck it up.

Imogen noted that Caitlin's face looked a lot better than it had the last time she had seen her. The bruising was fading and coming out, and there was no more swelling. Even knowing that the girl had lied, Imogen felt pity towards her. Whatever part she was playing in this mess, she was not the mastermind. She was sat up in bed, watching the television, when Imogen and DI Walsh opened the door.

Caitlin looked instantly guilty as soon as she saw Imogen, and the tears started to flow. She picked up the TV remote and flicked off the telly. She scooched up a little in her bed, wincing and instinctively reaching for her side.

'Miss Watts, I hear you wanted to speak to us. Do you wish to change your statement from earlier?' DI Walsh said.

'Please don't be angry with me. I was only doing what I was told,' Caitlin said.

'What are you talking about?' asked Imogen.

'That day, when you came to the university and you asked questions about Doctor Norris. Gillian was really angry about that. And then when she saw that I knew you both, she told me that I had to do something for her. She said she needed some time and that I was to derail your investigation. She told me that I had to get DS Miles alone; she wanted me to sleep with him. After I had slept with him, she wanted me to claim that he had raped me.'

'Why would she do that?' DI Walsh said.

Caitlin just shook her head and looked down.

'Why didn't you have sex with him then? What went wrong with your plan?' Imogen asked, trying to ignore that part of her that didn't want to know the answer.

100

'I tried. I flirted with him. I was attracted to him and I thought he was attracted to me. But when I asked him inside for a drink, he said no; he didn't even hesitate. At that point I knew he wasn't gonna take the bait. He was just being nice, and I fucked him over,' Caitlin said, tears hovering at the corners of her eyes, the blue magnified under the glaze.

Imogen found those tears annoying; after what Caitlin had put Adrian through, she didn't have the right to be upset.

'Do you know what Gillian Mitchell's involvement was in Doctor Norris's murder?' DI Walsh asked.

'I can't talk to you about that. I shouldn't have even said this much. I just wanted to make sure that DS Miles wasn't still in trouble,' Caitlin said.

'What do you mean? Why shouldn't you have said this much? What aren't you telling us?' DI Walsh said.

'I'm already in deep shit for saying as much as I have. But, now that she's gone, I just had to tell you the truth about DS Miles. He never touched me. I'll tell whoever you want me to tell.'

'Has someone been putting pressure on you to change your statement? Has DS Miles contacted you or threatened you in any way?' DI Walsh said.

Imogen shot DI Walsh a look. She knew he was only doing his job, but she hated every part of this investigation. The questions needed to be asked and she was glad that she didn't have to do the asking. Just the thought of Adrian pressuring a vulnerable witness was making her angry on his behalf. It just wasn't in him.

'No, he hasn't done anything wrong. I was lying before. He never touched me, I swear,' Caitlin cried.

'Do you have any idea what you've done?' Imogen fumed. She was finally allowing some of her rage to surface. Now that DI Walsh had heard the statement she felt there was some room to express her anger.

'I know and I'm sorry. If there is any way I could take it back, then I would!'

'So, what did happen to you then? Who raped you?' DI Walsh asked.

'No one. I wasn't raped. I phoned Gillian as soon as Adrian turned me down. She said she would sort it, but I had to do something too.'

'What kind of something?' DI Walsh asked.

'I had to hurt myself . . . Down there. I had to make it look really bad.'

'How was she making you do that?' Imogen said. She was finding it hard to believe that anyone would tell someone else to do that, let alone a woman.

'She said if I didn't, then she would get someone else who would. She gets people to do things, that's what she does.'

'What about all your other injuries, they aren't self-inflicted, someone else did that. Who hurt you?' Imogen said.

'I'm sorry, I can't tell you. Please tell DS Miles how sorry I am.'

'I don't suppose he cares much how sorry you are. Do you have any idea the kind of damage you've caused? People like you disgust me. It's hard enough for women and men who have been sexually assaulted to come forward. To use that as some kind of power play, to get what you want, to hurt others? How can you live with yourself? Every time a person reports a rape, there are plenty of people who call them liars. Not to mention the fact that false claims are investigated with the same attention. Attention that could be used elsewhere. What you have just done has made it ten times harder for the next person who walks through the door and says that they were raped.'

Tears were streaming down Caitlin Watts' face now, but Imogen didn't really care. She could go on about this for hours.

'OK, DS Grey, you've made your point,' DI Walsh said. 'How did you find out Gillian had died?'

'I got a phone call, not long after you all left earlier. I didn't recognise the voice. It was a man. Maybe he was part of it. I don't know. But he told me I didn't need to be afraid any more, that Gillian was dead and that I could tell the truth about DS Miles now.'

'The person didn't identify themselves?' Matt Walsh asked.

'No, they just told me what I've told you,' Caitlin replied.

'You're going to have to make an official statement to the officer who is investigating DS Miles,' Imogen said, a little calmer now that she had said her piece.

'Of course, he was nice to me; he didn't deserve any of this. Usually if I make a pass at someone, they don't even think twice before accepting. It's kind of my superpower.' The words sounded like a guilty confession rather than a brag.

'Is that what happened with Doctor Norris? Were you the student he had an affair with?'

Tears started to form in Caitlin's eyes once more; she wiped her cheek with the back of her hand and exhaled deeply.

Before she could answer Imogen, the door opened and two men stepped inside – an older man in clerical dress and a younger man in a suit. He looked like a lawyer. Caitlin seemed to be relieved that they had turned up, stopping her from carrying on talking. She composed herself before speaking again.

'Am I in trouble?' Caitlin asked.

'Your grandfather has asked me to represent you, Miss Watts, and I'll have to advise you not to say anything else at this point. Not without going over it with me first.'

Imogen took one look at the girl and responded; she didn't want to leave her hanging. 'I suspect not. We tend not to pursue charges in cases of false rape claims. Right or wrong, it actually adds further damage to a situation that's already complicated enough. You may have to have some counselling or something. We will have to see what our DCI wants to do.'

'Thank you,' Caitlin said, looking up at Imogen.

'Don't you dare thank me,' Imogen said to Caitlin. As far as Imogen was concerned, she wanted nothing more to do with Caitlin, bar exonerating Adrian, and she certainly didn't want her gratitude for not smacking her one. Imogen turned to DI Walsh. 'I'll be outside.'

She left the room, wishing, not for the first time in recent days, that she hadn't given up smoking. She would have to go outside and stand among the other habitual users and see if second-hand smoke made her feel any better. She hoped Caitlin's statement would be enough to exonerate Adrian as quickly as it had implicated him. She hoped everyone in the station knew that Caitlin had lied about her partner. Imogen couldn't imagine how horrible it must have been to be accused of that crime, to know that at least some of your friends thought there was a possibility that you did something as inhuman as that.

Chapter Sixteen

Adrian and Imogen were in the incident room, with pictures spread out over the walls and tables. They had photos from the Norris murder, the Mitchell murder and some of the images of the attack on Caitlin Watts. Adrian seemed to be fixating on the images of Caitlin's bruised and battered body.

'Snap out of it, Miley.'

'People looked at these photos and thought that I did this, Imogen. People I work with.'

'No one who mattered thought you did that.'

'Tell that to Professional Standards,' Adrian said.

'That's their job. The DCI has spoken to DCC Sneddon and he has taken a statement from Caitlin, so all charges against you have been dropped. Once the hospital gives Caitlin the all-clear they are going to videotape her testimony and that will be that.'

'What are the hospital doing?' Adrian said.

'Her legal counsel wanted her to get a psychiatric

evaluation before anyone else spoke to her; she only agreed to have one done if they let her speak to me first.'

'What the hell was Gillian Mitchell playing at? Why would she tell Caitlin to do that to herself? That's one of the most fucked-up things I have ever heard of and whoever went to town on her face wasn't playing. She could have been killed,' Adrian said.

'You obviously made quite an impression on someone. They really wanted to take you down.' Imogen tried to lighten the mood.

'Don't even joke about it.'

'Do you think that's why Gillian Mitchell was killed? Because of what happened with Caitlin?' Imogen said. This was obviously much bigger than they could wrap their heads around. 'Maybe it was revenge or retaliation.'

'There's no way it's not connected, but who would do that for her? How does this tie in with Norris? Look how different the murders are. Mitchell's is so clean and calculated, almost artistic, like something from a film. It just feels so—'

'Familiar?' Imogen finished the sentence; she knew what he meant.

As if by magic, Gary entered the room with another stack of paperwork under his arm. He had that look on his face – the excited look that was going to blow their minds. He was about to show them something that would either open this case up or make everything a shitload more complicated. DCI Kapoor followed behind him; he had obviously called her to join them.

'Tell me things,' DCI Kapoor said to Adrian.

'OK, so we have the bodies of the two professors, neither of whom seem to have been killed by the same person. One scene is frenzied, one is a lot more controlled. According to forensics, it's possible this second murder, Gillian Mitchell, was committed by someone who had previous experience. Or maybe it was just far more premeditated and the Norris murder was a spontaneous decision. It's not confirmed that its two different people,' Adrian said.

'Thank you, Adrian, it's good to have you back,' DCI Kapoor said. 'You did everything PSD asked of you and you have been cleared, but still, we have to tread carefully as far as your involvement with this case goes. Please don't give me a reason to take you off the case.'

'We still don't know how Caitlin Watts fits into all of this,' Imogen said. 'She said the professor told her that she had to falsely accuse Adrian to derail the investigation into Hugh Norris's death. So, all three people are definitely connected, we just don't know how.'

'OK, so I have news,' Gary said, beaming.

'What's your news, Gary?' DCI Kapoor said.

'Well, these aren't the only two professors who have died recently.'

'What? No one mentioned another professor dying when we were up at the uni,' Imogen said.

'That's because it didn't happen there.'

'Where did it happen?' DCI Kapoor asked.

'Bristol.'

'How did the victim die?' Imogen asked.

'Violently. It wasn't in the news because of all the batshit North Korean stuff dominating the agenda at the time. I like to read all the local stuff and so I tried to remember where I had seen something about a uni professor dying.'

'Professor of what?'

'Genetics.'

'Right. That's not a humanities subject, is it?' Imogen said.

'No, you are correct. It's not. But the genetics professor at Exeter, Helen Lassiter, takes some of the humanities classes as she is mega-qualified in, like, everything.'

'Was she one of the professors you spoke to about Norris's murder?' DCI Kapoor asked Adrian.

'She's away currently,' Adrian said. 'They said she would be back by the end of the week.'

DCI Kapoor turned to Gary. 'So, tell us about this other professor, the one that was murdered in Bristol.'

'His name was Professor Robert Coley.'

'Coley? Like the fish?' Adrian said.

'That's right and get this . . . he was filleted,' Gary said.

'What do you mean?' Imogen said.

'His spine was taken out.'

'Say what now?' Adrian said.

'His spine was removed.' Gary nodded with his eyebrows as far up into his hairline as they would go.

'Removed?' Imogen asked, unsure what that meant, even though Gary wasn't exactly mincing his words.

'A precision affair, too. No messing around. I spoke to the coroner briefly and she's sending over the full report. She spoke to our own coroner and they compared notes. The long and short of it is, we think there's a connection.'

'Do we think the same person killed Hugh Norris?' Imogen said.

'Maybe, maybe not. There could be various reasons why his crime scene was so different.'

'What do we know about Hugh Norris?' DCI Kapoor said.

'We know one of his students committed suicide a few months back. Owen Sager,' Imogen said. The more she tried to connect the dots, the further apart they seemed to get.

'Was that a genuine suicide, do you think?' Gary asked excitedly.

'I guess there's only one way to find out.' DCI Kapoor stood up gathered her papers. 'I'll order an exhumation and you see if you can find a way to connect all of these dots together. Someone knows something. Re-interview people and I will get on to Bristol and see what their DCI has to say about their murder. Great work, guys.'

DCI Kapoor left the room.

'Are those photos of the spineless professor?' Adrian held his hand out towards Gary.

Gary handed them over. Imogen peered over Adrian's shoulder as he looked through the pictures.

'What the hell is wrong with people?' Imogen said; it seemed to be becoming her mantra.

'So, what do we do now?' Adrian said.

'We keep trying to connect these things together. It just can't be a coincidence. Maybe if we interview that genetics professor when she gets back we can get ahead of this thing. Are we looking for two killers, one methodical and one inexperienced? Are they a team? Or just someone who is all over the place?' Imogen said.

'I think we are looking at maybe a team or a copycat, God knows. Maybe it's one person with an MO we haven't figured out yet. I'm so fucking confused,' Adrian said.

'You can say that again. All we do know is that this all centres around the university.'

'What do you need me to do?' Gary asked.

'Gary, you are always ten steps ahead of everyone, just do what you do.' Imogen smiled; aside from Adrian, Gary was the only person she could absolutely rely on.

She was grateful that things between her and Adrian had resumed their normal level of discomfort. Adrian had managed to file the kiss between them as irrelevant; he barely even flinched when he saw her, and she had been expecting some extreme awkwardness. The last thing she needed was for this to become a problem. She was still adjusting to being alone, still adjusting to losing her mother. She really didn't need any other complications.

Chapter Seventeen

The pathologist stood by the body of Owen Sager; it had completely broken down already and Adrian couldn't see how they would be able to get any useful information from this. Bits of him were in bowls and the smell was incredible. Three months might have been the worst time to exhume a body, it certainly smelled like it. Adrian resisted the urge to throw up, but he decided when he was done here he would phone up and cancel dinner with his family.

'The body of Owen Sager,' the pathologist said. 'On further examination, it seems unlikely this was a suicide.'

'What makes you say that?' Adrian asked.

'In suicidal hanging there is scarcely ever any internal evidence of neck injury at all. Suicidal hanging is usually pretty gentle as the person is compliant with their own death. Apparently, it's painless and can practically be done lying down,' the pathologist explained.

'But that's not the case with Owen Sager?' Imogen

said, her voice cracking a little as she tried not to inhale any more than necessary. At least Adrian wasn't the only one struggling in here.

'His hyoid and his mandible were fractured. This suggests someone else was involved. The hyoid is well protected in the neck. It takes an amount of force to break it.'

'Was there an autopsy of this kid before?' Adrian said.

'No. The investigators at the time were confident it was suicide.'

'His mother didn't seem to think he was suicidal,' Imogen said.

'There is some clear evidence of historical abuse and self-harm on his body. It's also quite well documented in his medical files. He had spoken to his GP about depression only a week before. It's entirely possible they looked at that and decided the kid just wanted a way out, didn't want to put the mother through any more trauma.'

'OK, thanks. Let us know if you find anything else unusual,' Adrian said, eager to get out of there. He still hated being around dead bodies.

Adrian and Imogen left the pathologist's office and went to grab a coffee. Adrian hadn't been round to Imogen's house since she had turned up at his and they had kissed. He felt quite lucky that he was able to compartmentalise and push his feelings to one side for the time being.

'So, we've gone from two murders to four murders, probably connected but not the same killer,' Imogen said.

'Who do you think killed Owen Sager?'

'I don't know. Maybe someone else entirely. The other three murders are nowhere near as ambiguous.'

'So, we have four murders and two or three murderers. Seems unlikely,' Adrian said.

'I think we need to speak to that genetics lecturer at the university. She was due back in today, wasn't she? Maybe she can shed some light on all of this.'

'Let's swing by there now then,' Adrian said.

Imogen put the car into gear and they pulled away. Adrian liked to watch Imogen drive – she got a look of intense concentration mixed with complete control, it was a little mesmerising.

'How are you?' he asked.

'Excuse me?'

'You haven't really spoken to me about your mother,' Adrian said, noting her back straighten slightly at the mention of Irene Grey.

'You've never really spoken to me about yours,' she threw back, jarring him a little, too.

'Mine didn't just die.'

'There's nothing to talk about really. I don't have anything to say. If I do, I promise I will talk to you about it.'

'Well, I might understand is all.'

'Thank you. In all honesty, Adrian, I don't think it's sunk in yet. Part of me feels like she is still on holiday with Elias and that she will be back soon.'

'Grief can be a bit like that, 'til it smacks you in the face every now and again to remind you what you've lost.'

'Do you still think about your mother?'

'Of course I do. I kind of hope she found some peace.'

'We've spoken about your dad loads, but you've never told me much about her.'

'Well, maybe one day I will, but not today. Nice diversion though, making this about me,' Adrian said, his tone a little sharper than he had anticipated. She had hit a nerve he forgot he had.

They pulled into the uni car park near the humanities block and Imogen cranked the handbrake loudly. Adrian got out and walked ahead. When he got inside there was no one at the reception. He dinged on the bell repeatedly until an exasperated old man appeared from a back office.

'Can I help you?'

He pulled out his warrant card and showed it to the woman. 'I am DS Miles and this is DS Grey. We want to speak to Helen Lassiter. She was due back today.'

'She was, yes, but she didn't turn up for work this morning. I have been trying to get hold of her. I was about to send someone over there to see if she was all right.'

'No need, we'll find out for you. What's her address?' Adrian said.

The old man scribbled an address down on a piece of paper and slid it under the glass.

'And what's your name?' Imogen asked, flipping open her notepad ready to write it down.

'I'm Doctor Marcus Pike, one of the ethics professors here at the university.'

'OK. We'll be in touch.'

* * *

Outside, Helen Lassiter's house was quiet. Her car was parked in the driveway, but there were no signs of anyone being inside. Adrian and Imogen walked to the side of the house and looked through the window. There was a dirty coffee mug on the side near the sink – but no Helen Lassiter. Adrian noticed some of the drawers were open in the kitchen, which was odd. People didn't generally leave several drawers open at a time in their own house. He glanced at the back door; the glass was smashed.

'Call it in. I think someone's broken in.'

He found the back door and opened it. Adrian hated walking into properties like this. You never knew what you were going to find and on occasion he had seen things that he wished he could forget, but the memory of them was almost tangible, so horrific that his mind had remembered every detail right down to the taste in his mouth at the time.

He made it up the stairs; the house was silent, too silent. Adrian knew that he was going to find the professor dead before he even entered the bedroom. It was no surprise to him when he saw her lying on the bed, eyes closed. What was surprising though, was her skin. It was a bright cherry red.

Chapter Eighteen

Adrian had just come back in after a smoke when Denise came bounding over. Apparently, Helen Lassiter had died of carbon monoxide poisoning, which is why her body was that colour, diagnosed at the scene, unmistakeable apparently. It wasn't something Adrian had ever seen before, but it wasn't something he would forget in a hurry.

'There's someone here waiting to speak to you.'

'Who?'

'She wouldn't tell me who she was but refused to speak to anyone else. Asked for you by name.'

'What was it about? Did she say?'

'Her husband has gone missing.'

Adrian was far too preoccupied to deal with this at the moment, but the fact that the woman had asked for him by name made him feel like he had to. Even if he just had a quick conversation with her now, he could deal with her case later on, maybe much later on.

'And she didn't say how she knows me?'

'No, but she was adamant that you were the only one she would talk to. I put her in liaison room two.'

'Cheers.'

He rubbed his head. He hated missing persons cases and in the case of marriages it was more often about making a clean break than anything else. He grabbed his notebook and walked over to liaison room two, wondering where Imogen was. He looked around, but she was conspicuously absent.

As he approached the liaison room, he caught a glimpse of the woman through the glass. She was heavily pregnant. He stepped inside. She had long black hair tied in a side ponytail and red lipstick that looked out of place on her pale olive skin. There was something a bit fragile about her, the curve of her shoulders maybe. She stood up when she saw him, recognition on her face. His was not a name she had picked out of a hat. He didn't recognise her at all.

'I'm DS Miles, I believe you wanted to speak to me?'

'Yes, thank you for seeing me.' He noticed she didn't say her name.

'What's your name and how can I help you?'

'My husband is missing.'

'How long has he been gone?'

'A few weeks now.'

'What makes you think he is missing? Is it possible he's just . . . taken some time out?'

'No, that's not possible. He's not like that,' she said emphatically, brows furrowed in concern.

He had seen things like this before though, especially

when a pregnancy was involved. Husband decides family life isn't for him and takes off.

'So, what do you think has happened?' he asked.

'Something terrible.'

'Do you think he is in danger?'

'Not him, no. Not exactly.'

She reached down for her bag, which was on the floor by her feet. She pulled out an envelope and started to thumb at the edges nervously. Adrian saw something then, a flash of something familiar on her face, her dark brown eyes, so lost and vulnerable. He had met this woman before, but where did he know her from? *Ask her for a name.*

'What is that?'

'I found it on my doorstep this morning. This is his writing. He obviously wanted me to deliver it to you.'

'Can I see it?'

'Can I trust you?'

'Why did you come to me if you can't trust me?'

'He said I would be able to, he seemed to think you would know what to do if he went missing.'

That was a strange thing to say. Her husband had told her what to do if he disappeared? That changed everything. Why was her husband expecting to go missing? *Ask for a name.*

Adrian watched her for a moment, trying to remember her. His long-term memory for faces was exceptionally bad. She was different though. Her hair hadn't been black before, and it hadn't been long like this; he saw shoulder-length hair in his mind, a mousy brown. A mousy girl. His skin recognised her before his mind had caught up, his hairs standing up on end and a creeping chill up his spine. *A name.*

'Can you tell me your husband's name?' He held out his hand, ready to accept the envelope from her. His name was written on the front. Some of the questions he had had about this case had suddenly been answered. Her face changed too, knowing now that he had recognised her. The air got thicker as she lifted the envelope and placed it in his hand.

'It's Parker.'

Part Two

Chapter Nineteen

Adrian's hands stuck to the paper as he read through the short note inside the envelope. He was sweating. He had always suspected he might hear from Parker again, but had hoped he wouldn't. Although in truth Adrian couldn't help but admire the man a little, despite the fact that Parker was an undocumented serial killer. Some of the most horrific crime scenes Adrian had ever been to were the result of Parker's handiwork.

Adrian realised now where he knew the girl in front of him from: she was Abbey Lucas, and they had met a couple of years ago when she handed him a photo album that documented the systematic and relentless abuse Parker had endured as a child. It had reports and images of torture inflicted on Parker that included electrocution, suspension, cutting, branding and much more. After looking through it, neither Imogen nor Adrian could pass judgement on the man he had become. When faced with the opportunity to arrest Parker, Adrian just couldn't do it. He let him go. Parker was crafted into a killer; he wasn't born one.

They deserved it. Three down, one to go.
P.

Adrian wasn't sure what he was supposed to do with this information. If he handed it in, there would be a lot of questions. Questions whose answers would get both Adrian and Imogen fired. The murders that Parker had committed the first time they encountered him were attributed to a couple of different people and so no one was particularly looking for Parker, but that wasn't to say that the scrutiny of DCI Kapoor might not blow the case wide open again.

'And you can't get in contact with him?' Adrian said to Parker's wife.

'No. He knows how to disappear.'

'Fair enough. Did you know about this?'

'I figured it out, when I heard about the first murder I knew that it was him. I didn't want to believe it.'

'Where have you been since I saw you in the museum two years ago?'

'We moved to Bristol.'

The pieces started to fall into place. The spineless man. 'Of course you did. Professor Coley?'

'I went back to university. I used to go to Exeter, but I left several years ago, for one reason or another, I never finished my course. I started working in the museum, where I met Parker . . .'

'Did you know what Parker was when you met him?'

'I knew he was special.'

'That's one word for it.'

'You saw what they did to him. The fact that he even survived is a miracle. Those men he killed tortured him physically and mentally. Can you honestly tell me that you would have turned out any different?'

'You haven't seen the bodies he left behind. I did, and they still haunt me,' Adrian said. He should have put Parker away but he just couldn't. Parker had saved Imogen, saved his son, Tom. Adrian owed him.

'You know, sometimes, when he thinks I'm not looking, I see him cry. He tried to hide it from me because he doesn't want me to worry, but I do worry about him.'

'If anyone can look after themselves, it's him,' Adrian said.

'The people who hurt him made him that way. They burned him, cut him, electrocuted him and so many more things. How can anyone be right after going through that?'

Adrian didn't want to admit she was right, so he changed the subject instead. His empathy for Parker had got him into trouble before. 'So, you went back to university, in Bristol?'

'That's right. I went to study to become a vet.'

'Was Robert Coley one of your teachers?'

'He was, he taught genetics.'

'When you were at Exeter, was Helen Lassiter your genetics teacher?'

'Yes.' She looked confused. 'Why?'

'We found her body this morning. She died of carbon monoxide poisoning.'

125

'Did she die naturally? I mean, do you think it was murder?'

'Any idea why he would target the genetics teachers?' Adrian said, ignoring her question.

'They must have been bad. Parker isn't a bad person, he doesn't just kill people.'

'He does just kill people,' Adrian corrected her.

'You know what I mean.'

The scary thing was Adrian did know what she meant.

'You can't just take the law into your own hands like that. If everyone did that then everything would fall apart. Who gets to decide who deserves to die and who doesn't?'

'Everything is already falling apart, we just choose not to see it. Bad people get away with terrible things every single day.'

Abbey started to shift nervously in her seat. Considering how sweet she was, he found it hard to believe that she was OK with the things that Parker was doing and yet she seemed to believe it was completely justified. Was it just a case of love being blind? He didn't think so.

'What about Gillian Mitchell, have you ever heard that name before?'

'No, I'm sorry, I haven't.'

Adrian thought for a second; what the hell should he do? What could he do?

'I'm going to have to tell my boss about this.'

'How? You'll get in trouble if you admit what you did. Won't you?'

She had a point. They had captured Parker before, but when Abbey had shown Adrian evidence of Parker's abuse, it had made him question whether Parker deserved to be punished any more than he already had been. Adrian decided he had suffered enough. Adrian was a hypocrite; he had taken the law into his own hands and now Parker was free to commit more sadistic acts. No judge. No jury. He needed to speak to Imogen.

'I'll at least have to tell my colleague about it. I can't just let him go around killing people – we need to find out why. If this is all retribution for something else, something bigger, we need to know.'

'If I knew I would tell you. He must have found something out about Professor Coley.'

'You didn't notice your professor doing anything strange that might warrant him becoming a target?'

'He was a strange man, he seemed to favour me in class. A few weeks in, he started to become overfamiliar with me. He didn't know I was married and I wasn't showing then.' She gestured to her stomach. 'People have a tendency to underestimate me.' She said the last part rather ominously.

'Do you think he was interested in you . . . sexually?'

'No, that wasn't it. I felt like I was being groomed for something, I'm not sure what. Coley made me very uncomfortable though and I have learned to trust my instincts about people. I mentioned it to Parker and I think he did some background checking.'

'And then killed him. What did he find?'

'I didn't see him after that; he left me a note telling me not to worry. Then a few weeks later I found this note for you posted through my door.'

'So, you've had no contact with him since it started?'

'No. But I am scared. I don't want him to go to prison. He doesn't deserve it.'

'That's debateable.' Adrian tried to ignore the rising panic inside him. Was there any way out of this? What concerned him the most was that Imogen would get in trouble too, never mind himself. It was never as simple as just making that one decision to break the law, it was all the lies that came after, all the other decisions that just pushed you further and further into a corner.

'Whatever is going on, they must have done something to deserve it,' Abbey pressed.

'That's not really up to him.'

'I'll make him promise never to hurt anyone again. I can't do this alone,' she said, immediately holding onto her pregnant stomach.

'When are you due?'

'Seven weeks.'

'Look, I won't do anything just yet. I'll have to speak to my partner first. How do I get in touch with you?'

'I'll contact you with a number you can reach me on.'

Adrian stood up and opened the door, adrenaline coursing through him. There was no time to spare. Yet again he was watching this woman walk away, knowing she had answers but feeling powerless to stop her. It was almost the same as the last time he had met her. She had provided him with information back then that blew his case wide open. Photographs of historic abuse against her husband and the motive for his crimes. Now that Adrian knew Parker was involved, the case filled him with a strong feeling of dread. God only knew what horrors they would see before it was over.

He followed her to the exit and watched her walk out of the station and across the forecourt until she disappeared out of view. The further away she got, the harder his heart beat until he could hear it echoing in his ears.

'You all right, Miley? You look like you've seen a ghost.' Imogen was standing behind him eating a bar of chocolate from the vending machine in the corridor.

He grabbed her by the arm and pulled her back to the room where he had been talking to Abbey.

'You're hurting my arm, what's going on? Who was that?'

Adrian felt winded – the full repercussions of what he had done just over a year ago were coming back to bite him in the backside after all. He tried to speak, but he couldn't think of how to tell Imogen what was going on. This was massive, and somehow, he felt paranoid even trying to explain it in the station.

'That was her,' he finally said. He was breathless. Was this what a panic attack felt like?

'I'm going to need more than that.' Imogen seemed both annoyed and concerned at the same time.

'Her. From the museum.'

'Again, no idea what you're talking about.'

'That was *the* girl from *the* museum. Abbey Lucas, the one I spoke to that time . . . It's him, he's back.'

'What do you mean he's back?' Imogen said, although Adrian could tell she was starting to understand.

'Parker,' Adrian whispered. 'It's him, he's been doing this.'

She had finally got it.

'How? Why?'

'It seems he killed Robert Coley and I would guess Gillian Mitchell. They both match his MO. It also explains why those crime scenes felt so familiar. I don't know about the others.' Adrian handed Imogen the note.

She looked at it and sighed a deep and heavy sigh.

'What are we going to do? How the hell do we explain this to the DCI?' she whispered.

'I'm not sure we can explain it without losing our jobs.'

'Don't say that.' Imogen blew her cheeks out.

'If it comes to that, you need to let me take the heat,' Adrian said. 'I should have brought him in and I didn't. I won't let you get in the shit because of a decision I made.'

'I'm not agreeing to that right now. I would have made the same decision if it was mine to make, he saved my life. Let's think.'

'There is one good thing, I suppose.'

'What's that?'

'We know Parker is involved, now we just have to figure out why. If we can figure out his motivation, then the case should open up.'

'Then I guess we need to find out more about Robert Coley. He must have been up to something. Parker didn't pick these people at random, did he? There is a reason, we just need to find out what it is.'

Chapter Twenty

Imogen and Adrian huddled together over Imogen's desk. She had been feeling sick since she had heard that the most violent and undocumented serial killer they had met was killing again. Although thinking about it now, she wasn't sure what she had expected him to do with the rest of his life. She had hoped he would finally find some peace. Can you really go on to live in a normal way after you have exsanguinated and dismembered someone? Obviously not.

Now that they knew, it seemed so obvious. The parallels between Robert Coley and Gillian Mitchell's crime scenes were there. Parker's style was very much all over it, a mixture of primal rage and precision. He had confessed in the note to killing three people. In terms of timing, it seemed likely that it was Helen Lassiter who was the third victim. Although they still had no way to connect her to whatever the motive was, she was connected to Parker's wife Abbey Lucas. Carbon monoxide poisoning was more subdued than his normal blood driven murders, though. One to go? Why was he targeting four people specifically? How were those four people connected?

'Are there no clues on who the fourth victim could be?' Imogen said.

'It's got to be someone at Exeter; if it was Bristol then he would have stayed there and dealt with it. It seems likely that it would be another professor.'

'Are you sure Abbey wasn't lying about having no contact with him?'

'She didn't have to come forward at all. She's just trying to protect him, I think. Just like last time.'

'And she had no idea why he's doing it?' Imogen said.

'She said Robert Coley took a special interest in her. A bit like Gillian Mitchell took a special interest in Caitlin Watts,' Adrian said. 'I think we need to speak to Caitlin again. Well, someone does.'

'We might struggle to see her right now since the grandfather got a lawyer. He said she's not fit for medical reasons; her therapist has also said that any conversations about the case right now would be damaging for her mental state. The DCI is pushing to get her statement recorded,' Imogen explained.

'Covering their backs?' Adrian said.

'She was never going to get charged with a false report. She recanted really quickly, before you even got charged. Usually there is only a prosecution of the complainant if the accused has done jail time. Even then there have been less than a hundred and fifty women prosecuted for false claims in the last five years out of over five thousand reported rapes, and at least half of those hundred and fifty getting a conviction, that's still pretty low,' Imogen said.

'I know. It's frustrating, because I don't want her to be prosecuted, but I can't help feeling a little angry about it,' Adrian admitted.

'Of course you're angry about it. Are you OK now, though? Relieved that it's over?'

'Yes, of course, but we both know shit sticks and people are still going to think some kind of deal was made to make her retract her statement, unless we can figure out why she did it. It's going to be following me around for a while.'

'I'll see if I can get in an interview with her. All we can do is put in a request. I'll take DI Walsh with me. I don't think taking you would be a good idea,' Imogen said.

'Agreed.'

Imogen hated this. Everything inside her had always conditioned her to believe the victim first and then move on from there, but she had never believed Caitlin. That's not to say Caitlin might not have been telling the truth, just that she was so sure that she knew Adrian, beyond a shadow of a doubt. She knew that he wasn't guilty of rape. They had seen it time and time again though, a woman absolutely adamant that her husband wasn't a pervert only to then be shown a snapshot of his hard drive containing thousands of depictions of child abuse. Or the woman with the nice new husband she loves and trusts beyond reason, enough to leave her teenage daughter alone with him for long enough for

133

him to groom and exploit her. Those women had been wrong, but they had been so sure, as sure as Imogen was about Adrian. She wondered if she'd have accepted a guilty verdict for Adrian. Would she have insisted it was a frame job? These things scared her, new situations and her reactions to them. When Imogen's knowledge of herself was put to the test. When she didn't behave in the same way she would theoretically assume she might behave. Not knowing yourself was quite terrifying at times.

She watched Adrian study the pictures for hints and clues. She had to admire his resilience. You could tell the people who had written him off as guilty because they had a sheepish look on their faces around him. There were others who clearly didn't believe he would be accused without some possibility of truth behind the accusations.

'You go home if you want, Grey, I'll speak to the DCI, I've got a few things to do here.'

'You sure?' she asked, but the truth was she was happy to go; she was so tired. She hadn't slept since this case had started; somehow the news that Parker was back had made her feel a little safer, which was admittedly an odd thing to feel about the presence of a serial killer. Sometimes when she was half asleep she could hear him whispering into her ear, telling her everything was going to be all right, half memory, half imagination. A remnant of the last time she was with Parker as he held her hand, comforting her, making sure she was OK as they waited for an ambulance after a bullet had ripped through her. Knowing that they had at least some answers also took the heat off, even though Parker being linked to this case could complicate things dramatically. If anyone found out they knew he had killed people and let him go, they would have bigger problems than a disciplinary hearing.

Chapter Twenty-One

Six months earlier

Abbey sat eating her sandwich on one of the marble benches opposite the fountain near the statue of Cary Grant by the harbourside area in Bristol, posed to look as though he was walking through the square. She watched a little girl as she splashed in the fountain, up to her ankles in the water. Her father sat nearby on a bench, looking at his phone, occasionally mumbling encouragement at his daughter. Abbey remembered days with her father in the park, no mobile phone to distract him, his attention on her, making sure she had fun. With no mother to look after her, she had always been very close to her father, until she wasn't. She hadn't seen him in over a year now, and that wasn't even unusual any more. They had lost each other, and they couldn't find a way back after everything that had happened, after everything they had done. She couldn't forgive him for the actions he had taken after she had left university and he struggled with who she became after she was sexually assaulted.

It was a warm day in late September and people were still desperately clinging to the last trails of summer. Abbey had her university books next to her. She heard a loud scream as the little girl fell face first into the water. The girl's father came rushing over and pulled her out. As her little legs left the water, they started to bleed in little starbursts. She had fallen in some broken glass. The square was surrounded by pubs and someone must have tossed a bottle into the fountain. Panicked, her father dumped her in the pushchair and rushed away, presumably to get her to a doctor. Silence descended on the square again and Abbey was pulled from thoughts of her broken relationship with her father.

'Miss Lucas?'

Abbey turned around and saw her genetics professor, Robert Coley, holding a cup of coffee. He sat on the bench next to her. This wasn't the first time she had bumped into him outside of class; she was starting to think maybe it wasn't an accident.

'Professor Coley,' Abbey said, unsure why he was sitting with her.

'Lovely day, isn't it?'

'Yes, very warm for September.' Abbey wasn't an approachable person, which made her immediately suspicious of people who were nice to her. In her experience, those people always wanted something.

Robert Coley was an older man, in his sixties, with

tufts of white hair above his ears and a smooth rounded head. He had a dark grey moustache and brown eyes. He was clean and smart, and he did seem friendly, but she had met friendly people before whose kind faces had turned out to be nothing more than masks.

'How are you enjoying the course so far?' he asked.

'It's good.'

'You seem to have a knack for it.' He sipped on his coffee; his smile seemed disingenuous.

'Thank you,' she said. She didn't want to tell him that she had studie the module before when she went to university the first time in Exeter, she didn't care if he knew she had an advantage, but she didn't want the questions about why she'd left. She had put that part of her life behind her. She had come here for a fresh start. A new life.

'I'm going to be starting a study group after Christmas for my most promising students and I wondered if you might like to be involved?'

'I'll have to see if I have time,' she said, aware this was an opportunity she shouldn't dismiss out of hand purely because of her trust issues. 'I have some evening commitments.'

'You're not from Bristol, are you?'

'No, Devon.'

'Devon is a pretty place. How are you enjoying the city?'

'It's been very welcoming. Lots of nice places to walk,' Abbey said. She stood up and picked her backpack off the ground. 'I have to get to a class now, Professor.'

'Please, call me Rob.' He stood up and held his hand

out for her to shake. She didn't want to take it, but she did anyway. She felt uncomfortable and she didn't know why. He was just being friendly. Was she being over-sensitive or was something deeper at work here?

She pulled away and he sat back down. She could feel him watching her. Did he know that she had lied? She didn't have a class, but she wanted to get away from him as soon as possible.

She had been manipulated and misused before, and she found that it clouded her every relationship. Every judgement she made of people was tainted with the idea that they may want to hurt her in some way. She was distrustful, but that didn't mean that she was wrong.

She started walking away and could feel the professor's eyes on her. No, there was something very wrong with Professor Coley.

Abbey hadn't disclosed much about herself to her classmates. They knew she had a labrador, Sally, but that was about all she had mentioned. What they didn't know was that she was married. She wore her ring on a chain around her neck, under her top. It wasn't for the world to see, it was for her to have close to her heart. Her relationship was no one else's business. She would have to speak to Parker about the professor. It was nice having someone she could trust on her side. Them against the world. She would talk to him now, not wait until later. He was at home. To the outside world Abbey was vulnerable, alone, quiet and timid. They didn't know that she had someone in her corner, and not just anyone either. Someone brilliant, someone resourceful, someone ready to die for her. Ready to kill for her.

She unlocked the door to their home to be greeted by Sally, tail thumping against the ground in excitement.

'You're home early,' Parker said, appearing in the hallway in his vest and boxers a few seconds after her arrival, a smile across his face. She would never tire of that smile, of his face. He had a paintbrush in his hand and splatters of green paint on his legs. He was painting the hall a dark mossy colour.

'I bumped into my genetics professor again.' She scrunched her mouth up, like a shrug without shrugging. Was she making a big deal of this? Too late now, she had said it out loud.

'Again?' He picked up on the word. 'How many times is that?' He put the towel on the console table and folded his arms.

'Seven. I don't think it's right. There's something quite strange about him; I can't explain it.'

She had been nervous about telling Parker and had waited until she was sure that it was more than just a coincidence. Knowing who her husband was and what he had done in the past meant she had to think carefully before telling him her concerns. She was sure though, after careful consideration, that Professor Coley's intentions were not innocent. She wasn't about to let him ruin her happy ever after. They had been here in Bristol for a few months now; Parker had bought a small three-bedroom house with some of the money he had left from his inheritance. He had been left a large sum when his grandfather died. They had a second chance; she wanted everything to work out.

'You think he's following you?'

'That's silly, isn't it? Why would he follow me?' she said, even though that was exactly what she had thought, too.

'I could look into it. You need to trust your instincts. Tell me now if you want me to check it out.'

Abbey knew that when it came down to it she could look after herself, but she relished the fact that she didn't have to any more. She had also learned to listen to that part of her that told her something was wrong, and something about Coley was setting her alarm bells off. She had closed a big part of herself off when she left university the first time, after the attack. Parker had found that part of her, she had trusted him with it and he hadn't betrayed that trust. She had never spoken about what had happened at the university, what she had been through. It didn't seem to matter; he had been through enough horrors of his own and so she kept her secret. None of those things in the past mattered any more. From the moment they accepted their feelings for each other it was like the rest of the world came second, all that mattered was their little world and keeping each other safe. She knew that Parker didn't have the same boundaries as other people, but that wasn't his fault. He would never hurt anyone again, though, not unless they really deserved it.

'You could look into it,' Abbey said. 'As long as all you do is look. He's starting to creep me out.'

Parker walked up the stairs quickly, Abbey following.

He pulled his trousers on and grabbed a jacket. She wet her thumb with her tongue and pressed hard on his cheek, wiping away the streak of mossy paint smeared across his cheekbone. He smiled again and leaned in to kiss her. Every time it had the same impact as the first, a sharp intake of breath before their lips met and a dizzying moment of adjustment afterwards. As though the universe had entirely narrowed its focus into that one moment of time, passing through the neck of an hourglass. For those few seconds when their lips touched, nothing else existed.

'I'll walk back to the university with you. Would I be able to sit at the back of your lecture without being noticed?'

'Probably. It's a big place and it's usually at least ninety per cent full. He tends to focus on the first few rows.'

Parker grabbed a cap from a hook on the back of the door and put it on. He lifted her top slightly and placed his hand on her stomach. There was no bump there yet as she was barely three months pregnant, but she liked the feeling of his hand touching her, the sight of his scarred knuckles against her smooth white skin.

'I'll keep a low profile. Best to keep to not telling anyone about us just yet. I'll walk with you a bit of the way then you can go on ahead.'

'It's probably nothing,' she said, knowing it didn't matter now. It was out of her hands. She had told him and he would look; something about Coley's behaviour told her Parker would find something.

'Then let me check. Where's the harm in that?'

The harm was if it wasn't nothing. If there was some nefarious agenda at play, Parker would find it and deal with it accordingly. Abbey knew he saw the world through a different lens to most people. She wondered if she had just handed Professor Coley a death sentence.

No. The only way that would happen was if he deserved it. Parker didn't kill for the sake of it, that's wasn't who he was.

Chapter Twenty-Two

Present

Adrian and Imogen sat in the front of Imogen's car; they had taken to having meetings in there, in case anyone else was listening inside the station. They couldn't risk being overheard.

'Where do we even start with this?' Imogen said.

'It's going to be pretty hard while we are playing catch-up. We need to anticipate his moves and not turn up after the bodies,' Adrian said.

'These professors, they must be connected in some other way. What is it that they're doing exactly? Why are they being targeted?' Imogen said.

'So, Abigail Lucas said she got the heebie-jeebies from her prof? Because he was being nice to her? Caitlin Watts' relationship with Gillian Mitchell seemed to have a strong mentor vibe about it. Did Hugh Norris have someone like that? What do we know about Owen

Sager, besides evidence of abuse and some past mental health issues? How about Helen Lassiter?'

'You think Abigail and Caitlin were being groomed for something? Do you think it was something sexual?'

'Why not? Both attractive young women, in their own way.'

Abbey had a vulnerability about her that had made Adrian want to look out for her on both the occasions they'd met. Some people got off on that. Over the last few years, they had seen a rise in home-grown amateur pornography – local girls being persuaded into a film or two to help pay for uni fees, rent, food, whatever else they might want. Caitlin had a similar pull, not just because she was stunning but because she seemed lost, hurt, a little abandoned. Knowing that her parents had left when she was young was no surprise to Adrian. He had noticed that she was trying for his attention, trying to be good enough, something that came with parental abandonment. Always searching for others' approval, until cynicism takes over and you don't care any more.

'I'll ask the sex crimes guys to run the girls' faces through their system. Maybe they have something. They've just uncovered four porn cam houses in the St Thomas area.'

'Charming,' Adrian said; his neighbourhood wasn't getting any better. 'And Parker?'

'We've just got to hope we can stop him from hurting anyone else, which means figuring out what's going on here. At least this is an avenue to explore.'

'Right now, the best lead we have is Caitlin,' Adrian said, although he hated saying her name after what she had accused him of. He had to keep reminding himself that she was a victim in all of this, too.

'And Owen Sager. Someone killed him. That makes our body count three and two,' Imogen said. 'There's something we're forgetting here.'

'What's that?'

'You were attacked the night of Caitlin's attack. That can't have been a coincidence, can it? Do you remember anything about the person who attacked you?'

'Young. Male, around twenty years old. A little shorter than me, around five ten, I reckon.'

'Did you see his face?'

Adrian closed his eyes and tried to remember anything about the man who had attacked him. Sometimes it was hard to know if your mind was playing tricks on you or not. If your mind wasn't just putting things together because you were forcing it to. Trying to perform.

'He was Caucasian and he had really dark eyebrows; I remember that because his eyes were quite blue. I think anyway. I wouldn't swear to it. He was definitely white though and I got the feeling he was quite young.'

'That doesn't really narrow it down much around here. But, given the age, it does sound like it could be a university student.'

'Another one. What do you think is going on?'

'I'm guessing the murder of Hugh Norris is where we start. That was the reason Gillian Mitchell had Caitlin claim you raped her, maybe that's why you were mugged that night. He has to be the centre of the investigation. Now that Parker is involved, and presumably he killed those three teachers, I'm inclined to assume they were up to something. From what we know of Parker, he has only ever killed people who have done horrible things. We need to find out what those horrible things are.'

'How are the students connected to the professors? If we can establish that, then maybe we can find a pattern and find the final person Parker is planning on killing.'

'I'd put money on it being a professor.'

'We'll get Gary to go through their computers with a microscope. Maybe they left some evidence.'

'Let's speak to Gary then.'

They both got out of the car and walked into the station. Adrian could feel eyes on him from his colleagues. Were they still convinced he was a rapist?

Denise smiled sheepishly from the front desk. He knew she had given a statement to DCC Trevor Sneddon and he knew she would have told them about the nature of their previous sexual relationship. He couldn't be angry with her about it, but it did complicate their friendship. He wondered if she even thought that he did it. He couldn't assume she didn't. A part of him wanted to hate everyone who might have entertained the idea for even a second, but then he had to consider what he would have done in the same position.

Adrian noticed a silence descending as he walked down the corridor towards the room Gary worked in. Imogen was behind him and he could almost hear her annoyed discomfort with the situation; he was grateful at least that she had never wavered in her belief of him. Gary looked up as they approached.

'Did you get anything from the professors' personal computers?' Imogen asked.

'I was just about to come and find you. It all looks like it was on the up and up. Without trawling through each document and file individually, which will be done in time, there was nothing particularly innocuous on the hard drive. Mainly just lesson plans, assignments, first drafts of letters. Nothing especially exciting. They are old and well-used computers, though. Lots of info on there and lots of random stuff filed incorrectly, there's a lot to go through.'

'No mention of Caitlin or Owen?'

'There was a paper written by Owen Sager for the first philosophy term. "Is there a moral obligation to obey the law?" I thought that was pretty odd. He was the only one in the class who picked that topic.'

'And Caitlin?' Imogen asked.

'A standard nature versus nurture essay. Same as the rest of the class,' Gary replied.

'Any behaviour reports or anything like that?' Imogen pressed.

'Nothing,' Gary said.

'What about emails?' Adrian asked.

'Well, that's the suspicious part. There are no emails between Norris, Lassiter and Mitchell. Not one. I know they worked in the same building, but it's still strange, considering,' Gary said. 'And the thing is. I don't think they didn't email each other. I think the emails have been deleted. I think someone got into the system.'

'Maybe they connected through a different email provider,' Imogen said, quickly looking at Adrian, obviously thinking what he was thinking: Parker.

'I checked. The college has a block on all outside

email providers. The rule was brought in a few years ago to stop the sharing of illicit pics through the college.'

'What kind of illicit pictures?' Adrian asked.

'Revenge porn mainly, colleges are rife with it,' Gary said. 'Boy and girl have sex or send each other nudies. They break up, then one of them turns into a raging dickhead.'

'That's depressing,' Imogen said.

'The college has free, unlimited Wi-Fi and everyone can access it; it's a good service. But certain sites are blocked. It's a shit-hot firewall and would take some skill to bypass. Not that it matters, people share shit on Snapchat and WhatsApp these days,' Gary said. 'The university can't control what people do with their mobiles.'

'So if the emails have been deleted, can they be recovered?'

'Possibly, depends how it's been done. Who do you think might have done it?'

'A mutual friend,' Imogen said.

'How good is he with a computer?' Gary said.

'I don't know, but he seems to be very adept at covering his tracks, so I would assume he is good. Not as good as you though, mate,' Adrian said.

'Flattery will get you everywhere.' Gary grinned.

'Is there any way to find out if any emails were sent? Through the metadata or something?' Adrian asked.

Both Imogen and Gary turned and looked at him as though he had just sprouted flowers out of his nostrils.

'Maybe,' Gary said.

Imogen turned to Adrian. 'Metadata, Adrian? Do you even know what that means?'

149

'It means data about data, or something, I don't know, this is not my area,' Adrian said, shrugging.

'No shit,' Imogen said.

'I'll keep digging through, but for now that's all I have,' Gary said.

'OK, we're going to see if Sex Crimes have anything on Caitlin, maybe her face popped up somewhere. We need to find out how she is being manipulated, and why,' Imogen said.

'My money would be on Grandad,' Gary said.

'What do you mean? You think he's controlling her?' Imogen said.

Gary continued, 'No. If you want to control someone it's much easier if you blackmail or threaten someone they love. From what I understand, Caitlin Watts doesn't have many people in her life that would fit into that category, so I bet whoever is doing it is using the grandad to control her. He's a rev or something, isn't he? So many ways to go with that. A gay scandal, an inappropriate relationship with a parishioner, or maybe the most terrifying of all – pictures of kids on his hard drive.'

'That would explain a lot of her behaviour. She doesn't seem to care about herself much and yet she won't say anything about who attacked her,' Adrian said.

'And when DI Walsh and I pushed her for more information she freaked out and said she couldn't say any more, which means there are definitely other people involved. Or at the very least she thinks there are,' Imogen said.

Chapter Twenty-Three

Two months earlier

Parker waited for Professor Robert Coley to leave the office before he broke in. The hallways were clear of students and other personnel. This wasn't the first time Parker had broken into an office, or anywhere in fact. He pulled his kit out of his pocket and pushed the pins inside until he felt the mechanism click. He was in.

Parker had been following the professor for several weeks. He had seen Robert Coley looking Abbey up and down when she wasn't looking. It wasn't an attraction thing, it was a predator/prey thing. Parker knew the difference. He had seen that look before; the people who abused him had looked at him like an object, a pawn in their game. Parker had already been through Coley's house with a fine-tooth comb and found nothing of any interest, and so now it was time to check out his office. There was definitely something off about the man; Parker knew when someone wasn't 'right'. Robert Coley lacked humanity when he thought no one was looking. Unlucky for him, Parker *was* looking. A hunch wasn't enough for Parker though, he had to verify. He didn't want to become one of the 'Inhumans', the killers who took lives without giving it so much as a second thought, the people who walked among them just like everyone else. He had met several of them in his lifetime and they had no remorse; he supposed they would be referred to as psychopaths. That's not who he was. He wanted justice, nothing more.

Parker sat down at Coley's desk, opened his laptop and turned it on. It was slow to boot up, an old clunky model. Coley's office was full of books, floor to ceiling, piled high and doubled up on the bookcases. It smelled of dusty paper. Parker loved that smell. He couldn't imagine a life where he wasn't surrounded by books. Books had helped him come to terms with the psychological damage left by the men who had unravelled him and made him into what he was today. A killer.

When the computer fan had finished labouring and the screen stopped twitching, the computer finally asked for a password. Parker's eyes went to the painting on the wall. There was a large ornate framed picture of a golden lion with eagle wings above the desk. People were usually not as imaginative as they thought they were. He typed in the word CHIMERA, an organism that contained two or more sets of DNA, like a lion with eagle wings. Parker rolled his eyes as the computer unlocked.

Looking through the files, he didn't see anything

particularly interesting. Abbey's assignments were in among the others, she hadn't been singled out for any special treatment in any way. He opened the email folder. The inbox was clear, apart from one or two interdepartmental emails. He looked through each folder, but there was nothing out of the ordinary – letters to and from other colleges, other teachers.

He clicked on the search bar within the email account and typed in 'Abigail' to see what came back. There were twenty-six emails about Abbey – that couldn't be right. He started at the beginning. The first couple were standard messages about her entry onto the course. One mentioned her previous UCAS application to Exeter University for the same course. The next email was sent from Coley to an H. Lassiter asking for information on Abbey. Lassiter had come back almost immediately; the email header was 'candidate material'. Parker frowned. A candidate for what? Lassiter told Coley that Abbey would be a great fit for 'the programme' and that she had some more information on her that she would reveal in time.

When pushed for information in further emails, Lassiter told Coley about a serious sexual assault claim that Abbey had made, which the university had tried to make go away. There had been photographs of her in a compromising situation that could be construed as evidence of consent on the university social website and Abigail had left the college without pressing any charges. Lassiter had copies of the pictures, which were attached in a zip file. Parker had always suspected that Abbey had been through something traumatic, but he had never pressed her for the information because he didn't see what difference it made, and she could speak to him about it if she wanted to, when she was ready.

He understood that it took time to open those wounds; it clearly hadn't been long for her, she was still dealing with it on the inside, and he would be there if she ever decided to talk about whatever it was. But reading this enraged Parker; Lassiter was telling Coley how easy Abbey would be to manipulate, how she had been easy to dissuade from bringing her attackers to justice. She didn't say it in so many words, but Parker could feel the excitement and camaraderie between them.

Parker moved the cursor to the zip file and hovered; he couldn't open it, not least because it wasn't fair to Abbey. He knew from the documentation of his own assault that every time a person looked at the photos, you were plunged back into the shame; as long as the photos existed, you could never get away from what happened. As if that were even a possibility. He deleted the email without looking. He didn't need to see Abbie that way, not that he would love her any less, but it didn't matter, it wasn't an itch he needed to scratch.

Lassiter proceeded to say in further emails that her candidate was a wily tomcat who was up to any task put in front of him. *Candidate for what?* Further emails mentioned other candidates, but no one by name. There were several different people involved; this was obviously bigger than Parker had first thought. If Parker hadn't searched for Abbey specifically he wouldn't have found these emails. He found two other accounts that spoke about what had happened but nothing that could be construed as anything other than concern for a new student.

Anger pulsed through Parker; he hadn't felt this incensed in a long time. He struggled to concentrate, to stay in the present. Since Abbey had fallen pregnant he had been concerned about this side of himself, he wanted to prove he could keep it at bay. He worried that this badness he had was genetic, passed from his grandfather down through his father who had died when he was young. He had a fear that this child would be born broken, something he had often felt about himself. He had never been formally diagnosed with post-traumatic stress disorder because he never trusted anyone enough to subject himself to psychotherapy. He knew though. It was always there, in the background, the ability for the switch to be flipped and suddenly he was being pulled backwards into a place where he had no control over himself. It always started with an excess of saliva in the mouth, then a swirling head, not a pain so much as a jumble of thoughts and bad memories all shouting to get to the surface first. If you were lucky, you got a memory that was unpleasant but manageable; if you were unlucky, you were thrust into a nightmare where it was impossible to hide from yourself. He gripped onto the desk, trying to stay in the moment, trying not to disappear into the past, where he was vulnerable and weak. Exposed and alone. Like looking for shade in a desert, impossible to get respite for even a second.

Footsteps approached and Parker slammed the laptop shut. Darkness descended. The doorknob twisted, but

155

then a conversation started on the other side of the door. Coley was telling the cleaner that he didn't need his office servicing tonight and that he had just forgotten something. Parker stood up as quietly as he could and slipped behind a large mahogany bookcase situated in the corner of the room. He heard laughter from the other side of the door, which only seemed to exacerbate his fury. The men said their goodbyes. Parker's chest was heaving, and he was still trying not to have a flashback.

The door opened and Coley walked in, still laughing until the exterior door closed. After the cleaner had left, Coley closed the door and locked it before exhaling and throwing his folders onto the workbench at the back of the room. He rested his walking stick against the wall next to the door and turned the lamp on. Parker peered at him from the darkened corner. His nerves were finally settling as he felt his focus come back; he had gone from prey to predator yet again.

He moved forward silently and waited for Robert Coley to spot him. This was risky and not something he would ordinarily do, but he was just so angry. He couldn't live with this anger; he needed to act. He hadn't touched anything with his bare hands and he knew he hadn't been seen on the way in.

'Hello,' Parker said.

'Jesus Christ!' Coley jumped. 'What are you doing in here? How did you get in? The door was locked!'

'You should keep your voice down,' Parker said.

'You need to leave. Who are you? I've seen you in my lectures. Are you a student here?'

'No, but my wife is.'

'Look, I don't know what you've heard, but I don't do that kind of thing anymore. Whoever your wife is, I promise I didn't touch her.'

'Abigail Lucas is my wife.'

Robert Coley's face changed, he looked confused and surprised. 'Your wife? She's not married.'

Parker held his left hand up and showed Coley the ring. 'What is she a prime candidate for?'

'What?' The colour drained from Coley's face. 'What are you talking about?'

'I've been reading your emails. I'm going to ask you one more time, what is she a prime candidate for?'

'I can't answer that,' he said, his breath heavy.

'You really should.' Parker smiled at him.

'You don't know who you're dealing with.' Coley's eyes darted over to the phone on his desk.

Parker reached forward and grabbed the phone cord, pulling it out of the wall. 'Neither do you.'

'I'll scream, someone will come.' He looked at Parker's hands and saw the gloves. 'Listen, you don't want to do anything stupid. You can rough me up as much as you want, but I can't tell you anything.'

Parker pulled a knife out of his pocket and removed the sheath, exposing the blade. 'Who said anything about roughing you up?'

'This is insane. What do you want?' Coley's eyes fixated on the shiny serrated edge.

'What's a laminectomy?' Parker said, knowing it would strike a chord with Coley. He had been inside his house, seen his letters from the doctor. Robert Coley

157

was waiting for confirmation of an appointment after seeing a specialist about his ongoing back problem. He was going to have a couple of the flat bones next to the spine removed in order to stop the pain he was experiencing.

'How do you know about that?'

'I've been watching you for a while now; you gave Abbey the creeps and I had to find out why.'

'I'll leave her alone. I won't tell anyone you broke in here.'

'No, you won't. But you will tell me what's going on. Who are these candidates? What do you want them for?'

'I can't tell you that.'

'Why is that? You're not worried about what I will do to you?'

'I'm dead if I speak to you, so it doesn't really matter.'

'Death is the least of your worries. If you don't tell me what I need to know, you will be begging me to take your life.'

'I can't run, and I can't tell you what is going on. What you do is up to you.' Robert Coley seemed to resign to it too easily. Whatever he was afraid of had made the decision for him.

'I found an article in your house, tucked away in one of your drawers. A student died a couple of years ago in freak car accident, he was driving the wrong way up the M4. Was that one of your students? Did that have anything to do with this?'

'I can't talk about it. Do what you have to do.' Coley was resolved; even the threat of death didn't have the desired effect.

Parker moved closer and pressed the blade against his neck. 'I warn you, this won't be pleasant.'

Parker punched Coley in the stomach with force. Coley recoiled but made no attempt to fight back. Coley's behaviour was strange, and Parker couldn't understand it. It was unusual for someone who had no guilt not to plead their way out of a situation. Was he doing the right thing? He had never hurt anyone without being absolutely certain of their guilt before, never without bearing witness to their crimes first-hand. He had a feeling something big was going on, something he needed to get to the bottom of. There was a trail of student deaths going back years, from suicides to car accidents – all seemingly random, and yet they couldn't be. That in itself wasn't proof enough of Coley's involvement, but from what Parker had found during his investigation, at least one of his students every year could have been part of whatever was going on. Parker didn't understand how or why Coley was doing this, but he would figure it out, hopefully before anyone else got hurt. This was no time for Parker to get a sudden attack of conscience, if that was even possible. He would get Coley to confess, even if he had to torture him to do it.

With Coley still reeling from the punch, Parker swept the contents of the workbench onto the floor. He would clean it up when the professor was secured. He lifted Coley with ease and threw him face down onto the surface. Parker looked around the room and saw a scarf on the hat stand. He pulled it off and passed it under the table, across the professor's neck, keeping his head down. He tied the knot hard and tight. The professor groaned. Coley was not a particularly quick or mobile man. Parker pulled his own belt off and looped it around the professor's ankles before securing it to one of the workbench legs.

'She will look for you. It's not too late,' Coley rasped.

'She, who? Lassiter? Don't worry about her, she will be getting a visit from me, too.'

'Not just Lassiter, there are others.'

'Keep talking. What do you have to do with Exeter University? Why do you have so much correspondence with Lassiter?'

'I used to work there. I moved to Bristol several years ago.'

Parker took the knife and cut a line through the central back seam of the fabric on Coley's jacket, then he cut through the shirt with a swift movement, exposing the professor's back. He could see the nodules of his spine poking through his almost translucent freckled and aged skin.

'What are you doing?'

'It's going to get messy in here. Where do you want me to start? If I start at the lower section of your spine, then you will most likely be losing the use of your legs. There's no guarantees I won't nick your spinal cord though, in which case it's curtains for you anyway. Or I could start on the fourth vertebra at the top, which controls your neck. Or how about six and seven? They control everything below the top of your ribcage. Death is one thing, but being a quadriplegic is something else entirely.'

'You wouldn't do that.'

'With all due respect, you have no idea what I would or wouldn't do and I can guarantee that I have done much worse than this. Now talk.'

'What is it you want?'

'I want to know what you had planned for my wife.'

'I just follow the rules, I'm not the one you want to speak to.'

'I'm not going to lie. This is going to hurt.'

Parker pushed the knife against the skin, increasing the pressure until it broke through and the smallest trickle of blood ebbed out. The knife could have been sharper, but that would make this easier on Coley and Parker didn't want that. He inserted the blade a few millimetres into the flesh in the centre of Coley's back and pulled the blade downwards towards his waistband; the skin split open as though someone had unzipped him. The blood started to pool and roll away from the cut. The spine was close to the surface and Parker could see the white sheen of the vertebrae. Coley started to sob and Parker waited for the begging to begin.

'I told you, I'm not going to talk.'

'Then I'm going to carry on until you do. No one will be here for at least nine hours. Do you have any idea what I could do to you in that time?'

'Get on with it then.' Robert Coley spat the words out.

With that, Parker pushed his knife into an intervertebral disc in Coley's lower back, the soft tissue between each vertebra that stopped the discs from rubbing together. Coley screamed with the discomfort and Parker tried to ignore the thrill he felt at causing pain. Parker knew all about pain; there wasn't a part of his body that hadn't been through it. He hated the people that had hurt him, and he made sure he hurt them back. With everything his abusers had put him through, he had become a master of pain. He knew how much pressure to exert and when, he knew where all the little nerve endings were. He had been prodded, poked, burned and skewered himself enough times to understand the intricacies of pain. He thought that his desire to cause pain had gone when they were no longer alive, but it hadn't. It wasn't a compulsion or something that he actively missed, but here, now, doing this felt more right than Parker had felt in a long time. He knew he was messed up, knew that he wasn't like everyone else. But he wanted to protect Abbey, and this was a part of that, wasn't it? Or was this his sickness raising its ugly head again? He had been determined to move past the person they had made him, but here he was again and as he watched the blood pool on the floor by his feet, he was excited. Had he really moved on or was this just the excuse he had been looking for?

He disconnected the vertebra and pulled it out, Coley's body spasming until he went limp, passed out from the pain. He should stop now, he should just get it over with. If Coley hadn't spoken up to save himself, then he wasn't going to talk now. Instead Parker pushed the knife in again and again, methodically removing each of the vertebrae.

Chapter Twenty-Four

Imogen rang the doorbell to Adrian's house. She couldn't remember if he had told her he was going out. There were no lights on downstairs, but it was late. She banged on the door in case he was just asleep. She had tried his phone, but it'd rung through to answerphone. Adrian hadn't been quite right since the accusations were made against him. She had told him the truth when she said she didn't doubt him, but she wasn't sure he believed her. Adrian was full of self-doubt at the best of times, convinced that he was genetically predisposed to be a shithead. The reappearance of Parker was a concern. This could be the end for them. If anyone knew they had concealed his identity from the rest of the force, from the investigation, then they would be in deep trouble, facing not only unemployment but also criminal prosecution and probably prison.

The hall light came on and Imogen banged on the door again.

'I'm coming, wait!' Adrian shouted from inside; he sounded drunk. He tripped over something in the hall and swore before opening the door and walking back inside.

'Nice to see you're behaving like an adult about all of this.'

'Spare me your sanctimonious crap tonight, Grey, I'm not in the mood.'

Imogen closed the door behind her and stepped over a black bin bag full of used rags that had spilled out onto the floor; the hallway stank of turpentine. 'What's wrong with you?'

Adrian took his mobile phone out of his pocket and pulled up a picture. Someone had painted the words *rapist pig* on the door in bright red paint.

'When I got home that was on the door. The paint was dry, so God knows when they did it. It was probably there all day.'

'That's vandalism. We can ask your neighbours if they saw who did it.'

'Do you think my neighbours are going to help me out now? Bad enough being a cop. Not many things less popular than a rapist.'

'But it's not true. You didn't do it. You need to snap out of this and start acting like someone who is innocent.'

'Yeah, well, maybe I deserve this. Anyway, I cleaned it off and then decided to drink myself to sleep. Chin chin.'

'You smell awful. Come on, you get in the shower, I'll tidy up your hallway.'

Imogen took her coat off and hung it on the end of the bannister. She bent down to pick up the stinking rags and put them back in the bag.

'What if this never goes away? This is one of those things that can't be taken back once it's out there.' Adrian's voice cracked. Imogen looked up to see tears in his eyes. 'I would never do anything like that. I couldn't. You know I couldn't!'

'People forget things, Miley, this is no different. It might take a couple of weeks, or months, but people will move on to the next thing – they always do. Besides, not all of us believed it in the first place.'

He was holding his breath, trying to stop himself from crying, but his eyes brimmed over and the tears fell. He wiped his face with the back of his hand and then winced, the turpentine fumes on his hands obviously aggravating his eyes.

Imogen tied the black bag up and pushed Adrian towards the staircase, both hands on his back, then up the stairs, along the hallway and to the bathroom. She left him slumped against the wall and went inside to turn the shower on. The bathroom was a mess. She picked his clothes off the floor and put them in the laundry basket, then waited until the water was warm before sticking her head back outside to find Adrian nodding off against the wall. She grabbed his arm, pulling him in, and yanked his shirt over his head.

'What are you doing?' he said, giggling.

'Get in that shower. You stink of turps. You can't sleep like that. The fumes will probably kill you.'

'Nonsense,' he barked before putting his own finger to his lips. 'Shhh.'

Imogen shook her head and smiled. She stared at his jeans. He could take those off himself.

'Take your trousers off and get in the bloody shower.'

'Fine.' Adrian fumbled at his flies and pulled his jeans down to reveal a pair of Spiderman underpants. He stepped into the shower and leaned against the wall.

Imogen watched for a few moments before she realised he may have actually fallen asleep in there.

'For fuck's sake.' She kicked her shoes off and pulled her own jeans down. Yanking her jumper over her head, she decided she didn't care if she got her tank top wet. She stepped inside the shower cubicle and turned the showerhead towards Adrian before turning the hot water off.

Adrian jolted awake with the feeling of the cold water against his back. He became breathless instantly.

'What are you doing? Turn it off!' He shrunk into the corner of the shower.

Imogen put the warm water back on and he relaxed again. She grabbed the shampoo and poured some onto Adrian's head, then reached up and started to work the soap into a lather, trying to get rid of the smell of turps. The water was cascading between them, drenching her, and she leaned away to stop it from going in her mouth. It occurred to her that she was half naked in the shower with him. It hadn't even registered before, but here they were. Noticing this development made her instantly self-conscious. She looked at Adrian; he had obviously noticed it too, the drunken look replaced with another look altogether. Oh shit.

Imogen was confused. She had been thinking about Adrian a lot lately, not in the same way that she normally did. The accusation against him made her feel defensive of him, his loss made her feel protective of him. Concern for him had pushed most other things out of her mind; even her mother's death had taken a second seat to Adrian recently. Not to mention the kiss, the kiss she had tried to push out of her mind a hundred times. Standing here, wet and half naked, his head in her hands, she realised that maybe she had feelings beyond anything she had admitted to herself before. He wanted to kiss her, she could see it, he couldn't take his gaze away from her lips. She looked down at his hands to see that his fists were clenched. She pulled him forward, so the water washed the shampoo out of his hair, and he gasped for breath under the showerhead that beat down on his face. Imogen grabbed the shower gel and handed it to him.

'You can do this bit yourself.'

She got out of the shower and grabbed a towel; they had already gone too far. She had slept with someone from work before and it hadn't worked, not in the long term. She couldn't risk losing her best friend over what could just be a desperate need for companionship. Losing a person you love made you feel your own mortality and the need not to be alone. She had lost her mother; he had lost Lucy. They had been through so much together already, and she couldn't take a chance on something that may be fleeting.

Imogen picked her clothes off the bathroom floor and left the room, then went downstairs and put the kettle on. She made two coffees and slipped her jeans back on over her underpants.

'Why did you come here tonight?' Adrian said as he walked into the kitchen moments later, his hair still wet from the shower.

'I couldn't sleep. Can't stop thinking about this case. We need to figure out what the hell is going on. We also need to find Parker before anyone else does, before he kills again.'

'Tell me something I don't know,' Adrian said.

He took the coffee from the side and sat at the table; she could see he was sobering up fast. The air was thick with the things they weren't saying. Was there any way past this without talking about it? Imogen had come here to discuss the case, but if she was honest with herself then that wasn't all she was there for. It wasn't about sex. Although sometimes she thought they should get that part out of the way because, until they had, this feeling wasn't going to go away.

'We should talk,' she finally said, the awkward silence a little too awkward to ignore.

'About what?'

'About us.' There was no avoiding it any more. If they didn't deal with it, they wouldn't be in control. Although it felt like control went out the window a long time ago.

'What about us? I mean, I know what you want to

168

talk about, but why are we talking about it?' Adrian asked.

'Because I'm worried that we are going to do something stupid and regret it. I'm worried we are going to ruin . . . this . . . us. In case you haven't noticed, I don't have an abundance of friends, and I'd hate to lose you, too.'

'Who says you would lose me?' Adrian said.

'I think I will unless we start being open and honest about what is going on here. I know neither of those things come naturally to either of us, but it's important. However uncomfortable this feels, I think we need to stop pretending it's not happening.'

'OK. So, let's talk.'

Imogen took a deep breath before speaking. 'I like you, Adrian, we have something special. You are the person I turn to when I need someone. I think it goes both ways. We look out for each other.'

'You've been there for me a lot more than I have been there for you lately.' Adrian's lips were trembling slightly and the excess water from his hair dripped onto his shoulder. He shivered a little and clasped his hands around the hot mug.

'It's not a competition, it's just . . . nice. It feels good to care.'

'It does, and I've got to admit that it makes me a bit crazy seeing you flirt with other guys.'

'What are you talking about? I don't flirt with any guys. Name one guy you've seen me flirting with,' she said, racking her brain to try to think who he might be talking about.

'Constable Jarvis for a start.'

'We have very different ideas of what constitutes as flirting. I am not interested in him.'

'The lady doth protest too much, methinks.'

'Blimey Miley, do you always quote *Hamlet* when you're drunk?' Imogen said.

She was deflecting; the truth was, PC Jarvis had asked her out on a date and she had refused. She hadn't told Adrian about it and she had assumed he hadn't noticed anything. At the time, she hadn't acknowledged the reason why she had said no or the reason why she hadn't told Adrian. Now, of course, it seemed obvious – it was because of this unspoken thing between them. Her feelings for him had been growing for some time.

Adrian put his cup down and stood up. He walked over to Imogen and reached for her arm. He took her hand in his and ran his thumb across the back. She wanted to kiss him, but she needed to think, too. It was against the rules for colleagues who worked side by side in the department to date. That's not to say it didn't happen, of course it did. But Imogen was already on thin ice and had lost out on a promotion because of her relationship with Dean. She had to tread carefully. All she knew right now was that her feelings for Adrian had changed.

'So, what do we do, Imogen? I know what you're saying and logically it makes total sense. I'd like to be grown up about this and say we can turn it off if we want to. But it doesn't really work like that, does it?'

'How does it work then?' Imogen said, frustrated that she didn't have an answer that meant everything could stay the same. She pulled her hand away from him and he went and sat back down; she sat opposite him and watched him drink his coffee.

'Maybe we should go on a date,' Adrian said, staring into his drink, refusing to look up. 'Get to know each other, maybe change perspective.'

'A date? Are you joking? I see you all the time. If it got back to the DCI, we could be in serious trouble.'

She wasn't sure what she had been hoping for. All those nights they spent together in the dark, in the morning, pretending it wasn't happening – it wasn't healthy. Maybe she wanted him to say it was all a big mistake and he was just using her to get over Lucy, but of course she knew she didn't want that. She didn't know what she wanted.

'There's something else we need to talk about, of course,' Adrian said.

'What's that?'

Adrian looked at her. 'Dean. What if he comes back?'

'It doesn't matter if he comes back or not,' she said, not entirely convincing herself.

She had finished with Dean because of his criminal tendencies being incompatible with her career choice. He wasn't about to change and neither was she, so there was nothing more to think about when it came to Dean.

'But you still have strong feelings for him, I know you do.'

'That's all in the past now, the relationship is over.'

'What about me?'

'What about you?' Imogen said.

'Do you have feelings for me?'

171

'You know I do. I don't know what they are yet, but yes, I do.'

'I don't think I can just pretend I don't feel the way I do.' Adrian looked up. 'At first, I thought that I was just hurting and didn't want to be alone, but it stopped being about Lucy a while ago. I don't think this is going to go away.'

'What are you saying?' Imogen asked.

'I'm saying I want more.'

Flustered, Imogen wasn't expecting it to go this way. 'You've been drinking, maybe we should talk about this when you're sober.'

Adrian reached his hand across the table and put it on hers. 'It won't change anything. Cards on the table, I've thought about this, about you, for a while – well, more to the point, I have avoided thinking about it, but in the back of my mind this has been coming for a long time. But, like you say, I would rather nothing happened if it means it's going to mess up what we already have. You're too important to me.'

'I thought maybe talking about it would make it clearer, but it hasn't.'

'I know. I want to wait until it does. Now that we have talked, maybe it will change, maybe the feelings were a manifestation of all the secrecy, maybe now that it's out in the open the idea will lose its shine.'

Imogen hesitated. 'What if it doesn't?'

Chapter Twenty-Five

Imogen woke up early at home, alone. She had left Adrian's with her head swimming. If she couldn't sleep before their chat, she certainly struggled last night. The last time they had met Parker she had almost died; maybe his return had made her feel vulnerable again. Perhaps that was what was bringing those feelings for Adrian to the surface. Imogen had seen enough of his behaviour around women to know that he was treating her differently, he usually jumped in and out of relationships without thinking, if you could even call them relationships. Until Lucy, of course, but she was gone now. Then there was the small matter of Dean, a man Imogen wouldn't be able to resist if he turned up on her doorstep. The only reason they weren't together was because he was strong enough to stay away for now.

After her morning run, Imogen showered and dressed for work. She paused when she realised she was looking through the chest of drawers and actually considering what suited her most. In an act of defiance against no one but herself, she pulled on a dark blue hoodie and a pair of cords. She hadn't cared yesterday, why should she suddenly care today? She pulled her wet hair up into a ponytail and checked her face. She looked fine. Imogen locked her flat up and got in the car; it took her a minute to compose herself before driving to the station. Normally she would swing by and pick Adrian up, but he had expressly told her that he would meet her at work after ushering her out of his house at one in the morning.

Things were awkward anyway; this was just a new level of awkward for Imogen. She walked into work and saw Denise, and for the first time she couldn't stop thinking about the fact that Denise and Adrian had slept together. After hearing some detail about what had happened between them, she couldn't help wondering what it would have been like. She said a quick hello and walked through the glass doors. Adrian was sitting at his desk, holding onto his head; she wasn't surprised if he had a headache.

'Good morning.'

'Hey.' Adrian smiled nervously.

It hadn't been her imagination; the conversation they'd had last night was written all over his face. Was she seeing him in a new light or was he looking at her differently? They couldn't go back to pretending that nothing was going on between them. That wouldn't help anyone. The time had come to confront this thing head on.

'Did you get any sleep last night?' she asked.

'I passed out as soon as you left. You?' Adrian said.

'I got about two hours. I went for a long run this morning to clear my head,' said Imogen.

'Is it clear now then?'

'I think we need to tell Gary.'

'Tell him what? About us?'

'No, about the case, about Parker. I trust him.'

'I trust him, too,' Adrian said. 'I also don't want to put him in a position where he might lose his job.'

'We need someone smarter than us to help find Parker. We didn't find him last time; Abbey came to us. What makes you think we can this time?'

'Fair enough. If you think he can handle it. Let's go.'

Thankfully, Gary was alone in the computer lab. Imogen explained as little as she could get away with, Gary's mouth agog as she spoke. Adrian filled in the parts of the story that Imogen wasn't familiar with or there for, and they described how and why they had come to find out Parker was involved in this crime.

'Are you going to tell the DCI?' Gary asked when they finally stopped talking.

'I'd rather not,' Adrian said. 'I realise that may not be possible, though. If it comes to it, then I will. Maybe the fact that I was under extreme emotional stress at the time will make a difference to how they choose to deal with me.'

'We need to find him. All we know is that he is really good at this. He was left a lot of money by his grandfather and so cash isn't an issue. His wife is staying in town. We only know he has anything to do with this because his note told us he did. We hadn't figured it out and there is no physical evidence that points to him,' Imogen said.

'So, he's good. But he's also dangerous. What if we get close? Are you sure he wasn't warning you off with that note?' Gary asked.

'As strange as this sounds, I don't believe we are in any danger from him. He's not evil,' Imogen said.

'Right. He's just fucked in the head?' Gary added.

'After what happened to him, who wouldn't be?' Imogen acknowledged, still feeling as though she should defend Parker. After all, he had saved her life.

'So where do I start?' Gary asked.

'We have two problems. We need to find Parker, but what concerns me more is the person who killed Hugh Norris. That wasn't him, so we need to know who it was,' Imogen said.

'How do you know it wasn't him?' Gary said.

'In his note he said three down and one to go. We know that those three were Coley, Mitchell and Lassiter. It makes no sense for him to lie about Norris, so it must be someone else,' Imogen said.

'I have a feeling that all has something to do with Owen Sager, that was the first death. I'll find out if his parents have his phone or computer still. He wasn't living in halls, he was still at home,' Adrian said.

'We'll go back,' Imogen replied. 'Gary, you can dig into Hugh Norris more. We are missing something.'

'What about the "one to go"?' Gary asked.

'We don't know who that is. We need to find out the motive, what's driving all of this. Without that I don't see how we could figure out who the final person is. Maybe Owen Sager's parents can shed some more light on the situation. Maybe they can tell us the connection between Owen and Norris.'

'Thanks for telling me all this,' Gary said.

Imogen detected a hint of annoyance in his voice.

'We didn't want you to get in trouble before. We made the decisions we did, and it wasn't on anyone else to lie for us. It was never about keeping secrets from you, Gary. It was about keeping you safe.' Imogen felt bad for not confiding in him, but confident that it was the right thing to do.

'OK. I get it. I'll see if I can find anything.'

'The wife's name is Abigail Lucas, and she was a student at both Bristol this year and Exeter a few years ago,' Adrian added. They hadn't known anything about her before, bar the fact that she worked in the museum. Her name hadn't been on any of the staff registers at the museum so she must have been paid cash in hand. After the case had ended they hadn't been inclined to find her, until now. 'See if you can find anything about her on any of the dead professors' computers. Or maybe the uni social media forums, they go back a few years.'

They stepped out of Gary's lab and walked back to their desks.

'We need to think of something to tell the DCI, she's not stupid,' Imogen said.

'I don't know how to tell her now. We've kept too much from her. There is no conclusive proof or material evidence pointing to Parker. So, at the moment, there's nothing to tell.'

Chapter Twenty-Six

Imogen woke up with a tight knot in her stomach. She was thinking about Adrian; he had even started making cameo appearances in her dreams. Something had changed between them. They had had the conversation now, too. It just felt so weird, like it was wrong in some way, although she didn't know why. In many ways, her friendship with Adrian was the healthiest relationship she had ever had. He was quite uncomplicated as a person; he didn't lie, and she never felt as though she wasn't getting the whole picture with him. The more she got to know Adrian, the more she liked him as a person. If anything, her original thoughts of him were unfair, not that she'd ever disliked him, but she hadn't fully appreciated what a good guy he was. He hid it well by being a bit crap at people. He had appeared to be vain and a bit in love with himself when they first met, but as they spent time together she realised it was nothing like that. He messed around for the same reason she ran. A little time pretending you could be better, be someone else. She couldn't judge him for that.

She tried to put a finger on why she found it so strange to think of Adrian in that way. Maybe because they were friends first and foremost. Many relationships start with lust and progress to friendship. To be fair, that had never worked out for her. All she knew was that when she was in that shower with Adrian she certainly wasn't thinking about him as a friend. Thank God he felt the same way. Could she wait? Were they past the point where they could get to know each other? Of course, she knew she still had a lot to learn about Adrian. She blushed at the prospect. Christ, she had to get ready for work and stop getting fired up like this.

At the station, Gary and Adrian ushered Imogen into the liaison room. If their goal was to seem nonchalant, they failed. She shook her head; they couldn't look more conspicuous if they tried.

'What is it?'

'We found something out about the wife, Abigail Lucas. Well, Gary did,' Adrian said.

'Go on.'

'She left the university because she claimed she was assaulted and the university basically didn't give a shit. Tried to sweep it under the carpet,' Gary said.

'Who assaulted her?' Imogen asked.

'That's never mentioned in any of the emails,' Gary said.

'And what's that got to do with this?'

'In the emails to Coley, Lassiter suggests using it as

leverage to get her involved in some kind of programme, but I think it's more of a game,' Gary said.

'Game?'

'Yeah, as soon as I saw that it all clicked into place. I saw a movie like it once, a French movie, fucking horrible it was,' Gary said.

'OK, so how does it work?'

'You start by getting a person you can control somewhat, either financially or with some secret they might have that they don't want to go public. In the movie, it was about winning a large sum of money, but I don't think that's what's happening here. Then you get them to do things they wouldn't normally do, immoral or illegal things, and escalate it until they are doing some properly messed-up stuff. Once you get people involved in the game, it becomes harder for them to leave when they have committed any of the acts. You get them on the hook, then when you have them there you threaten them with exposure in order to compel them to commit another slightly more heinous act.'

'How far does it go?'

'As far as they want. Who can say? There is a possibility the other killer we are looking for is one of the others, like Caitlin. That maybe the killings were part of the challenges being set. Or maybe they just pushed someone too far and they lost the plot.'

'Why am I surprised by anything that people do?' Imogen said wearily.

'Caitlin claimed she didn't know any of the other people involved, only Gillian Mitchell, who was the one who was controlling her,' Adrian said.

180

'It seems as though Coley and Norris both had someone to use as their pawn, which means Lassiter probably had one, too,' Imogen said.

'So, this Parker guy, do we think he's now after the final professor? Do we think he knows who it is?' Gary asked.

Imogen frowned. 'Where's the list of the faculty members?'

Gary pulled out a small brown file and handed it to her; it was a list of university staff.

'So, if we assume Owen Sager was Norris's pupil, Coley had his eye on Abbey Lucas, then we need to know who Helen Lassiter's pupil was,' Imogen said.

'Right. Well, I went through all of Lassiter's pupils and there's one that sticks out. He comes from a lower socioeconomic background; his grades didn't meet the requirements, but Lassiter pulled some strings to get him in. His name is Russ Beacham and he's been AWOL since Hugh Norris went missing,' Gary said.

'It's not uncommon for prestigious universities to let students with lower grades in if they fit the requirements in other ways. It's an effort to make them seem less elitist. It could be innocent enough,' Imogen said.

'His were lower than that, and realistically he didn't have anything going for him. No outside academic clubs. He hadn't taken part in any of the hiking challenges like Ten Tors or Duke of Edinburgh or any of that other extra-curricular stuff they look for.'

'You think he could be the attacker?'

'Well, Russ had lessons with Hugh Norris and Owen Sager,' Gary said. 'Also, Owen Sager got in trouble with the police a couple of weeks before he died for tagging on a church – he sprayed a giant swastika in broad daylight.'

'Jeez, that almost sounds like a dare,' Imogen said. 'What about Beacham? Has he been in trouble with us before?'

'He sure has. Shoplifting in that huge DIY warehouse down by the bus station,' Gary said.

'So, let's flip it. Let's look for all the uni students that have been brought in since September and try to ascertain for sure which ones had one of our twisted profs,' Imogen stated. 'Beyond that, look for the pupils who didn't have the required grades. Maybe we can find out who the fourth person is.'

'Do we have enough to show the DCI without getting in the shit? We just have to leave out Parker's involvement,' Adrian said.

'It all connects, so yes,' Imogen added. 'What happens if we catch Parker?'

'We arrest and charge him,' Adrian said.

'For everything?' Imogen asked.

'We'll have to deal with that shitstorm when the time comes.'

'I was hoping you would say that,' Gary said.

Chapter Twenty-Seven

Adrian knocked on the door to Imogen's flat. She opened it almost immediately. He held out the flowers he had bought for her and she ushered him inside with a puzzled look on her face.

'Why did you buy me flowers?'

'I literally have no idea. I was in the petrol station and they were there. It was flowers or charcoal.'

He didn't know what to do with this new stage in their relationship. There was her constant niggling presence in his mind and he had to come over – not just as her friend or colleague. Now that he was here with these flowers in his hand though, he felt foolish. He didn't even know if Imogen liked flowers.

'I'll put those in water.' She took the flowers and went into the kitchen, Adrian following. On the windowsill was a vase of what he supposed were dead flowers, although they looked more like a witch's binding of dusty twigs. She pulled those out and put them in the bin, then started to fill the vase with water. He had been wrong before; he couldn't take things slowly. That's why he was here, now, with these stupid flowers. This collision course had been coming for some time, maybe from the moment they met.

Adrian walked up behind her and brushed her hair away from her neck. He kissed her on the very most inner part.

'I can't stop thinking about this . . . about us,' he said, hoping he wasn't alone in his feelings, knowing that he probably wasn't. Now that they had put it out in the open, it had got worse. Maybe sex was the only way through it. Maybe once they had got that over with they could move on. Right now, it was at the very front of his mind and driving him to distraction.

Imogen turned and their lips met. Instead of the frenzied kiss they had shared before, this time he was slow and deliberate, soft and curious. She leaned back against the sink. Adrian reached behind her and turned the tap off that was running in the background. Imogen took a deep, heavy breath.

'Me either.' She put her lips on his and took his face in her hands.

The scent of coconut shampoo was all Adrian could smell as Imogen's hair brushed against his face. He had put his hands on her before, but this time was different; there was no secret any more. He pushed his fingers in between hers.

'Are you sure? We can't go back if we do this,' Adrian said.

'I don't think we can go back anyway,' Imogen whispered. 'Let's go in the other room.'

She led him into the bedroom and sat him on the bed. Adrian watched as she pulled her jeans off before leaning forward, kissing him again and straddling his lap. This closeness was unfamiliar but not unwelcome. The warmth of her legs around his hips stirred him and he fell back onto his elbows. She unbuttoned his shirt and he watched her hands travel down his body. Seeing her touching him made him breathless. There was no darkness now, no secrecy. It was still light outside and he could see her legs across his pelvis – the only thing between them was three layers of fabric. He put his hands on her thighs and slid them towards her waist, catching the edge of her sweatshirt and dragging it upwards so he could see more. Imogen pulled the sweatshirt off. She wore a tight black vest that clung to every muscle. He looked at her grey pants, pressed against him, the tail end of the scar that ran the length of her torso tucked into the hem.

He pushed himself into a sitting position, Imogen's body closer than they had ever been before. They kissed again and he shook free of his shirt. He put his hands around her, grabbing onto her backside, and then stood up before turning and lowering her onto the bed. It felt so strange to be together like this, but also so natural, so completely predestined. It was impossible to fight and now he was amazed they had lasted this long.

Reaching down, he unbuckled his belt and undid the top button of his trousers before he carried on. Just leaning over her like this, seeing her looking up at him made Adrian light-headed with hunger. He didn't know what to do, what he was allowed to do. The time for talking was over and so he just had to push past his fear. Fear of what? He couldn't keep asking her if she was sure. She was. He had permission.

Holding his breath, he leaned down and kissed her stomach through the fabric. As he exhaled onto her, she took a deep breath and pulled her top up to offer her skin to him. The silky white jagged line of her scar was so prominent against her olive skin. He could feel her tremble through his lips; she tasted exactly as he supposed she would taste. It still wasn't too late to pull back, to say this was all a mistake, to stay friends without the awkwardness of knowing what inhabited them.

One of them needed to make the decision and Adrian decided it would be him. He traced his finger along the edge of her underwear and ran his hand over her, the warmth from between her legs in his palm. He gently stroked the jersey fabric as Imogen's breathing became more uncontrolled. Raising himself up again, his hand still between her legs getting less and less gentle as he felt the fabric dampen, he kissed her on the lips, slipping his tongue inside her mouth. He heard the tiniest of sighs with each movement. As he kissed her neck, he pulled her underwear to the side and slipped his hand under the fabric. As he felt her wetness against his fingers, he had the strongest urge to be inside her. He couldn't breathe.

He pulled away and looked at her, there was no going back now. He pulled off her pants and knelt on the ground by the bed. From the corner of his eye, he could see her clamp her hands over her face and she moaned into her palms as he wet his lips with her. He wanted to bring her to the brink so that she was as overwrought with desire as he was, until she was pulling him into her and digging her nails into his flesh. He didn't want it to be safe any more, he wanted them to be overtaken with this energy that was desperate to be expelled.

With both hands on her thighs, he felt her legs quiver with each kiss. He reached up and slid his hand under the fabric of her top, his fingertips brushing against her nipples, her hand clutching his hair. He looked up and she was propped on her elbow, watching him as her chest heaved. Why had they waited so long?

He ran his hand along her forearm until she let go of his hair and brought her hand to meet his, interlocking fingers; she squeezed his hand as he drew her into his mouth. Her grip tightened as she bucked involuntarily before pushing him away and turning onto her side breathlessly. He climbed up next to her and she kissed him, slipping her tongue inside his mouth while reaching down and sliding her hand down the front of his jeans.

'Are you OK?' he whispered.

'No,' she laughed and pushed him onto his back.

She reached across to the bedside table and pulled out a condom. He unbuttoned himself and put it on as she watched impatiently. He could see the heat in her cheeks; he was sure he was blushing, too. She pulled her vest over her head and threw it on the ground as he removed his jeans.

'This is really happening, huh?' Adrian said.

'Last chance to back out.' But before he could answer, Imogen straddled him and guided him inside.

Adrian closed his eyes, trying desperately not to succumb to his body just yet. She felt so good. He rested his hands on her hips as she moved, her hands pressed firmly on his chest. He had been ready for longer than he could stand and so he closed his eyes again, the sight of her writhing on top of him only exacerbating the situation. *Just hold on a little longer.*

Adrian pulled her off and pushed her down onto the bed; he wanted to be in control, he wanted to feel her underneath him as pushed his way inside again and again.

It probably should have lasted longer than it did, but they had months of foreplay behind them, this was just the culmination of all those lonely nights teasing each other in the dark. When he opened his eyes again, he saw her watching him. The moment over, he rolled onto the bed next to her. He took her hand in his and kissed it.

'So, that happened,' Imogen said.

'Regretting it already?' Adrian said.

'Of course not. Don't do that, it's an insult to both of us. We know what we are doing,' Imogen said.

'Obviously.'

She kissed him on the lips again before getting off the bed. Everything had changed since he had last seen her. He couldn't believe they had gone there. The strangest thing about the whole situation was how natural it felt to be here in a room naked with her. He watched her pull her hair back into a ponytail, wondering when he would be allowed to touch her again. He sat up and pulled his jeans back on as she grabbed her sweatshirt and underpants.

'So, why did you come over?' Imogen asked.

'I um . . . I thought that was obvious?'

'Well, do you want some dinner maybe? I order a mean pizza.'

'If you don't mind me hanging around?'

'You're right, you should leave. We couldn't possibly share something as intimate as a pizza now. It wouldn't be right.' She grinned at him.

'I'm confused, OK? What happens next?'

'I say we try not to overthink it, Adrian. Let's eat some dinner, watch some TV and then you can stay the night. This is weird enough without us being weird with it.'

'You're being very pragmatic about the whole thing.'

'I know, it's disconcerting.'

Imogen left the room. Adrian followed her into the lounge, feeling like a lost dog waiting for instruction. He was used to being the one in control in these situations, but he knew that wasn't the case here. It occurred to him in that moment that every woman he had ever had strong feelings for was like this with him. Andrea, Lucy and now Imogen. Maybe he needed to feel submissive in order to feel love.

Imogen picked up her phone and went into her takeaway app. 'Pepperoni OK?'

'Sounds great.'

She paused for a moment and took a deep breath

before speaking. 'What do we do about work? The DCI will kill me if I get into another inappropriate workplace relationship.'

'Another one?'

'Dean, you know, suspect, witness . . . whatever you want to call him.' She put the order through and put the phone down.

'Oh, I thought you meant another copper.'

'No. Not at this station anyway.' She winked and pulled the vase of flowers out of the sink and put them on the windowsill to die.

Adrian had only recently started thinking about Imogen with other men. Even though he had known when she was with Dean, he felt uncomfortable thinking about it now. He didn't like to think of her with anyone else. He was jealous.

'How long 'til that pizza comes?' he said, walking towards her, knowing they had at least half an hour. He needed to confirm that this was real, that it was still happening. Now the first time was out of the way.

Chapter Twenty-Eight

One month ago

The train pulled into Exeter St David's train station and Parker stood by the door ready to disembark. His stomach churned as the landmarks came into view. He'd never thought he would come back to this place. He thought he was done. The train came to a halt and Parker stepped off. No one looked at him, no one noticed him, no one knew what he had done. What he was about to do.

He walked through the station and took the various roads to get to his old house, his grandfather's house. He held his breath as he opened the door to the smell of his childhood, not wanting to be hit with it but to let it in slowly. Everything was how he had left it. He would never sell this house, it wouldn't be fair. It was tainted and cursed. He had left a message for the cleaner not to come this month; he didn't want any unexpected visitors. He had work to do. He had to find out what the link between Helen Lassiter and Robert Coley was, he had to find out who else was involved and what this was all about, what they wanted from Abbey, Parker's wife, the love of his life. He got angry when he thought about the conversation he had read, angry enough to kill again.

The house was dark, even in the day, the woodwork all stained ebony, accompanied with dark blue embossed wallpaper. He flicked the switch and the hall light came on, barely illuminating the space. He remembered when he'd come to live here after his parents had died; it had reminded him of a haunted house ride that his father had taken him on at a theme park in America. Those days of freedom were a hazy memory – moving here was like being put in prison. The bad feeling ran through to the foundations; each floorboard that creaked sounded like a distant voice crying out for him to run away as fast as he could. He could never have anticipated how much evil was in this place, how much evil he would have to endure. Nature or nurture, Parker was a product of both. He would make sure at least that his child had a better chance in life. All he could do was hope the child would turn out like Abbey.

Every time he came to this house, he was a different person to the time before. Last time he'd come looking for revenge; this time he was looking for answers. The stairs groaned under his feet in the same way they always had done, the song composed of his childhood. Upstairs he switched the lights on to see an even darker, longer corridor with a large black rectangle at the end

– his bedroom door. A child's refuge, place of solace, somewhere to seek comfort and rest. Or so it should have been.

As he drew closer, he saw the familiar metal bar across the door, the large steel padlock that his grandfather had installed. Locked in every night, bars on the window, never quite sure if the door would be opened again, sometimes even praying it wouldn't be. Comforted by the fact that he might be left to die, alone, without malice or fear. Abuse and neglect to the extreme. Those thoughts and feelings flooded Parker's mind inside these walls. He couldn't bring himself to go inside the bedroom, not this time, not today. Some people moved on from pain, some people couldn't. Parker carried his pain with him, he couldn't imagine being without it. It was almost reassuring to him.

Parker opened the office door and turned the computer on. It had been a while since he had been in here, but everything was still working. After a few moments of inconsequential updates, the start screen finally appeared. He logged onto the virtual private network and secured his browser before he started to look up the people whose names he knew, researching both Exeter and Bristol university staff to see if there were any cross connections. He had spent a lot of money fortifying this system; these computers were protected by layers of security and encryption. No one knew about this house, not even Abbey, so he could conduct his investigation without disturbance. He found Helen Lassiter's home address. He had exhausted his search in Bristol – everywhere led to a dead end or a dead student. His search always ended in one place though: Exeter University. He had found out that Robert Coley used to work in Exeter, and that he still had family in the area and ties to the community. He didn't matter any more though – he was dead.

Parker scribbled down the information that he needed and went back downstairs. A police siren whizzed past the window and he briefly caught his breath. They wouldn't find him here; this house had been in the family for generations and his now dead grandfather was even less fond of the authorities than Parker had been. It was registered under a trust and had no named connection to the family at all. If the police looked it up, the owner was a local solicitor who had strict instructions not to disclose who the real owners were. Of course, when the property changed hands and Parker inherited the house, he had to pay restitution to the solicitor to keep the arrangement in place. He knew it wouldn't be an issue, as any person his grandfather was dealing with was more than likely corrupt and so all he had to do was find out where the corruption was and make sure the solicitor knew he was aware. As it happened, the solicitor was more than happy to take the bribe even without the threat of exposure, although Parker was sure that didn't hurt.

The kitchen had Italian marble floors in black-and-white tile and a deep French grey on the bespoke units. The conservatory backed onto the kitchen and the blocked stained glass was the only real colour in the room. The cupboards were full of the same crockery his grandfather had left behind. He found a tin of tomato soup and opened it, drinking the contents cold and straight from the can. He had no desire to stay in this room any longer than necessary, but he was hungry; late nights and lack of sleep were catching up to him. He saw the knife block by the side of the sink and instinctively rubbed the silky line on the back of his hand. The gash in the oak worktop was still there from when his grandfather had driven a knife through his hand and pinned him there to punish him for drinking a second glass of water. Grandfather was all about discipline.

Parker left the kitchen with a full stomach – an unusual feeling for him in this house. He turned the hall lights off again, wanting to soak in the feeling of the house in the dark, no longer afraid of it now that he had been inside for a while. The silence confirmed that he was the only occupant and that his grandfather was indeed dead. Even though he had been gone for several years now, his presence in this house was a constant. Every time Parker walked into a room here, he half expected his grandfather to be sitting there. When he was still alive, Parker had sometimes crept through the building at night when his grandfather had fallen asleep before remembering to lock him in his room. He knew every corner, every scuff on the floorboards, every loose thread on the rugs. He would return to his room before his grandfather awoke, too afraid to run away.

He would sleep on the sofa tonight; he couldn't sleep in the bedroom, the upstairs felt particularly haunted and while he had his wits about him right now it was manageable, but when he woke in the middle of the night, which he often did, then it became another matter altogether. The nightmares Parker had in this house were not nightmares, they were memories, even worse than most people could comprehend. Anyone who had been involved was now dead and the secrets of this house were deep inside Parker; though sometimes he felt as though the house were trying to pull them out again, make him relive it all.

He lay down and closed his eyes, focusing on the ticking grandfather clock in the alcove next to the bay window. He thought about Abbey and the baby they were due to have, the fear of passing on his genetic material, his deep-rooted badness, a real fear. He hoped that there was enough good in Abbey to override that. She made him a better person. She had always supported him and never made him feel like the monster he always imagined he was. Abbey was the light to his darkness. He tried to focus on his love for her and not the other feeling he was so desperate to ignore. It was excitement – excitement that he was hunting again, excitement at the prospect of killing again. He thought his anger would end with the death of the people who'd hurt him, but when they were gone the anger had stayed. There were other bad people though, other injustices he could avenge, other evils he could extinguish. His abusers had always told him he was rotten on the inside, maybe they were right. The malevolent whispers of the house lulled Parker to sleep, preparing him for the day tomorrow.

Chapter Twenty-Nine

Two weeks ago

It was easy breaking into Helen Lassiter's house. She had no security to speak of; not many people in this part of the country did. They felt safe without it. Helen's house was empty, the kind of empty that indicated a holiday and not just a day at work. There were letters piled up on the welcome mat. Parker picked them up and looked through them, but there was nothing particularly interesting. He went through the house room by room. He found her computer and turned it on. Lots of photos, her work calendar – she was away on a school trip to Johns Hopkins University in America, the leading university in the study of genetics and molecular biology. She wouldn't be back for over another ten days.

Frustrating as that news was, it meant Parker could spend time in her house without fear of detection. He went through every document folder and file in her computer, but there was really nothing suspect on there. He looked through the photographs of various school trips and conferences, away days and team-building exercises. Certainly nothing of any note. Each folder was labelled with a date and name of the occasion. The only folder that didn't have a detailed label was one called Hibiscus.

Parker opened the folder to find lots of photos of Hawaiian hibiscus flowers. Helen Lassiter didn't seem like the kind of person who would particularly be into tropical flowers. Her house was very neutral, almost monochrome. He looked into the properties of each picture; he needed to figure out the key. He could tell this was basic steganography – the art of concealing hidden messages inside files in order to avoid suspicion when handing the messages from person to person. It wasn't a particularly accomplished computing skill, you could get apps that helped you cover and uncover the messages and Parker had no doubt he would get inside them eventually. He looked through her desk and found an address book with passwords and codes scribbled inside it, clumsily scribbled between the details of actual contacts. He tried several but to no avail. It was a long shot, but he tried the same word he had used on Robert Coley's computer: Chimera. The files unlocked. Another unimaginative genetics professor.

The files contained correspondence between four of the lecturers going back several years: notes from Robert Coley, Helen Lassiter, Hugh Norris and Gillian Mitchell. There was another person whose name was left out of all correspondence – it was definitely a man, but apparently he would only speak in person about what they were doing. They each had a candidate and the professors were toying with their pupils, literally – manipulating them into a game of sorts. Parker couldn't figure out exactly what the stakes were, but it was obvious that the candidates were given risky assignments and for each assignment completed without complication and with evidence, the professors would gain points. The riskier the assignment, the more points the professors got. A fantasy psycho league. There were points for graffiti, points for stealing exam papers or important school trophies, points for intimate relations with certain untouchable professors, points for hurting people. There was something unspoken, too. The code speak they used was rudimentary at best, but to gain the biggest points of all there was a specific task: murder. Suicide was a deduction in points, and murder was the greatest point scorer of all. There were basically points for everything. Robert Coley was trying to recruit Abbey to be his candidate, to manipulate her into doing crazy things in order to win points for him. He had backed the wrong horse.

As Parker delved further into the details of the files, he was shocked to find that not only had this been going on for years, but it had gotten more extreme, with these people trying to outdo each other. He read through the correspondence and saw that they picked high-risk students with low entry grades, ones who had more to lose, and then leveraged something against them. With Abbey, it would have been something to do with the sexual assault. How low do you have to be to do something like that for entertainment? That's all it was to them, entertainment. There was no purpose here. They had tried to justify it under the guise of some sociological experiment, but it wasn't that, it was fun and games, nothing more. He had read about the Milgram studies on obedience and other experiments where children were taken to summer camps and forced to attack each other with knives, all trying to find out how far you could push a person against their own moral code. The success of these experiments lay in the small increments: start with something small, then build up to the big stuff. Many years later it had been discovered that many of the results had been falsified to prove the hypothesis, but that was less widely known; they left it out of the textbooks.

He had known people like this, he had killed people like this. You never heard about this kind of thing happening in the lower classes, it was always something that happened among the more affluent and educated people. People who thought they were better than anyone else. Before he had exacted his revenge, he had studied this kind of predatory behaviour. For, while he could understand one person deciding to kill someone, he wondered how these people met each other, how they approached each other and invited new members into the fold.

He read through the night, making notes in his black leather notebook, jotting down names and places. Although the names of the four professors were listed, the names of the students weren't. On its own this wasn't enough evidence for the police, but it was enough for Parker, enough to condemn them all. Tomorrow he would go and observe these professors and decide what to do next.

* * *

In the morning, Parker got up early. He had to think ahead. If he got caught by the police before he finished, then Helen Lassiter would go unpunished. There was a chance they would catch him and he had to be prepared for that. It was unclear from Helen Lassiter's correspondence whether she had been complicit in the sexual assault Abbey had endured at Exeter University. Had it been part of her game? Had she won points for what happened to Abbey? Had she told those boys to assault her? He wanted to ask her outright, but she wasn't here. Was he just reading between the lines and seeing things that weren't there? From what he could see, there was a chance, and with the way he felt about Abbey, that chance was enough. To break someone for sport was not a new concept, but the collusive nature of the game made Parker feel sick. It always amazed him that wicked people could find others like them. He couldn't risk letting her get away with it.

The pipes that led to the boiler were in the back of a corner cupboard. Parker pulled a wrench out of his backpack and started to loosen them. He grabbed some fairy liquid and smeared it on the edge, waiting for the tiny bubbles to appear, showing that there was a tiny hole where gas could escape. Hopefully the gas would build up enough before she returned, she wouldn't even know. He couldn't bank on the police not catching him before she returned and he knew she had to die, she was getting off easy though.

He walked from Helen Lassiter's place, making sure that no one saw him leave over the back fence. He had downloaded a map of the inside of the university and found out the internal layout. He marked Hugh Norris and Gillian Mitchell's offices. He was going to find out what he could about them.

When Parker arrived at the university, the sun had not yet risen, and the day was just beginning. The doors to the humanities block were unlocked, but it was a good three hours until lessons began. Parker slipped inside and walked through the halls, getting his bearings. The light to Doctor Norris's office was on. Parker made sure he was not seen before he knocked on the professor's door. There was no answer. He turned the handle and the door clicked open; he slipped inside.

When Parker turned around, he was confronted with the sight of blood, a lot of blood. He assumed the blood belonged to the body on the floor and he assumed that body belonged to Doctor Norris. It was hard to tell because his face had been obliterated. It looked fairly fresh and so it had happened in the last few hours. Who had done this? Was this part of the game? Or was this something else? Was there another person like Parker at work here, trying to ascertain the truth and dishing out retribution? He didn't know any of the answers, but he did know he had a limited amount of time now. The police would be involved soon.

Parker looked around the room for a computer, as it might have more information about who was in charge, but the computer wasn't here. He needed to find the other students before they were forced to commit any other crimes and asking Norris was no longer an option, so he searched in the drawers for any clues. He tried not to disturb the room too much, knowing the forensic scientists would be going over the place with a fine-tooth comb. Whoever committed this murder did a sloppy job.

He moved slowly and methodically through the room, making sure he didn't touch anything that had blood on it. He didn't want to transfer any blood to anywhere else. It was too difficult, and time was ticking on. He was angry with the person who left this mess. He couldn't do his job if things like this happened. Whatever their motivation was, whoever did this had made things more difficult for Parker. Or maybe he just couldn't admit to himself that he had been looking forward to confronting Norris. Maybe it wasn't about finding things out at all, maybe it really was all about the killing. He still had one shot left with Gillian Mitchell. She could prove to be the key to the case. He would follow her and watch for a while, from a distance.

Norris' death was bound to stoke up some frantic embers. He had to get out of there before someone walked in and discovered the body. He opened the door a sliver and looked into the hall. He could hear the clopping of heels approaching. Holding his breath, he waited for the woman to pass, hoping she wouldn't try to enter the office. He didn't want to hurt anyone that didn't deserve it. A minute later and she was gone. She might tell the police that she saw the professor's light on, but other than that she'd have seen nothing. He slipped out as quickly as he had slipped in, no one any the wiser. There was no CCTV inside these buildings.

As he was walking down the hill and out of the uni, he saw one of the maintenance staff unblocking one of the outside drains. He needed to get himself some blue overalls.

Chapter Thirty

Present

Imogen pulled the burned toast out of the toaster. It didn't matter what number she put it on, it always burned. It wasn't like it was the toaster's fault either; this was the third one she had bought. It was definitely something about her that was causing the problem. She felt Adrian's hands on her hips as he pulled her into an embrace, and she leaned back into him and huffed.

'I like it burned, it's good for you,' Adrian said.

'I'm pretty sure it's bad for you, actually.'

'Doesn't matter, I'm not that hungry anyway.'

'Who says it was for you?' She threw it in the bin onto four other slices of black toast.

'Do you want *me* to make you some toast?' Adrian offered.

'Yes, please.' She let him kiss her and then pulled away to make some coffee – something she rarely messed up. There was no denying that this was strange. Her there in her underpants and T-shirt, and Adrian with a towel wrapped around him after having a shower, having just spent another night at her house. It occurred to Imogen that it was even weirder because it felt quite comfortable. There was a slight cringe moment when they first slept together, but it was gone now, over with. He put a plate of perfect toast in front of her; she found this made her even more annoyed.

'What are you doing today?' she asked, knowing that Adrian had the morning off.

'I'm meeting Tom for breakfast. Second breakfast. He's on study leave for his mocks, so he wanted to meet up. I'll go into the station after that. What are you doing?'

'I'm going to go and see Caitlin today, see if we can get a link to the person who attacked you. She must be able to tell us who gave her those bruises and I'm betting it's the same person.' She saw Adrian flinch at the mention of Caitlin's name.

'Don't go alone, God knows what she might accuse you of,' Adrian said.

'I'll take Matt,' Imogen said, trying to gauge whether or not they were at the point yet where she could say what was on her mind. 'Listen, Miley, we still need her. Until this case opens up and we find out more. I know this is difficult for you, but she was as much of a pawn in this as you were.'

'I know.'

'I just hope this doesn't colour any further investigations.' She had said it. She braced herself for a

205

confrontation, but she had made a promise to herself that she wouldn't hold back on her thoughts now that they were in a relationship for fear of an argument.

'What does that mean?' Adrian turned and looked at her.

'You know how rare false accusations are. I don't want you . . . or me . . . to be jaded by this. We judge each case on its merits and try not to pass judgement before we have the facts.'

'Oh, I'm not jaded. My comment was only in reference to her, no one else.'

'OK, good. You're not upset, are you?'

Adrian walked over to her and kissed her on the lips; it was unexpected as she had been worried about broaching this subject with him. One false accusation tended to throw everyone's sensitivities out of whack. There would be some deep suspicion of everyone who reported a sexual assault once this was proven to be false, especially if it got into the newspapers. Sometimes it wasn't even a conscious thought, or a thought people wanted to have. It just crept in there. It was one of the reasons most police officers liked to downplay false accusations.

'I want you to always say what you're thinking. I hate mind games and I know you don't play them. I don't want us to have secrets. After everything that has happened I would rather have the truth and deal with the fallout of that.'

'You're a good egg, Adrian.' She kissed him back, mostly tasting the butter on her lips as he pressed against her, but unfortunately she didn't have time for this right now. She pushed him away. 'I have to get dressed. I have to be in in twenty minutes.'

'That's plenty of time.' He pulled at the hem of her T-shirt, guiding her out of the room. 'I'll help.'

Imogen didn't enjoy driving with someone who wasn't Adrian next to her. DI Matt Walsh was a nice guy; there didn't seem to be any ulterior intentions going on. He wasn't exactly open, but it didn't feel like he was hiding anything bad. He was quiet, reserved, but it just wasn't the same as having Adrian beside her. They made their way to the Reverend Nigel Watts' house to speak to Caitlin. The grandfather had granted them permission after they had assured him that no charges would be brought against her for the false allegation against DS Miles.

'Sorry I was late,' Imogen said.

'No need to apologise. Are you going to be OK with this interview?' Matt asked.

'Yes, of course. Why wouldn't I be?'

'Must have been hard to watch your colleague going through that.'

'It was, but I'm more interested in finding out who helped her stage the attack. It could be the same person who assaulted Adrian and made it look like a mugging.'

'Yes, just try not to let your emotional attachment to DS Miles affect the way you conduct this interview. It would be nice to get ahead of this. Figure out who is involved before they show up dead.'

'I think that's what we all want at this point,' she

said, angry at the implication that she would be anything other than professional.

She parked the car and opened the door, getting out before Matt had a chance to ask any more questions.

The faintest sound of sirens was somewhere in the distance, more than one vehicle, seemingly getting closer. Imogen walked up the path and knocked on the door.

A few seconds later, a frantic Reverend Watts opened the door.

'Please! Hurry!' he cried.

His sleeves were soaking wet and pink; it took Imogen a few moments to realise it was actually blood. She pushed past him and ran into the house, unsure where she was supposed to go.

'Where is she?' Imogen shouted.

'Upstairs, the bathroom,' Reverend Watts said.

Imogen knew, she knew before she even got to the room what she was going to find. She was going to find Caitlin Watts' dead body, in the bathtub, arms slit open from the inside of her wrist to the inside of her elbow. Imogen slipped on the polished floor, wet with a mixture of blood and water; at this point it looked like mostly blood. Caitlin lay in the bathtub, her skin whiter than the tiles and her hair floating in the deep pink water like tentacles. There was no need to check her pulse. She was dead. Any malice or anger Imogen may have felt for this girl disappeared in that instant. Caitlin had her whole life ahead of her – whatever mistakes she had made, she didn't deserve this. But Imogen couldn't shift the feeling that this wasn't what it seemed. Why would she do it now? Caitlin had already confessed to lying about Adrian. She had been afraid for her life, for her grandfather. It was possible that she had committed suicide in order to stop their control over her, whoever they were. But it was just as possible that this had been staged, that she had been murdered.

In the back of her mind, she tried to figure out if Parker would have any reason to kill Caitlin. The scene was artistic, like something he would have done, but far too messy. She couldn't think of a reason and decided that she would give him the benefit of the doubt for once. Unfortunately, the reverend had clearly been clambering around the bathtub, which had probably messed up any trace evidence of an intruder.

'Bloody hell,' Matt Walsh said. 'I'll call this in.'

'I'll do it. You'd better take the grandad downstairs for now as well. He doesn't need to see this again, not that it will make much difference, that image is already in there.'

'Poor kid,' Matt said before turning to the reverend and speaking softly to him. Imogen couldn't hear what he was saying, but it was working. She could hear the man calming down.

Imogen pulled out her phone and called the station. She wanted to call Adrian and tell him what had happened but thought better of it. If anything went awry with the investigation, they could pull up her records and see. She would call him later. She wasn't sure how he would take the news and she couldn't bear the thought of him being pleased about it in any way. She couldn't imagine he would be, but she didn't want to hear that in his voice. Why would she even think that of him? It occurred to her that she was either putting Adrian on a pedestal unduly or she was looking for ways to find fault in the relationship. She wasn't sure why. Maybe it was all moving a little too fast.

As she hung up to the station, her phone rang. It was her father, Elias.

'Imogen.'

'It's not really a good time right now.'

'I know you're busy and I'm sorry to bother you. I just wondered if you had given any more thought to meeting your brothers.'

She wished she hadn't answered the phone. With Caitlin lying dead before her, Imogen immediately started thinking about her dead mother, something she had been ignoring quite well so far. In Imogen's mind, her mother was where she always was. The sadness in Elias's voice forced her to face the truth.

'I'm sorry, I just don't think I'm ready yet. I know it's important to you, but I just need more time,' she said, aware that she was on the verge of crying all of a sudden. She could hear the ambulance sirens fast approaching. She needed to get back to work.

'I understand. I hope you are well.'

'I'll call you soon, I promise,' she said, hanging up the phone before she lost control of herself completely.

The ambulance Caitlin's grandfather had called arrived. Imogen shook her head at the paramedics as they ran past her. Caitlin was gone. There would be no resuscitation.

Chapter Thirty-One

13 days ago

Parker was wearing the university maintenance staff uniform. He found this made him entirely unmemorable if not invisible. He was able to walk in and out of rooms without suspicion, as long as he was careful not to bump into any of the other maintenance staff, who would have surely recognised him as not being one of them. He had been watching and waiting to scc how the faculty reacted to Hugh Norris's death. For the most part, everyone was suitably distraught. Gillian Mitchell was clearly not; he could see right through her. He had yet to determine whether she knew about the murder before it happened, whether she had orchestrated it in some way. He'd watched and followed Gillian all morning – she had stopped and spoken to colleagues about the tragedy that had happened, expressed her concern for her own safety and exasperation at the lack

211

of information from the police. There was something mechanical and rehearsed about her performance. She was almost definitely a sociopath. Playing to the crowds.

A part of the building had been cordoned off by police and the students were desperate to find out what had happened. He heard lots of whispers about a shooting, or terrorism, some other ludicrous conspiracy theories. The police were everywhere, searching the grounds; this was not a good time to be in the middle of it, and yet it was the best time, because it was when he might see the monsters. The way people reacted to a trauma was always very telling.

He followed Gillian Mitchell back to her office. She was just about to go in when Parker saw the familiar faces of DS Adrian Miles and DS Imogen Grey. He had known this was a possibility, but seeing them here like this made him feel vulnerable and exposed. One turn of the head and it could all be over. He watched from the corner for as long as he could. He had a bond with them; he didn't see them as the enemy but he didn't want to take his chances. He watched on affectionately as they approached Gillian Mitchell. She put her sad mask back on and answered their questions. He wanted to tell them not to believe her, to arrest her, but another part of him wanted to deal with her himself, to mete out his own brand of justice. He looked forward to it, but it scared him that he felt that way. He became increasingly annoyed at Gillian for lying to them and maybe even more annoyed at them for falling for it.

A young girl approached them and put her hand on Adrian Miles' shoulder. She was overfamiliar and Parker could see Adrian's obvious discomfort with the situation. He turned and looked at her, then looked away quickly. She didn't remove her hand straight away and Parker discerned that maybe she was playing the same game Gillian was. He saw Gillian's face change, both detectives preoccupied with the pretty young thing. Parker noted other students flashing glances the girl's way. She was striking; even from this distance, Parker could see how different she was. There was a Helen of Troy quality about her, the kind of girl that made the male students behave in a way that seemed a little desperate in her presence. He even saw it in Detective Miles for the briefest of moments. It wasn't so much beauty as a 'knowing' about the girl, as though she had the power to unlock some deep dark secret, not malevolent but curious and a little vulnerable.

It was Gillian who watched the girl the most intently as she batted her eyelashes at Adrian Miles; he pretended not to pay attention, but the girl wasn't even hiding the fact that she was flirting with him. Parker saw the machinations of Gillian Mitchell's mind whirring though. She had a plan and the girl was part of it.

Gillian walked away, leaving the detectives talking to the young girl. Parker saw the professor wait around the corner until the police left and then approach the young girl again, her skin shed. Parker was right about the girl; he could see that from their body language.

He got closer and listened to their conversation.

'I need them looking somewhere else. I can't have them snooping around here. At the very least I need them distracted. I think we need to give them something else to think about,' Gillian Mitchell said.

'I am already in enough trouble. I don't see what I can do without getting nicked.'

'You're going to get that good-looking detective to sleep with you. And then when you are done, you are going to say he raped you. With that hanging over them, they won't be able to concentrate on this at all and the media focus will definitely shift. The press will have a field day.'

'What makes you think he will even do that?'

'You're a pretty girl and I saw the way he looked at you. You can tell he likes you. Men can't resist something that's offered to them on a plate.'

'What will happen to him?' The girl looked genuinely concerned.

'That doesn't even matter, the whole force will be sidelined from this mess once the local news gets hold of it, which I will make sure of.'

The girl was being instructed to lure DS Miles into a trap, apparently because the investigation needed to be derailed. The girl wasn't as complicit as maybe Gillian Mitchell wanted her to be; Parker could see she was resisting.

'He's a nice guy. Isn't there some other way?' she asked.

Gillian grabbed Caitlin's arm, her fingers digging in. 'I've already told you. I need some time to deal with this and this is how I get time. You know what is at stake. You don't want your grandfather to go to prison, do you? Do you have any idea how easy it is to put unsavoury stuff on someone's computer? It's very easy. Just think about that.'

'Please, don't make me do this. You said you wouldn't ask me to sleep with anyone else. Not after Doctor Norris.'

'Norris needed to be brought back in line. He seemed to be under the misguided opinion that he could just stop whenever he wanted.'

'Did you have him killed?'

'Good lord, no. The last thing we need is a murder investigation on the premises. Now that we have one, you have to give them something else to think about.'

The girl seemed to be distressed at the suggestion, until Gillian reminded her of how much she had to lose. She was being blackmailed.

'It's your grandfather or the detective: you decide.'

'What if he doesn't want to? What if he says no?'

'Then we make it look like he did.'

Parker saw the girl wipe her cheek. She was in a situation she couldn't win, being forced to take part in this sick game. This was what they had planned for Abbey. His fist tightened into a ball. How many times had they done this before? It seemed to have been going on for years, judging by the things he saw on Helen Lassiter's computer. He wondered how many people had been caught up in their game. How was this fun? What was wrong with these people? He couldn't help but wonder what the prize was. What could possibly be worth this kind of manipulation? With every instruction Gillian Mitchell gave out, she forfeited a part of her soul, if she even had one any more. Maybe there was nothing left inside her but evil.

This whole scenario was making him so angry. What gave them the right to toy with others like this? It was the same force that gave him the right to kill them for it. Like an unspoken code, they were playing on his side of the tracks now and that was not a place you wanted to be. He would put a stop to this, not just because of what they had planned for Abbey, but because in his opinion, people like that didn't belong in the world. It wasn't for them, they didn't deserve it and they didn't really want it. They wanted their secrets and their lies, they wanted to feel smarter than the rest, they wanted to feel like gods. Parker had met people like that before and he had removed them from the game: not their game, his game. The only rule in Parker's game was that you didn't put yourself above others. No one should have the power to play with the rest of the world. Parker had proved this more than once. Power was not something you could own forever, you could lose it or it could be taken from you. That was why Parker believed he was here, to put those people in their place.

People like that know they are on borrowed time, he thought. *They know it will end badly for them, in a way that's what they want*. Parker knew that one day everything would catch up to him, he knew that he wouldn't live to grow old with grandchildren nipping at his feet. There would come a time when he would be removed from the game too.

216

Chapter Thirty-Two

Present

'Rather helpfully, we received a letter from Caitlin Watts, drafted by her lawyer, that cleared you of any wrong-doing. She said she was sorry for all the pain she caused you and that she was ridden with guilt over the allegations she made against you. It's being treated as a kind of suicide note,' DCI Kapoor said to Adrian, who was sitting across from her in her office.

'I don't think it was a suicide,' Adrian said.

'What makes you think that? Imogen said the same.'

'Mostly Owen Sager's body. We suspect whoever is orchestrating this may have staged a suicide before. These people think they are one step ahead of us all the time, they think they're clever. I think we can move forward with the assumption that maybe Caitlin's was staged, too.'

'Well, they *have* been one step ahead of us the whole

time. The good news is that you're now restored to full duties. DCC Sneddon and the Professional Standards Division are closing the investigation. I know it's been tough for you, but I'm impressed with how well you have handled it, and hopefully you will see things start to return to normal. Closing this case and finding out how the allegation Caitlin made against you fits into it will go a long way towards further clearing your name.'

'We are closing in and they know it. If Gary is right about the game, then we are only missing a couple of pieces of this puzzle,' Adrian said, not wanting to think about the investigation against him.

'How many people have to die before we figure it out?' Kapoor said disapprovingly.

'We need to find Russ Beacham, one other young male and, assuming we are correct about how this is working, one other lecturer. Those are the major players we know about. Assuming my mugging was also connected Beacham doesn't match the description of the guy who attacked me.'

'Are you sure?'

'Positive.'

'That still leaves the question of who is actually committing the murders?' DCI Kapoor said.

'We are chasing down some possible avenues. Nothing concrete yet,' Adrian lied. He couldn't tell her about Parker. Even if the DCI understood why they hadn't been able to arrest him, she would have no choice but to do something about it. Adrian wondered why he always managed to screw things up, even when he wasn't particularly trying.

'Well, keep me informed and stay away from this particular part of the investigation please, Adrian. If it does turn out that Caitlin Watts didn't commit suicide, the last thing we need is your name anywhere near it. No offence. You concentrate on finding the final players. Once the press hears about this there is no way they won't say it's some kind of conspiracy or cover-up. I'm really looking forward to that.'

'You don't think it's suicide either then?'

'I think from what you have told me so far then I have to be open to the possibility it isn't a suicide. It's strange timing for her to do it. She was essentially off the hook with us, as annoying as that is. Maybe she did feel guilty about what she accused you of, but she had already stated that she was in danger. We can't just ignore that or pretend she didn't say it.'

'What do I do now then?'

'Go through what we have already compiled on the case. After that, you can keep running through for any connections between Mitchell, Coley, Sager, Norris and Watts. That's five bodies; we simply cannot allow anyone else to die.' DCI Kapoor paused. 'I don't understand how Coley is connected, considering he was at a completely different university. I suspect if you track back far enough you will be able to find a connection between the professors. Maybe if we find out when it started we can find the final professor. Look for any leads on Beacham; I have a feeling he either knows what's going on and has disappeared to keep himself safe, or he is in it up to his neck and he's in hiding – from us.'

'Or he's already dead,' Adrian said.

'I love your unrelenting optimism, DS Miles.' DCI Kapoor waved him away and he left her office and went back to his desk.

The files on Sager and Norris were already lying next to his computer. He was more concerned with the other murders though. Understanding why Parker had killed Mitchell, Coley and Lassiter was key to finding out who was next. Maybe there was some kind of society or club they all belonged in together with Norris. In Adrian's mind, this game must have started as a conversation, which meant they must have all been in the same place at the same time at some point. Not only that, but they must have been close enough to even broach the subject with each other, most likely with prolonged contact. At some point Coley must have been with the others; Adrian was sure that was the key to unravelling this mystery. Maybe finding out when the game started was another possible key to figuring out who was next on Parker's kill list.

Adrian's phone vibrated on the desk. The number was blocked.

'Hello. This is DS Miles. Who am I speaking to?'

'Detective.'

It was Parker, even from those few syllables, Adrian knew. He was well spoken but his voice was soft, low. Adrian looked around him to see if anyone was looking.

'What is going on? You need to tell me.'

'I'm sorry about the girl. It wasn't me.'

'I didn't think it was.'

'I doubt it was suicide either.'

220

'Do you know about the game? Do you know who killed her?'

'Not yet. I think it was a student, but I haven't yet figured out who the final puppetmaster is. His identity seems to be the best kept secret of all.'

'You're sure it's a man?'

'I would be surprised if it wasn't.'

'You need to let us deal with it. When you find out who it was then you have to tell me.'

'I don't think I can. They are dangerous people, they don't deserve prison, they would probably thrive in there.'

'That's not really up to you.'

'I understand my return has put you in an impossible situation and I am truly sorry. I didn't want this. It came to me.'

'There is no way for me to protect you, or myself for that matter. If you get caught, then we are both in a lot of trouble.'

'They won't catch me, Detective. If they do, there is no way to connect me to the previous murders and I won't tell if you don't.'

'What if I hand you in?'

'You're not going to do that. These people are ruining lives, they have killed people. I just need to get the last of the professors and then it's over. The world will be a better place without them in it. They almost destroyed you, too. Think of all the innocent people they have hurt, including this girl. You know as well as I do that she didn't commit suicide.'

Adrian couldn't fault his logic, but if he stopped

believing in due process and people's rights then what was he? He had to do things by the book, no matter how much it pained him. There was a little part of him that wanted the people who made Caitlin Watts make those false allegations pay for what they did. As he walked through the corridors at work he could still hear whispers. He had a reputation with women, granted it had been a while since he had done anything like that, but shit sticks, and right now there was a definite stink around him, thanks to the group of people Parker was trying to eradicate. Maybe death would be too easy for them, but perhaps Parker was right, maybe they needed to just not exist any more.

'You need to let us take care of this,' Adrian said unconvincingly.

'I don't have any faith in your justice system, I only trust my own.'

The phone went dead. He was gone.

Chapter Thirty-Three

Adrian continued to look through the files, but his mind kept going back to Caitlin. He had tried not to think about her for a while now, since before she made the allegations against him. He had been attracted to her on some level; maybe if she was older and they were in another life, he wouldn't have hesitated to take the opportunity she had offered to him quite plainly.

When he was younger Adrian was quite a vulnerable teen himself, which was how he ended up being a father at sixteen. His parents were both preoccupied with their own problems; his mother virtually a ghost and his father an addict. He was left to fend for himself with no real guidance and a compulsion to seek refuge in the arms of his girlfriend, now the mother of his child, Andrea. She was the closest thing to love that Adrian had ever known. Although looking back now, he realised it wasn't love, just lust and, more than that, a desire to belong to someone, to be wanted by at least one person in the world. Caitlin had her grandfather; he was her home and her family. He could understand how she would do anything to keep hold of that and to keep him safe, and so Adrian couldn't be angry with her for what she had done. She really was a victim in this, too. He had been lucky enough when he was a teenager not to fall in with the wrong people. His father's experience had made him hate anything to do with drugs, and so he never touched them and stayed away from the dealers that used to hover by the back gates of his secondary school.

Sick of thinking about himself, Adrian opened the report on Owen Sager's staged suicide. The pathologist had told them that it would require some force to break his hyoid bone. Assuming it was the same person who had then attacked Caitlin, there should be some physical evidence on her. He wanted to get justice for her, even after what she had been forced to do to him.

Imogen walked in and sat down, letting out a huge sigh.

'Bad?' Adrian said.

She was wearing a police-issue tracksuit and her hair had been washed. Her clothes were obviously being processed to look for any evidence that it was foul play. He hadn't actually spoken to Imogen since they parted after breakfast this morning. DCI Kapoor had informed Adrian of what had happened at Caitlin's. He still hadn't been cleared to leave desk duty.

'We need to find out who is doing this and quickly,' Imogen said. 'I don't want to walk into anything else like that as long as I live. Her grandfather is a hollow shell right now. He just sat there staring into space, her blood on his hands and face. There was nothing I could say. I couldn't wait to get out of there.'

'Why didn't you call me?'

'So many reasons, most of all to protect you: you can't go anywhere near that place right now. You're too close to this case. I thought it would be better coming from the DCI anyway. Don't be mad.'

'I understand. I'm not mad, just worried. Are you OK? That must have shaken you up.' He wished he could go and hold her but that was out of the question here in the station.

'Just seemed like such a waste. All of it, you know? Why does life shit on some people more than others? For all her faults that girl was chosen because she was vulnerable and easy to manipulate.'

'I don't know. I'm sure there's some higher reasoning behind it, but as a lapsed Catholic I can't tell you what it is. Free will or something.'

'Don't even go there.'

'Exactly.'

'What have you been doing?' Imogen asked.

'Looking into Sager and Beacham. Realistically, I'm not getting anywhere. I feel like I'm missing something obvious, but I can't tell you what it is.'

'Maybe you need to step back a bit.'

'I don't see how.'

'Rather than looking for connections, focus on Beacham. We need to find him,' Imogen said. She had that haunted expression they all got sometimes when you see something you wish you hadn't seen. She was putting on a brave face, for him. Her mind was some-where else.

'How did she look?'

'Dead, Adrian, she looked dead.'

'You know what I mean. Did she suffer, do you think?'

'We spoke to Nigel Watts and he said she was fine when he left for his morning service. He got back to the house at around nine thirty, by which point she had been left alone for two hours. We arrived there soon after and she had been dead a while. If someone else did it, they must have been waiting outside for the reverend to leave. I think it was quick; there was a lot of blood though.'

'Was there any evidence of a struggle?' Adrian couldn't stop himself from asking.

'No, but she was clothed and the force with which her wrists were cut points to someone else being involved. She could have perhaps cut one, but I don't see how she then would have had the strength to do the other one with the same effort and precision.'

'What was she cut with?'

'A vegetable knife, one of those small serrated ones. It was on the floor in the bathroom. Can we talk about something else?' Imogen shuddered.

Adrian knew how to distract her. 'He called me.'

'Who did?'

'He did – Parker. Told me he didn't kill Caitlin.' Adrian could see Imogen visibly tense as he spoke.

'Jesus Christ, and you waited 'til now to tell me?'

'There's nothing to tell. He said he doesn't know who

the others are, but he was sorry about the girl,' Adrian whispered, aware that there were other people close by.

'Did you believe him?'

'He doesn't seem to lie, so I don't see what he would have to gain from starting now. Yeah, I believed him. He said he is trying to find the puppetmaster.'

'So maybe we can find out the final players before he does.'

'What are the chances of that?' Adrian said, unsure whether he wanted to find the person first. Maybe Parker was right and prison wouldn't stop them from manipulating people for their own entertainment. There were plenty of vulnerable people in prison. The only saving grace was that now all their playmates were dead. He probably shouldn't feel that way, but Adrian was fresh out of sympathy this week.

'Let's go and see Russ Beacham's parents. We have more information now at least. Maybe we can find out what hold the professors have over him,' Imogen said.

Chapter Thirty-Four

Russ Beacham's mother, Judith, answered the door to her apartment set among a small, low-level red-brick council block. Her eyes wandered up and down the detectives, then she walked back inside the house and left the door open for them to follow, obviously clocking that they were police immediately. Imogen always wondered what it was that gave them away; neither she nor Adrian particularly dressed like the rest of CID. She was always in her baggy trousers and Adrian generally looked like he had just got off a bender of some kind.

Judith Beacham sat on the sofa and lit a cigarette straight away, facing the window and crossing her arms. Here was a woman at the end of her tether.

'What's he done now?' she said, nervously sucking on the cigarette as soon as she had finished speaking.

'Do you know where your son is, Mrs Beacham?'

'Ms,' she corrected Imogen.

'Have you seen him?' Imogen asked.

'I haven't seen him for a couple of weeks now,' Judith Beacham said.

'Is that unusual?' Adrian asked.

'Probably means he is sponging off someone else for a change.'

'Did your son get a scholarship to Exeter University?' Imogen said.

'Someone else is paying for him, if that's what you mean.'

'Has he been in trouble before?' Adrian asked.

'Never had the police round before, but it's not really a surprise, not with the way he's been the last few months.'

'What's he been doing?'

'He nicked a load of booze from the shop on the corner, but luckily the man who runs it decided not to press charges. He knows me, knows us.'

'Anything else?'

'Took my mum's car for a ride when she was visiting one day, and he doesn't have a licence. He's stolen money from me, broken things. He beat some kid up in the park, but I managed to convince the mum not to report it.' She took a long drag before looking up at them. 'So what has he done now?'

'We need his assistance with our enquiries on a case,' Adrian said, ever the diplomat.

'I am sorry, I have no idea where he is. I don't even know him any more. He's always been a good kid, doesn't make any sense. I've tried talking to him, but nothing seems to get through. They always said he was too bright at school, that that would mean he got bored.'

'What are his grades like at university?' Adrian asked.

'Good, as far as I know. He didn't quite get the right grades to get in, but we had a few problems while he was doing his exams, so they said they would give him a shot.'

'You said someone else was paying for him,' Imogen probed.

'Yeah, my stepdad. Well, my mum's boyfriend. They're quite close, have been since Russ was about five.'

'Have they seen him? Your parents?' Imogen asked.

'No, and now they aren't talking to me any more. Said I've ruined him and I need to sort it out. I don't know what to do.' Judith Beacham's eyes glassed over, and she sniffed before wiping her eyes with her sleeve.

'Do you know if your son was hanging around with anyone new?' Adrian asked.

'He stopped telling me anything a couple of months into uni. Only got in touch when he wanted something. He was seeing a girl for a bit, but I don't know her name. I saw them together in town once and he practically ran away from me.'

'What did she look like?'

'Black hair, blue eyes. She was really pretty; I wondered if she was the reason he went off the rails.'

Imogen pulled out her phone and found a photo of Caitlin Watts. She showed it to Judith Beacham. 'Is this her?'

'Yes. Definitely.'

So, Caitlin and Russ had a relationship. Had she been

230

the worm that got Russ Beacham on the hook? Imogen wondered what they had threatened Russ Beacham with, how they got him to do the things he did. Had Russ Beacham been involved in Caitlin Watts' death? Had he killed her? Imogen's mind flashed to the image of Caitlin's black hair in deep pink water and she shook it off.

'You don't know of anyone else your son might have been involved with?' Adrian asked.

'No, I'm sorry.'

'If you hear from him, or if you think of anything else, then give me a call.' Imogen handed her card to Judith Beacham.

'Is he in a lot of trouble?' she said, a hint of defeat in her voice – as though she already knew the answer.

'We just want to eliminate him from our enquiries.' Imogen smiled, the stock reply when you didn't want to give the game away.

In a way, it was the truth, it would be great to be able to take him out of the equation, but from what Judith Beacham had said about his escalating bad behaviour, it seemed entirely possible that he was involved. Was he involved enough to have killed Caitlin, though?

They had linked the pair together now, which was at least something. They still needed to find the person who assaulted Adrian. Adrian had been certain it wasn't Russ Beacham and Imogen couldn't imagine he would feign any kind of certainty if it wasn't true, so that meant there was at least one other student involved.

Imogen and Adrian said goodbye to Ms Beacham and walked back to the car. The sky had clouded over

231

since they had been inside the flat. Imogen found herself shivering; she still kept seeing Caitlin's ashen face and she needed to get it out of her mind somehow. She couldn't help feeling like they had failed her, even after what she had done.

She looked over at Adrian as she got in the car. His face was screwed up in a mixture of concentration and concern.

'Thoughts?' Imogen said.

'He was in it, wasn't he? Even the fact of the one-parent family unit makes him a slightly more vulnerable person.'

'Hey! I was in a one-parent family.'

'So was I for the most part. I'm not saying anything other than, in terms of vulnerability, that leaves him a little more open to manipulation.'

'I suppose.'

'Do you think Caitlin was part of the manipulation?' Adrian said.

'How do you mean?'

'Beacham was an average-looking kid, Caitlin was not; maybe one of her tasks was to make Beacham fall for her. It certainly wouldn't be out of character for her to use her looks to get someone to do what she wanted.'

'I hadn't thought of that. That would make sense,' Imogen said, aware that Adrian was talking about himself.

'See, I'm not just a pretty face,' Adrian smiled.

'So, they get Caitlin together with Beacham, maybe to control him somehow. Then they draw him in by telling him that she is going to get hurt in some way.'

Imogen could see quite plainly that Beacham and Caitlin were not evenly matched in terms of looks. He wouldn't have ever had a relationship with someone like her before.

'Do you think he found out the truth and killed her for it?' Adrian asked.

'It's possible I suppose,' Imogen said.

'Maybe he killed Norris when he found out the truth as well.'

'So, Beacham just got promoted to suspect number one?'

'By default, if nothing else,' Adrian said.

'So, he's just gone rogue and is cleaning up?' Imogen said.

'Or someone is saying the right things to make him do what he's doing. We have at least one more major player and one more kid. It could be either one of them. What about if we get Gary to look through university student social media accounts? See if he can find any pictures of Beacham, either in the background or something – even without access to private accounts, there are plenty of public pictures.'

'That sounds like it would take a ridiculous amount of time.' Imogen groaned internally.

'He loves that kind of thing. At the very least, he could round up as many pics as possible and we could look through them. We might be able to find out who Russ Beacham was hanging out with. See if we can see which lecturers he was engaged with the most. It's got to be worth a try.'

'Blimey, Miley, do you need to lie down now? Those were a lot of thoughts.'

'Lying down sounds good.' He smiled at her.

The heat rose in her cheeks as she realised what he was implying. It was strange; she forgot a lot of the time that things had changed between them, mainly because so little had changed in the day-to-day. So far, he had been completely work-focused when they were on duty, which is why that comment had caught her so unawares.

'Right then, I'll let Gary know what we need,' Imogen said after the briefest moment; the foray into flirtation was short-lived. Back to work.

Chapter Thirty-Five

Adrian stared at the big monitor as Gary put up picture after picture from the university campus. Knowing that Russ Beacham had only started that previous September meant they didn't have to go back that far, but still, the amount of information was ludicrous. Between Facebook and Instagram alone, Gary had found over five thousand pictures, all public. It was like looking for a needle in a haystack. After three hours staring at the screen, Adrian wanted to poke his eyes out. Imogen returned to the room with hot coffee and some bagels.

'Any luck?' she said.

'What do you think?' Adrian groaned; maybe a bagel would keep him awake. They had to get ahead of this, though. They couldn't wait until someone else turned up dead and so it was a night of coffee and junk food for them.

'Well it was a long shot.' Imogen sighed and sat down, looking at the screen.

'If I stare at these screens any longer, I'm going to go crazy,' Adrian said as he massaged his own shoulder. A sharp pain ran across the width of his back and he was trying to get rid of it.

'Spoiler alert. You already are,' Imogen said.

'We've got plenty more to go. When I click through to friends and their friends, I just keep finding more,' Gary offered with a little too much enthusiasm, considering how dull the task was.

'No one connected with Beacham though?'

'He's not on social media. Bizarrely,' Gary said.

'I'm not on social media, what's bizarre about that?' Adrian asked. He had been thinking about joining, for about ten years now if he was honest. He just didn't want to get sucked into that world. He heard all the conversations in the station of things people did online and he was utterly baffled by it. It made the world feel so much smaller. So he stayed away from it. Maybe now Tom was a bit older he might consider it so that they could stay in touch.

'Couldn't he just be on there under a fake account? Or a parody account or something?' Imogen said.

'He could.' Gary nodded.

Gary pulled up a picture someone had taken of a person asleep in the lecture hall. Adrian spotted Russ Beacham sitting in the background, staring ahead.

'There he is – if he is in lessons with these people, then maybe this is the circle of people we need to focus on.'

Gary pulled up a few more pictures from the same social media account and from accounts linked to it. Nothing.

At least they had seen him once, that was a start.

The time passed slowly, and it became increasingly difficult to stay focused. A picture of some girls with Caitlin popped up and it was like a kick in the face for Adrian. Gary skipped past it to the next. It showed the same girls, only this time, Caitlin wasn't with them, she was in the background talking to someone. It wasn't Russ Beacham, but Adrian knew the face.

'Wait!' Adrian said before Gary skipped past. 'I've seen him before.'

'The guy talking to Caitlin? Where?' Imogen asked.

'Here. He was in here for something. Something really minor.' Adrian tried to think back to when he had seen him. 'Driving over the limit.'

Adrian stood up. It couldn't be a coincidence, could it? Was this kid the missing link? He remembered his countenance at the time of his arrest. He hadn't seemed particularly fazed by the experience.

'Can you remember when or what his name was? Or do we have to go through all the drink-driving offences?' Imogen sighed.

'Give me a second. It's on the tip of my tongue.' Adrian closed his eyes, searching for the name of the student that had made enough of an impression to secure a place in his memory. 'Finn. Finn Blackwell.'

'I'll pull up his file.'

Moments later, Gary pulled up an image of Finn Blackwell and put it next to the image of Caitlin with the young man. It was the same person.

'Do you have an address for him?' Imogen said

with a mouthful of bagel. She stood up and put her coat on, ready to go.

'We had better speak to the DCI first. Appraise her of the situation,' Adrian suggested.

'She's got an early meeting with the press, so she went home. We can't wait until then. Finn Blackwell is either dangerous or in danger. I'll tell Matt to let her know. We need to pick him up now,' Imogen said. 'Does Blackwell have any priors, Gary?'

Adrian could tell she was still thinking about Caitlin's dead body. He was glad he hadn't seen it himself but sorry that he couldn't have been there to support Imogen. She had always fiercely identified with the victims in their cases, especially young and vulnerable females. He wondered if she was remembering close calls in her own life; even since he had known her she had had more than her fair share of them.

'I'll see what I can dig up about him while you're out. And I'll let the DCI know what's going on,' Gary said.

Chapter Thirty-Six

Imogen and Adrian knocked on the door to Finn Blackwell's room in the halls of residence. The security officer had shown them inside and left them standing there, having gone back to his night watch. Adrian knocked again. The corridor was silent, and the lighting was dim, enough to light the way, but actually the semi-darkness felt quite imposing. There was the sound of various types of music coming from behind the many doors; it was a strange atmosphere. Adrian had expected it to be buzzing.

The door opened and Finn stood in front of them eating a bowl of cereal.

Finn was wearing pyjamas, he had music playing in the background and there were books pulled out across his bed.

'Can I help you?'

'Finn Blackwell?' Adrian asked, knowing the answer because they had met before, although there didn't even seem to be a remote spark of recognition on Finn's face.

'Yes. What is it?'

Imogen held up her warrant card and Finn leaned forwards, squinting to read the words.

'We need to ask you a few questions. Would you mind coming to the station with us?'

'What is this about?'

'I think it's better if we speak down at the station,' Imogen said.

'I'm not even dressed.'

'We can wait.'

At the station, they put Finn in an interrogation room and left him there for a few moments, watching him on the security cam to see how he was dealing with the situation. Finn was different to the last time Adrian had met him. He couldn't quite put his finger on it, but it was like he was less confident or cocky in some way. Maybe it was the alcohol in his system when they met the last time, but this boy didn't seem like trouble at all.

'Do you think he was the person who attacked you?' Imogen asked.

'He doesn't seem the type, does he?'

'No, he doesn't. Actually, seems quite nice. Quite sweet.'

The door opened and DCI Kapoor walked in. She crossed her arms and looked at the monitor.

'We thought you went home?' Imogen said.

'Well, I came back. Would be nice to have a suspect

name to take into my meeting tomorrow. Caitlin Watts'
death, aside from being a tragedy, is very bad optics
for us,' DCI Kapoor said. 'Which one is this?'

'This is Finn Blackwell. We haven't questioned him
yet, we're just watching him for a little bit, to see what
he does. He seems quite distraught.'

'Why haven't I heard that name before? Who is he?'

'We saw him talking to Caitlin Watts in one of the
social media images and I recognised him. I remembered
that he was brought in when I was on the desk with
Denise on Valentine's Day. Gary looked into him a little
and he could well be a part of whatever this is. He was
in Helen Lassiter's class. We thought we should question
him, see if he's involved.'

'OK then. Let me know what happens. Adrian, I
think you should take the lead on this interrogation as
you have some history with the boy.'

'Hardly.'

'Still, it makes more sense.'

'Fine, if you say so.'

'I'll stay in here and observe you both. No pressure.
See if you can find out if he knows Russ Beacham and
if he does know him, see if he knows where he is.
We don't have enough for a warrant yet. Everything we
have on Beacham is circumstantial. And the only thing
we have that connects this boy to this case is a photo
of him talking to Caitlin? Knowing what she looked
like, I expect there are plenty of pictures of her talking
to plenty of guys or at least guys trying to talk to her.
That's really not enough.'

'OK, I'll see if I can dig deeper,' Adrian said.

Adrian opened door and left the room, Imogen following closely behind. The DCI stayed.

There was something strangely innocent about Finn. Adrian found it hard to believe he could have murdered Hugh Norris; at the very least he didn't seem to have the physical power it would have taken to smash his face in in that way. Adrian wasn't one hundred per cent sure that Finn wasn't the person who had attacked him on the night of Caitlin's alleged assault though. It could have been him, but all he could really remember were the attacker's eyes. Blue eyes, the most common eye colour in Britain, displayed by almost half the population in the South of England, higher the further north you went. It was hardly a lead. Maybe Finn was just a really good actor. One thing was certain, though: whatever he knew, they would find out.

Chapter Thirty-Seven

Adrian crossed his arms and leaned on the table. Finn fidgeted nervously in front of him and his eyes darted around the room. Adrian could feel the heat of Imogen's body next to him; he could feel her concentration and knew that her stare was making Finn uncomfortable. She was good at that.

'Why am I here?' Finn asked.

'I think you know why you're here, Finn. Do you remember me at all? We met on Valentine's Day.'

'Look, this is a mistake. I don't know what you think I've done, but I haven't done it.'

'Caitlin Watts? What do you know about her?'

'I heard that she died, that she killed herself. I didn't really know her though.'

'How did you hear that? It's not common knowledge yet. Who told you?'

'It's all over the uni. You can't keep a secret in that place. No one can.'

Finn's agitation seemed to be increasing and Adrian could feel a gulf between them. There was no connection. Adrian shifted his gaze to Imogen, who took his cue and leaned forward as Adrian pulled back.

'Do you know Russ Beacham?' Imogen asked.

'I'm not friends with him, he's weird.'

'Weird how?' Adrian pushed. The mere mention of Beacham's name and Finn's face had turned white: he was afraid.

'I don't know how to explain it, he just sets my teeth on edge.'

'In what way? What is it that he does that upsets you particularly?' Adrian said.

'I just steer clear of him.' Finn's eyes darted as the questions continued.

'So, are you better friends with Caitlin or Russ?' She slid the photo of Finn talking to Caitlin in front of him. He looked down. His thumb traced across Caitlin's face. He looked confused for a moment and pushed the photo away.

'I've hardly ever spoken to Caitlin before. She's way out of my league.'

Adrian watched Finn. His eyes moved from the picture to Imogen to Adrian and back again as though he were trying to assess the situation. He had that look on his face, the kind you get when you just can't remember something, when it's on the tip of your tongue. Or maybe it was something else.

'How about Russ? Can you tell us anything about Russ?'

'He was aggressive, he drank a lot and he used to

do those codeine drink combo things. You know, that "Purple Drank", that's what they call it, I think. I've never tried it myself, but it's when you put a load of painkillers and cold medicine crushed up in a caffeine drink. You can chuck all kinds of shit in there. Russ used to put Fruit Polos in his.'

Adrian had heard of this before, new highs with over-the-counter drugs mixed in with high-sugar, high-caffeine energy drinks and anything they could find in the medicine cupboard at home. There was no recipe per se, but that was part of the fun. Some people called it 'Lean' and others use the American nickname of 'Purple Drank'. Cases at the local hospital were on the rise, but there had been no local fatalities yet, just a lot of stomach pumping. He wondered if the high was worth it.

'So how much time would you say you spent with Russ?' Imogen said.

'As little as possible.'

'Do you know about the game?'

'What game?' Finn's eyes widened momentarily and he looked down to conceal the panic. He knew what she was talking about.

'When I first met you, you were brought in for drink driving. You don't seem to have a history of that sort of thing.' Adrian glanced at Imogen, who had put her elbows on the table, leaning forwards. She had noticed Finn's reaction, too. It was hard to hide in a tiny room when all eyes were on you.

'I think my drink was spiked, I don't remember too much. I remember waking up in a holding cell.' He wasn't convincing anyone.

'So, you weren't asked to do that? Forced to do it?' Imogen pushed.

'What are you talking about?' Finn said, getting more agitated and looking at the door as if he wanted to try to make a run for it, or perhaps he thought someone was coming to save him.

He clearly hadn't accounted for this situation. Wasn't prepared for it. Whatever was going on with him, he seemed to be under the impression that this was all a big mistake. Had someone promised to keep him out of trouble?

Adrian decided to take a risk; after all, Finn wouldn't know he was lying.

'Caitlin told us about the game. About what you were being asked to do, by Helen Lassiter and the others. The drink driving, the attack on Caitlin.'

'I didn't attack her. I wouldn't do that,' Finn cried.

'Was that Russ?' Imogen asked.

'It must have been. It wasn't me. Russ was a psycho, you have no idea the things he was capable of.'

'But you know what we're talking about, don't you?' Imogen said.

'I didn't do anything. I swear to God I don't know what you're talking about!'

'What other things have you been asked to do?' Adrian said.

'I don't feel very well.' Finn rubbed at his neck, which had gone an angry red colour; it looked more like a rash than embarrassment. He was sweating.

'Did they make you hurt people?' Imogen said.

'Please, I need to lie down.'

246

They were close to breaking him, but they were also close to shutting him down completely. Adrian didn't want to stop him from talking altogether, so he pulled it back a little. 'OK. We'll come back to that. Let's talk about Russ some more. Do you know where he is?'

'I don't feel very well.' Finn's face had gone pale, exaggerated by the redness of his neck. He looked like he was going to throw up.

'*Do* you know where Russ is now?' Adrian repeated the question.

'I don't know,' he said unconvincingly, the intonation at the end of the statement going upwards as though he were asking a question.

'You don't have any idea where he might be?' Imogen pushed further.

'His mum would probably know. She was always on his case to do better, to make sure he didn't blow his chance at university. He would tell her things just to upset her, especially when he was off his face. Just to stop her thinking of him like he was her little boy still. He wasn't a nice guy.'

'I've noticed something,' Imogen said. 'You've been talking about Russ in the past tense. Why is that?'

Adrian couldn't believe that he hadn't noticed. Imogen was right.

'I haven't seen him in ages and I don't want to see him again. He is not part of my life any more. The guy is nuts.'

'We're going to go and speak to his mother again, see if they can tell us anything.'

Adrian finish the recording and nodded to the constable to take Finn back to holding.

'What do you think?' Adrian said. 'He's weird, right?'

'Seems OK to me. All over the place a bit, but that could be nerves. Then again, I have no point of reference. If you say he's different to the last time you met him then maybe he is.'

They walked into the observation room where DCI Kapoor was waiting for them.

'It's late or early depending on how you look at it. Should we go and see Judith Beacham now?' Adrian looked at the clock – it was three in the morning.

'Go home, grab a couple of hours' sleep, get showered and then go and see the mother at first light,' the DCI said. 'I wish I could offer you more than that, but we don't know when the next body is going to turn up and as you seem to have the firmest grasp on the facts of this case, better if you do the interviews at this point – we need continuity right now. You might spot something someone else doesn't.'

She was right, there were some cases you just couldn't walk away from until they were done and dusted. When the threat of people being hurt was imminent, a good night's sleep was the furthest thing from your mind. You just wanted to make sure that no one else died on your watch.

Chapter Thirty-Eight

Imogen pulled up outside Adrian's house and stopped the car. Adrian paused before turning to her. Still in the very early stages of a relationship, she had no idea what the protocol was now when they were driving each other home, as they always had done. It didn't make much sense for both of them to drive into work. They were saving the environment. Now maybe the environment didn't matter as much as setting boundaries.

'What are you going to do now?' Imogen asked.

'Sleep. It's been a while,' Adrian said.

'Oh, okay,' Imogen tried not to sound disappointed.

'You're welcome to come in. I don't want you to feel that you have to hang out with me all the time. But you should know that I would be fine with that.'

'I might be OK with that as well.' She smiled.

'Come inside for a bit then?' he said; he had that concerned look on his face.

She switched the engine off. She didn't want to be

alone right now, the image of Caitlin was still fresh in her mind.

They both got out and went inside. The house was cold; the heating had obviously been off for several hours. As soon as they were inside, Adrian put his arms around Imogen and held her close.

'You smell like the station soap.' He gently touched her face and she looked up. She liked the way Adrian looked at her now they were together. She could feel him studying her face and wondered what he was looking for.

'Thanks. I haven't been home since . . . earlier.'

'You know, I could use a shower. Come in with me?' He kissed her.

She followed Adrian upstairs and he handed her a towel as she got undressed.

In the shower, she stood with her back to him, his hands working the hot soapy water into her neck and shoulders, and she felt glad that he was grounding her like this, stopping her from thinking about that poor dead girl. She turned and pressed against him, water running between them. She just wanted to hold him for now.

Afterwards, they lay together on the bed, her hair wet on the pillow. Occasionally he would kiss her forehead and stroke her arm, but other than that they just let the tension of the day slip away from them.

'What are you thinking about?' Adrian said as she dozed.

'Isn't that supposed to be my line?'

'Don't avoid the question.'

'Sorry, officer,' Imogen said.

'Still avoiding. What's on your mind?'

'Just wish the world wasn't so unfair sometimes, you know?'

'We can't control that,' Adrian said.

'If we had got there sooner then we might have been able to save her,' Imogen admitted. It was a pointless thing to say because you could say that about almost every turn in every single case. You just had to follow the case and go where it took you. Not every crime was premeditated, some things you just couldn't stop. Imogen knew all of that and yet she still couldn't help feeling somewhat responsible.

'I'm sorry I wasn't there.'

'I'm glad you weren't.'

'We don't have a crystal ball. You just have to know that you're doing the best you can.'

'Am I though? Half the time I'm thinking about my own bullshit.'

'You're a good policewoman, Imogen. Don't tell yourself otherwise. It's been a rough time, both of us have had a lot to deal with over the last couple of years. It won't always be like this.'

'After everything that's happened, how can you be so optimistic? My mother spent her whole life alone and when she finally got the man she wanted, she died. These kids are being manipulated as part of someone's sick game. Not to mention what happened to Dean . . . and Lucy.' She felt his muscles tighten at the mention of Lucy's name. 'Sometimes it all feels so futile, like whack-a-mole or something. Get rid of one bad thing and another two pop up in its place.'

251

'You miss him, don't you? Dean.'

'If I wanted to be with Dean, I could be with Dean, Adrian. You need to believe that I am choosing you, you are not the booby prize,' Imogen said. She wasn't lying; she had chosen the job over Dean and part of the reason she'd chosen the job over Dean, she realised, was because of her friendship with Adrian. Maybe she hadn't admitted to herself that there had always been something more between them. When she'd transferred to Exeter, she had promised herself never to get involved with a colleague again, so she had never even entertained the idea of being with Adrian, until she couldn't run away from her feelings any longer.

She let out a big sigh and closed her eyes, hoping to drift off for a few minutes. It had been an exhausting day.

Adrian broke the silence. 'We'll get the people responsible for this.'

'Do you ever think that he's right? Parker?' Imogen asked.

'Yes, I do sometimes, but then I remember why I chose to join the police. Because I believe in due process and not vigilante justice. I guess it's just hard with the things we have seen to be clear-headed sometimes,' Adrian said.

'You can say that again.'

'I feel bad for Caitlin Watts, too. Even after what she did, I don't hold her responsible, I know she was forced to do it.'

'Small consolation, I expect,' Imogen said.

'The idea of someone deliberately doing that to anyone,

252

making a false claim like that, is hideous. I could almost understand it if it was just one messed-up person looking for attention or something, but to think this was a premeditated and orchestrated accusation made to derail an investigation seems a lot more callous and inhuman.'

'Which is why we have to get those involved. What's left of them anyway,' Imogen said.

'We will. And if we don't, Parker will.'

'How do we keep him out of this?'

'We don't. If he gets linked to the investigation through the evidence, then we have no choice but to go after him. He knows that.'

'But we're not going to actually look for the evidence?' Imogen asked.

'I don't know about you, but right now I'm glad he's out there doing what he does. I'm scared that if he wasn't and if we don't find whoever is responsible, they would be able to set up shop somewhere else and ruin God knows how many more lives.'

'Doesn't it bother you that you're OK with it?' Imogen said.

'It does,' Adrian said before kissing her again. Obviously in a move to stop her talking. She was fine with that. She pulled him onto her – his weight on her felt good. They had some time before they had to go to work again.

Chapter Thirty-Nine

For the second time in as many days, Imogen and Adrian were visiting the Beacham residence. Russ's mother looked surprised to see them. More surprised than she had the first time. Imogen knew when someone was keeping secrets; either something had happened since the last time they spoke, or she had neglected to tell them something important and knew they were back to get the information.

Judith Beacham welcomed them into the house and showed them into the lounge again. She seemed almost put out by their reappearance, but that wasn't going to stop Imogen from getting to the bottom of this. This case was really doing her head in.

'Is there something you haven't told us about Russ?' Imogen said, getting right to the point.

'Like what? I don't know what you mean.'

'Do you have any idea where he is?' Imogen asked.

'Can I get you a cup of tea? Or some water maybe?' Judith said.

'Do you think Russ is in trouble? Do you think he's done something he shouldn't have?' Adrian asked.

'He's a good kid, he's just been . . . Different lately. Whatever he's done is not his fault, someone must've made him do it.' Judith seemed to have changed her tune since yesterday.

'So, you do know something, something you haven't already told us?' Imogen said.

'Please know that I was completely honest with you yesterday, but . . .'

'But you got some new information?' Adrian said, his voice softer than Imogen's. Adrian was always the good cop.

'My parents knew I'd been having problems with Russ and so they didn't tell me that he'd taken their car again. It's been missing for over a week. I phoned them last night to tell you had been. They just didn't want to get him into trouble either. I was going to call you first thing this morning, I swear.'

'You said yesterday that he had taken the car before?'

'Him and that girl had taken it and driven out to the reservoir at Kennick. I think they went skinny dipping in there.'

'Caitlin Watts? The girl we showed you the picture of?'

'Yes, her.'

'Did Russ have any male friends? Do you know who this boy is?' Imogen pulled out her phone and pulled up the picture of Finn Blackwell.

Judith Beacham looked at the picture for a good few seconds before shaking her head. 'No, I don't think I ever saw this boy with my son.'

'Just the girl?'

'What is all this about? What do you think he's done?' she said, her eyebrows knotted in confusion.

'We're just trying to eliminate him from our enquiries,' Imogen said.

'Do you know the registration number of your parents' car? Do you think you could write it down for us?'

Judith leaned forward and scribbled on a notepad that was on her coffee table. She tore the page out of the book and handed it to Adrian. Imogen had noticed plenty of times before how women much preferred dealing with Adrian than they did with her. She had never particularly got any feelings of solidarity from any females in her life. She didn't even have a best friend, never had done, unless you counted Adrian. Which she did.

Five minutes later, they were stood outside the Beacham flat, the door firmly closed.

'I think I can get more out of Finn Blackwell. We already know they knew each other. I don't know what it is that bothers me about that Blackwell kid, but there's definitely something. I think I should talk to him again,' Adrian said.

'Are you sure? What about this Beacham lead?' Imogen said.

'Call DI Walsh and ask what he wants to do. If we find the car we will probably find Russ Beacham.'

Chapter Forty

Adrian and Imogen got back to the station just as Gary was arriving. They all walked straight in to see DCI Kapoor to let her know what they had learned. DCI Kapoor was putting the phone down as they entered. She had the look of someone who had just been reprimanded. Adrian was all too familiar with that feeling.

'Please tell me you have something,' she said.

'We spoke to Russ Beacham's mother again and she said that he took his grandparents car a while ago and hasn't returned it,' Adrian explained.

'So, we need to look for this car then. What is it?' Gary asked.

'Nothing too fancy, just a silver Ford Focus,' Adrian said.

'Oh good, there aren't many of those around,' Gary rolled his eyes.

'It is what it is,' Adrian shrugged.

'Do we have any possible ideas about where it might be?' DCI Kapoor asked.

'Well, the mother said the last time he'd taken it with Caitlin they drove out to Kennick in it, so I guess anywhere around there might be a good starting place, plus the surrounding area too,' Adrian said.

'By surrounding area do you mean Dartmoor? Roughly a thousand square kilometres of land? Brilliant,' Gary said.

'Can I get you a coffee or something? You seem unusually irritable,' Imogen acknowledged.

'Am I not allowed an off day?' Gary asked.

Adrian leaned against the wall and folded his arms; he hadn't dealt with bad mood Gary before, but he imagined it worked a lot like bad mood Imogen, who he had much experience with. If Gary was going to share what was bothering him, he needed the space to do it in. Badgering people for information only ever worked when you had them in an interrogation suite and even then, it wasn't a given.

Gary opened his laptop and started tapping away. He pulled up several videos on the screens and pressed play on one of them.

'I've got something, too,' Gary said as the video started playing.

'What's this?' DCI Kapoor asked.

It was Hugh Norris's office and after a few moments it became apparent that it was the murder. The resolution wasn't great and it wasn't from a particularly helpful angle.

'What do you think it is?' Gary said, looking at Adrian.

Adrian watched as the murder unfolded in front of him. The killer was wearing a hoodie and his face was covered, so there was no way of telling who it was, but still, this was a great piece of evidence, if only to understand the logistics of the crime.

'Where did you get this?' Adrian asked.

'Gillian Mitchell's computer. The crime techs didn't mention there being any hidden cameras in the offices, but there must have been and Gillian had the videos encrypted and hidden inside a ridiculous amount of subfolders – it took me a while to find it. I've passed this information on and Karen Bell went to check for the camera. Unfortunately, whoever the cameras belonged to has had them removed. Someone with access. There is more footage though. Most of it's pretty dull – just a bloke in his office. Still got a fair amount to get through, but I thought you would want to see these.'

Gary pulled up the murders of both Robert Coley and Gillian Mitchell in split windows. Same figure, same coldness.

'Fuck,' Adrian said.

The Coley murder was particularly long and hideous. The videos were all terrible resolution and in all of them the killer's face was obscured, even though Adrian knew who the killer was. It was one thing to theoretically understand where Parker was coming from, it was another thing to witness the calm cold-bloodedness of his crimes.

'Whoever this guy is, he's messed up. He shouldn't be on the streets,' Gary said, shooting yet another dirty look at Adrian.

'Can you enhance the resolution at all?' DCI Kapoor asked.

'I've been trying. Crap hardware and lens means it's not necessarily something that can be enhanced,' Gary said.

'We'll never get a conviction from it, even if we knew who was doing it. The resolution is terrible and if you say you can't enhance it then we definitely need much more than this. You can't even tell if it's a male or a female,' DCI Kapoor said. 'If we are to believe Finn Blackwell then this could be Russ Beacham. We need to find him. That's assuming Blackwell can be trusted. What do we really know about him?'

'Didn't get the right grades, same as the others. Been picked up twice by us before, once when I saw him and another time for causing a bit of a scene in Princesshay Shopping Centre; he urinated on one of the statues and someone called the cops. He wasn't charged either time.'

'Maybe you should go and speak to the other kids in the halls and see if they know anything about him. They might be able to tell you who has been visiting him or what hours he keeps, when he goes out, who with, if he is an easy neighbour or a troublemaker, et cetera. We need a more complete profile of this boy,' DCI Kapoor said.

'OK, Ma'am.' Adrian said.

'Get to it, then,' she said, beginning to usher them out.

Gary picked his laptop up and left the room. Adrian shot a questioning look at Imogen, who nodded for him to go after Gary. Adrian rushed out and down the corridor, grabbing hold of Gary's arm.

'Is this what you're upset about? The video?'

Gary leaned forward and whispered, 'Aren't you? You're covering for this guy.'

'No, I won't cover for him. He knows I will bring him in if needs be,' Adrian said, letting go of Gary's arm.

'I'm not sure I believe that.'

'What does that mean?'

'I don't know,' Gary said. 'I wish you hadn't told me about him.'

'First you're angry because we didn't tell you and now you're angry because we did?' Adrian said.

'Did they really deserve this? Does anyone?' Gary pointed at the screen where Coley's body lay strapped to the desk, his back sliced open, what was left of his spine exposed.

'Maybe. I don't know. Maybe some people do deserve it,' Adrian said.

'If you really believe that then you're not the person I thought you were.'

'All I'm saying is that it's not always black and white. If you had seen what they did to that man as a kid, then you would have thought twice about arresting him, too. They photographed most of the torture they put him through; we can go down to evidence and look at it, if you want? You wouldn't want to punish him any more than he has been.'

'But I would want to protect everyone else,' Gary said.

'He's not a danger to everyone else,' Adrian said, even though the video in front of him said otherwise. Who was Adrian trying to convince? 'What else did you find on the computer?'

'A lot of stuff. If Gillian Mitchell wasn't actually in charge, then she was the next best thing. She had an external hard drive that was found when they searched her place. There were a lot of files on it that I hadn't got from any of the other victims. I have to turn all this over into evidence once I catalogue it. I made a start last night, but I wanted to make sure you heard it from me first. And there's something else I wanted to show you.'

'Great.'

Adrian could feel Gary's disapproval and he didn't like it. He understood and respected Gary's point of view, but he didn't like being at odds with him, even though he couldn't change the way he felt any more than Gary could change his views.

Gary put his laptop on an empty hot desk, the ones they used for visiting staff. He plonked himself in the chair and pulled up another video; it was the high street late at night. This time the footage came from a camera phone. The video followed a young man in a hood as he walked. The person holding the camera stopped and kept filming as the other man ran across the road. Adrian recognised the area in town and then he saw himself, just before the camera zoomed in on the younger man swiping an open claw across his face and then punching him to the ground. Adrian got up and threw a couple of swings himself before he gave chase, but then the video stopped.

'That video is time- and date-stamped and completely exonerates you of any wrongdoing in the Watts attack. I suspect the DCI might want to release this to the press after we catch this Beacham guy, as there are still some people who are calling for your job.'

'You should have started with this video.' Adrian tried not to sound pissy.

'There's barely a glimpse of the guy's face as his friend filmed him from behind, but I am trying to get an ID. Now let's have a look for this bloody car.' Gary typed in the reg number to see if there had been any notifications on it over the last few weeks. 'I'll get on to traffic and see if they have anything.'

'I'll check with the university and see if it's on any of the campuses.'

'I'll do it,' Gary said, the knot in centre of his forehead visibly tightening.

'It's fine, you've obviously got enough on your plate. Sorry if I expect too much of you.'

Adrian felt guilty; maybe he did ask Gary for too much. He never usually seemed to mind; in fact, Adrian thought he liked it.

'God, it's not that. I'm just worried that you and Imogen are in over your heads. I don't know why you think you can trust this Parker guy, but you shouldn't. What he's doing in those videos shows a complete lack of empathy or human feeling. He's doing it because he enjoys it. Maybe it's all about justice for now, but what happens when he runs out of bad people to dissect? Those urges don't just go away.'

'I know,' Adrian admitted reluctantly.

'And what happens when you decide to drag your heels so that he can get to the bad guys before you?'

'What are you suggesting?'

Adrian knew what he was suggesting and it was a thought that had crossed his own mind. Where did this end? Wasn't Adrian already complicit by not putting Parker away? What was worse was that he was making his friends complicit, too. His head hurt.

'I'm saying that every time you let him cross a line, you cross a line yourself and who knows where that ends up? What if one day you start helping him?' Gary said.

'That's not going to happen,' Adrian insisted.

'You're on a slippery slope, my friend.'

'Are you going to tell the DCI about him?'

'And get you both fired, or worse? How is that going to help? I don't need that on my conscience, thanks.'

'You're right. I don't know what to do.'

'There's no way of knowing who is in these videos, they are all quite useless in terms of identification, so you got lucky there. The definition is very poor, but from what I can see the perpetrator has got generic clothes on, no identifying labels, average height and weight like the other suspects. This could be Beacham or Blackwell as far as we know,' Gary consoled Adrian. 'We just have to hope that your friend knows when to stop.'

The only way Adrian could think of this ever working was if Parker came forward and handed himself in. What were the chances of that?

Chapter Forty-One

Imogen had never been to university herself and so walking through halls was reminiscent of a life she'd never had. She couldn't imagine it for herself, being in close quarters with all these other people day and night. Growing up as an only child to a single mother meant she was not used to this amount of company. Imogen had never felt like she missed out and being here today confirmed that fact. Soon university would be a part of becoming a police officer; she was glad to have bypassed that.

Adrian was trailing behind her, on the phone to his son who was in the middle of intensive revision for his exams. She knew Tom well, but not as Adrian's girlfriend, and so what had been a fun and interesting friendship with her partner's son was now looking like it might get extremely awkward. Adrian rightfully hadn't told him yet and she wasn't sure how he would react to the news. Did she even want him to know yet?

Was this serious? It certainly had a weight about it, as relationships went – they already knew each other's baggage, and so the usual small talk at the start of a relationship had never happened and they'd been thrust straight into stage three. After flirtation but without the usual ceremony of the first or second date, here they were.

She waited patiently for him to hang up and then knocked on the door to the room next to Finn's. A small, waspish blonde girl opened the door and peered through, her tight smile dropping when she saw it was two 'older' people looking very serious indeed. There was no need to pretend to be friendly.

'Hi, we just wanted to ask you a few questions about your neighbour, Finn. If that's OK?'

'Um, sure. I don't know him very well though,' she said.

Imogen wasn't sure, but she thought the girl was blushing at the mention of Finn. She pulled out her notepad.

'What's your name, please?' Adrian asked, anticipating Imogen's next question.

'I'm Heather Randall.'

'Did you ever see Finn with this girl?' Imogen said, holding up a picture of Caitlin Watts with her free hand.

'Yes. A couple of times. He didn't spend a lot of time in halls though, to be honest.'

'Did he hang out with anyone in particular here?' Adrian asked.

'He had a fight with the guy down there. I think his

name is Scott.' She pointed to a door at the end of the hall. 'Number seven.'

'Thank you.' Imogen smiled at Heather, who shut the door as quickly as she had opened it. Imogen scribbled down everything the girl had said before they walked down the corridor to the room she had pointed at.

Scott had music thumping and the unmistakeable aroma of weed permeated through the door. Adrian banged on it hard. The music stopped and after a few moments of clattering, the door opened. Scott had unruly curls that hung in front of his eyes; he was young-looking, they all were. Imogen had to face the fact that she wasn't a teenager any more, even though in her mind she had never considered herself a grown-up.

'What?' Scott said.

Imogen held up her warrant card; she didn't need to, but all things considered she wanted to see the look on his face as it slipped into a panic about whether he looked stoned or not. He did look stoned. He looked very stoned.

'What's your full name and course, please?' Imogen said.

'Scott Joseph Woodlaw, I'm reading economics.'

'Finn Blackwell. We heard you had an altercation with him,' Imogen said.

'That psycho? He tried to fucking choke me.'

'Why?'

'I didn't know she was his girlfriend, that Caitlin girl, she certainly didn't act like she was. She came in here for a . . . for some . . . help with something and he practically dragged her out and then started punching the shit out of me, then got me in a headlock,' Scott explained. Caitlin had probably gone in there to get high without actually paying for her own supply.

'Did you report it?' Imogen asked.

'No, I just stayed away from both of them. I used to keep my door open, but now I lock it. I haven't seen him since. He ain't right.'

'What about this boy? Do you know him?' Imogen said as she scrolled until she found a picture of Russ Beacham and then held it up to him.

Scott shook his head. 'No, never seen him before.'

'We may need to talk to you again, Scott. You might want to ease off on the hash until we do,' Adrian said with a little wink in Scott's direction.

A fleeting look of fear passed across the boy's face, but he relaxed when he realised they weren't going to do anything. He closed the door and Imogen turned to Adrian.

'That doesn't sound like the Finn we've got in holding.'

'None of that means we can hold onto him for any longer though.'

'No. We're just going to have to find something else.'

'I'll find Gary when we get back and see if there is anything else we can use. We're running out of avenues right now. Where the hell is Russ Beacham? If we didn't have a photo of him I would almost swear he and Finn were the same person. How has Beacham stayed a ghost for so long?'

Chapter Forty-Two

Imogen couldn't keep her eyes open in the station. Two hours' light sleep really wasn't enough. Everyone had been working round the clock to try to find out where Russ Beacham was before another body turned up. Adrian was still in with Gary, and she didn't want to go and find them. It's not that she needed a break from Adrian, but she was worried that she was getting too dependent on him; she had to remember how to work alone. Adrian could just relay any information to her when he got back. In the meantime she wanted a coffee and couldn't face the tepid mud from the machine. There was a little cafe near the station. She could go and pick up some coffees and pastries for everyone before it closed; she could use the fresh air as well. Grabbing her bag, she left the station.

Ten minutes later the cafe owners had put all the coffees in a box and the owner's son was carrying it back for Imogen, when she saw a pregnant woman standing outside the station, pacing. She was clearly very anxious and looked as though she had been there some time. Imogen knew who it was. She waved to Constable Ben Jarvis who was standing near the entrance; he came over and took the box from the cafe owner's son.

'Hand these around will you? Can you put two black coffees on my desk and a couple of pastries before they all disappear? Thanks, Ben.'

She tried desperately not to be flirtatious with him, remembering what Adrian had said to her previously about the way she was with him. She didn't want to give him the wrong idea.

'You're a star. Thanks, DS Grey.' He smiled.

She waited for Ben to go back inside before approaching the woman.

'Are you Abigail Lucas?' Imogen asked.

The woman looked startled and her eyes darted to the road; Imogen could see she was considering making a break for it.

'I prefer Abbey, but yes.'

Imogen spoke again. 'I work with DS Adrian Miles. Do you need to see him?'

Abbey paused before speaking to Imogen, obviously trying to decide if she could trust her or not. 'I came to see him the other day about my husband. I just wanted an update.'

'Do you want to come inside and I'll see if I can find him for you?' Imogen said.

The woman clearly needed to sit down. She seemed exhausted and quite nervous.

Imogen led her inside and took her to the family liaison

room before pulling out her phone and texting the letters FLR to Adrian, hoping he would understand that she needed him to come to the family liaison room immediately. She watched the woman nervously scratching the back of her hand in a bid to control her nerves.

'Could I get some water?' Abbey asked.

Imogen stood up and poured her a cup from the water dispenser in the corner. The door opened and Adrian walked in, but it did nothing to decrease the tension in the air.

'Detective Miles, I still haven't heard from my husband and I have a bad feeling.'

'I spoke with him a couple of days ago,' Adrian said.

'It's unlike him to go this long without contacting me.'

Imogen noticed Abbey shoot a questioning look at Adrian, obviously concerned about speaking freely in front of her.

'I know about Parker. He saved my life and, for that, I owe him,' Imogen said, removing the option for Adrian to try to lie to protect her. She had made her decisions, just like he had made his; she didn't need him to try to cover for her.

'I don't know how much you know about what Parker is into,' Adrian said to Abbey, 'but he has uncovered a group of lecturers at the university who have been manipulating students, using unfavourable personal circumstances to control them.'

'For what reason?' Abbey asked, her eyes narrowing and shifting as though she were trying to understand what they were saying to her.

'It seems as though they have some kind of point-scoring

system depending on what they can convince their students to do,' Adrian explained.

'During the course of this investigation we found some emails from one of your old lecturers at the university to Robert Coley about you,' Imogen said.

'About me?'

'Specifically about an incident that took place while you were a student at the university. I'm sure I don't need to go into the details now. You know what I'm talking about.'

'Which lecturer?' Abbey said, losing colour from her face.

'Helen Lassiter,' Imogen said.

'And what did she say about the incident?' Abbey asked, her voice barely under control.

'They were going to use it to try to coerce you into doing things,' Imogen responded.

'What kind of things?'

'Petty crime, escalating into bigger things, maybe even murder by the end of it,' Imogen said.

'How much did she say about the . . . incident in the email?' Abbey asked, immediately holding her breath afterwards, bracing herself for the conversation.

'Enough.'

'Who saw this email?'

'If you're worried about Parker, he probably did see it. They had been deleted from the computer around the time of the professor's death, but our tech managed to recover them. I take it Parker didn't know about the attack on you?' Adrian said.

'No, he didn't. I didn't feel as though he needed to

know. He's got enough of his own issues to deal with,' Abbey said, her voice shaking, the panic rising as her breaths got closer together. 'That's what all this is about? Why did they choose me?'

'They didn't just choose you, it was other students, too. We think that's what Parker is doing now, trying to track the rest of them down,' Adrian said.

'Is there any chance that Helen Lassiter was involved in your attack? There doesn't seem to be any mention of the perpetrator's name in her emails, but it's possible that your original assault was part of this – for want of a better word – game,' Imogen explained.

'What are you saying?'

'Maybe your attacker was coerced into assaulting you in the same way they planned to coerce you into doing whatever Coley was going to make you do,' Imogen said.

'You think my teacher, someone I trusted, someone who was supposed to look out for me actually told someone to rape me? To score points as part of a game?' Abbey's tone contained a mixture of anger and distress.

'If you tell us who it was, then we can investigate further. We might be able to get more information on who was behind it. It might lead us back to Parker,' Adrian said.

'If I thought it would help Parker then I would tell you, but I don't think it will. I'm not willing to talk about it. I tried to report it at the time and it was ignored due to lack of evidence, and so I don't see the point in dredging it up again now,' Abbey said firmly, her face whiter than usual.

Imogen couldn't imagine what she must be feeling

upon hearing this. Probably similar to how Adrian had felt upon learning that the false accusation against him was not just one misguided person's decision but an action by committee.

'We have reason to believe this game has been going on for several years. It's possible whoever attacked you was doing so under her instruction,' Adrian said.

'That's horrible. Why would anyone do that?' Abbey asked.

'If we can just interview the person who attacked you—' Adrian tried.

'I'm sorry, but I can't help you. I have put that all behind me and I don't want to talk about it ever again.' Abbey was clearly upset by the conversation.

'Maybe Parker has gone after that person – it's possible he figured it out, isn't it?' Adrian pushed.

Imogen put her hand on his arm, a gentle reminder that pressing Abbey for this information was likely to push her away. Not to mention the fact that forcing a rape victim to share that information felt completely wrong. She hoped he understood without her having to spell it out.

'He wouldn't do that without speaking to me first. I'm telling you, there is something wrong. I have a bad feeling that something has happened to Parker.'

'You don't think he can take care of himself?' Adrian said.

'I don't know what he is up against. Doesn't sound like you do either,' Abbey said.

She was right about that.

Chapter Forty-Three

Adrian and Imogen were the last ones to the team briefing. Adrian was still stuffing the last of a Belgian bun into his mouth when he walked into the room; Kapoor looked at him disapprovingly and continued talking.

'We have three hours until we have to release Finn Blackwell. Please tell me you have something we can keep him here on.'

'We have looked through a lot of the data on the professors' computers, but there is still loads to go through. So far, he hasn't told us anything that we didn't know already. As confused as he is, he has managed to avoid implicating himself,' Imogen said.

'We found a few more images of Russ Beacham on social media. We are trying to identify the locations in the photos, because maybe that's where he will be. People generally tend to hide out in places they already know,' Adrian said.

'Do they?' DCI Kapoor said sarcastically before rolling her eyes.

They had been going through emails and photos all day, trying to tie anything to Finn Blackwell, because all they had at the moment was that he knew Russ and Caitlin. That wasn't nearly enough to keep him in custody. They had no evidence that he was anything to do with the game, apart from the fact that he had been caught drink-driving and done for a minor drunk and disorderly in the city centre.

'We'll keep checking,' Imogen said.

'What about the car?' DCI Kapoor asked.

'I got in touch with transport,' Gary began. 'There was a ticket issued for the Beachams' car for illegally parking near the Watts' house on the morning of her death. Making the probability of it being a murder even more likely.'

'So, he is still in the city most likely,' Adrian added.

'Maybe he's sticking around to take care of Finn Blackwell. Finn seemed genuinely scared of him,' Imogen said.

'Did forensics place anyone else at the scene?' DCI Kapoor asked.

'Only the grandfather, who contaminated it massively by trying to get her out of the bath and slipping over in there. They processed his clothes and the scene, but there was nothing to indicate anyone else had been there. Water in crime scenes is always a nightmare, as you know. A lot of evidence was destroyed. Nothing we can do about that now though,' Adrian said.

DI Walsh spoke next. 'Russ Beacham also has some

sealed psychological evaluations from the last twelve months.'

'His mother never mentioned those,' Adrian said.

'I spoke to a teacher at his sixth-form college and she said he was quite isolated during his A levels. Worked hard but didn't really have any friends. Not particularly outspoken or even that noticeable in any way. He was never really late and always turned up, just wanted to get into uni. She said he was smart but really struggled in exams. He didn't get the grades he would have got had they been based on his overall performance and not just on the day of exam results,' DI Walsh said.

'I think we need to look back over any fatalities of university-age kids over the last ten years at least. Maybe even minor crimes, too. See if we can't work out how long it's been going on for,' Adrian said.

'I could try to get that information together, but it might take some time,' Gary said.

'I can do it,' Adrian chipped in, aware that Gary was still a bit on the frosty side towards him. 'We might be able to get some information on who the lecturers were once we have some student names, and then we can cross-reference and see if there are any overlaps. Maybe we can find the final puppetmaster that way.'

'Right. Matt, see if you can get access to those psychological evaluations. Gary, keep doing what you're doing. DS Grey and DS Miles, keep looking for connections between the three students. If you don't find anything in the next couple of hours, then you need to let Blackwell go. I've got to make a statement to the press in the morning, so it would be good to actually have some progress to report. I'm going home now, but run any developments past DI Walsh until I get back,' DCI Kapoor said. They all stood up as the DCI left and then followed her out.

Adrian stood back and waited for Matt Walsh to leave before grabbing Gary's arm.

'Gary, can I have a word?' Adrian pulled Gary to one side.

'Uh-oh,' Gary said.

'Have you found anything on the computers that could link back to Parker?'

'I'm not hiding evidence from the DCI, if that's what you're after,' Gary huffed.

'No, God, of course not,' Adrian said hurriedly.

'Then what?'

'It seems his wife is worried that something bad has happened to him.'

'Aside from what I showed you earlier on the VT, I don't know about that. The professors obviously know it's not one of their guys on the tapes, but whether they knew who he was is another story. To be honest, I have no idea what pertains to him and what doesn't. Finding Russ Beacham before he kills anyone else has to be a priority right now.'

'That's the plan.'

'Well, if he is as good as you say he is, then if we look for Russ Beacham, we might find him anyway. He might know where Russ is; he could be with him right now.'

'Good point,' Adrian said.

'Anyway, I better get on with it,' Gary said.

'Are we all right?'

'I'm just very uncomfortable with lying. I'm not annoyed at you though. I completely understand why you made the decisions you did.'

'I'm sorry we put you in this position.'

Adrian wasn't lying. He was sorry he had put himself in this position too. Although he didn't think he had been wrong, the fact remained that there would be a strain on their friendship until Parker stopped actively killing people, and probably for a while after that, too. Every single death that happened from this point on was Adrian's fault. That wasn't an easy thing to live with. Adrian knew though that back in that moment when he decided to let Parker go at the end of the museum case, he had made the right call and that it hadn't even felt like a decision at all at the time.

'It'll all work out in the end. One way or another,' Gary said before leaving the room.

One decision, that's all it had been. One decision to not go after one person and look at everything that had happened since. More people had died and that blood was on Adrian's hands. Why hadn't Parker stayed away? Why hadn't he got on with his life and just left well alone? There was no way this was going to end well for Adrian, and he couldn't take Gary and Imogen down with him. He had to sort this out. He didn't know what he was going to do, but he would think of something. He just hoped that whatever it was didn't make things worse.

Chapter Forty-Four

There was less than an hour left before they had to let Finn Blackwell go. Adrian wanted to talk to him alone and see if he could get through to him. If he could get him to tell them where Russ Beacham was before Parker found him, then maybe he could stop any more bloodshed. Finn must know more than he was letting on; there was just something about him that seemed dishonest. Especially after what Scott Woodlaw had told them about his violent outburst. Adrian didn't know whether it was gut instinct, experience or subtle micro-expressions that gave away when someone was lying, probably a combination of all three, but after years on the job you just get a feel for those things.

Finn Blackwell was lying and Adrian didn't know how he knew that, but he was. This was what happened when you lied. You had to lie again in order to cover up the first lie, then again and again until you were in a hole so deep you couldn't see a way out of it. Adrian hoped that he would learn from this experience if he got through it; although learning from his mistakes was never his strong suit.

His biggest problem now was Imogen. There was no way she would let him try to fix this on his own. He knew she felt equally responsible, but she wasn't; she had gone along with his decision, but she hadn't made it. He hadn't given her the choice. Now she was stuck with the consequences, too. That just didn't sit right with Adrian.

Gary approached. 'I've got a lead on a possible location for Beacham,' he said to Imogen.

Adrian could tell that Gary held him responsible, too, and it was doing nothing to assuage his guilt in the matter. You never know how high you hold someone's opinion of you until it drops. Being in Gary's bad books made Adrian feel like shit.

'Where?' Imogen stood up and grabbed her jacket, ready to go.

'I was looking through the few pictures of Russ Beacham we found online and several of them take place outside the same building. After some cross-referencing and working out the date of the building, I managed to figure out where it was. It's in Scarborough Street in town. It's a building that used to belong to the sixth-form college that Russ went to,' Gary said.

'Used to?'

'It's scheduled for destruction, so it's been empty for a while now – seems like a good place to hide out.'

'How do we get in there?' Imogen asked.

'It's being sold as a land prospect and so the local

estate agents are in charge of the site. I'm trying to get hold of one of them to meet you guys down there. As you can imagine, it's not easy at this time of night,' Gary said.

'Anything else that links to him?' Imogen said.

'There was a call about a disturbance out there a few days ago, but when the uniforms did a drive-by they didn't see anything out of place.'

'Sounds like a good lead,' Adrian said.

'Let's go.' Imogen nodded.

'I've already spoken to DI Walsh and he said he will meet one of you guys at his car. I think he's going a bit stir-crazy in here.'

'You go. I'll stay and see Finn Blackwell off,' Adrian said.

For the first time, he saw Imogen narrow her eyes and look at both him and Gary. She had noticed the tension between them.

'Is something going on with you guys?' she asked.

'No,' Gary answered quickly. 'I'd better keep trying this estate agent.'

Gary walked away and Imogen folded her arms, raising her eyebrows.

'Spill it,' she said to Adrian, knowing them both better than they had given her credit for.

'He's upset about lying to the DCI and I don't think he trusts that the Parker situation won't get us both fired.'

'He's not alone there,' Imogen said.

'If it comes down to that, I am taking the blame and I won't have any arguments from you.'

'We'll see.'

'It's my fault. I should have taken him in when I said I would. You weren't a part of that decision, Imogen, and so you shouldn't take the fall for it.'

'But I agreed with you and I would have made the same decision had I been there.'

'I don't think I would have made that decision if you had been there. I don't want to get you in trouble. I've been such an idiot, thinking I was above it all. I get it now.'

'You get that the rules are there to protect you as much as anyone else? That they aren't just there to inconvenience us?'

'I'm sorry I dragged you into this.'

'I can take care of myself, Miley. You didn't force me into anything.'

'The DI is waiting for you, you'd better go,' Adrian said, glancing at the clock.

He could see her eyes flit to his lips and that was enough – she wanted to give him a reassuring kiss and just knowing that was reassuring in itself. He watched as she left and then looked over to the door that led to the holding cells. Finn knew more than he was letting on and Adrian was going to find out what that was.

Chapter Forty-Five

Adrian waited outside the station around the corner and out of view from the main exit, checking that no one else was around. Finn Blackwell stepped out of the station, with a furtive glance at his surroundings before proceeding. His twenty-four hours were up and they had released him. It was dark, but Finn had a light denim jacket on, so he was easy to spot from a fair distance. Adrian waited for him to get a few hundred yards from the station before he started to follow him. Finn walked slowly, occasionally checking behind him to see if anyone was following. What was he so paranoid about? Adrian managed to stay out of sight for the time being. Finn wasn't a particularly fast walker and so it was easy not to lose him. Although he wasn't walking back to his halls of residence; he was going somewhere else.

Adrian had been following Finn Blackwell for around twenty minutes; they had gone back on themselves a couple of times and through some very small alleyways. They started to walk towards the Cowley Bridge. Finn's pace had changed, this was clearly where he had planned to go; they were headed for his final destination. He reached the periphery of the Taddyforde estate inside the conservation area outside the lower end of town. All the houses here were well known for their architecture. Neo-Gothic, like many of the other properties in Exeter. These particular houses were built in Victorian times from local stone in the mid-nineteenth century. Knowing what Adrian knew about Finn Blackwell, he couldn't imagine he had any family in this particular area and so maybe he was going to see someone else, someone who had something to do with the case. He hadn't requested for anyone to be informed of his whereabouts when he was at the station and he had not asked for any legal advice either. Everything they knew about Finn Blackwell was in the very thin file they had on him at the station and that didn't amount to much at all. His family – a single mother and sister – lived in another county and he didn't have any familial links in Exeter. So where was he going?

Finn stopped at a house with a roughly seven-foot wall surrounding it, then disappeared down the passage that ran alongside the building. Adrian heard the wheezing creak of a gate opening. He had gone inside.

Adrian waited a few seconds before following Finn down the path. He peered in through the gate and saw the house. It looked to be empty, for all intents and purposes; there were no lights on. The moon lit up the grounds, which were a little on the dishevelled side;

basic maintenance had been done on the garden, but nothing with pride or love. The house itself was very imposing; it had steep pitched roofs and small gables. There were two octagonal turrets that made Adrian think of a castle in a fairy story.

The sinister feeling grew worse the closer he got to the actual property – it was almost like a low hum. Adrian was both relieved that Imogen wasn't with him because he would be concerned for her safety, but he also kind of wished she was because he was concerned for his.

He took a deep breath before stepping inside the gate into the garden. Luckily Finn had left the gate open, so Adrian didn't have to worry about the noise as he squeezed himself through the gap. The house itself gave off a coldness, if that was even possible; there was a bad feeling here. It was the kind of feeling that would have made Adrian's mother insist on getting a priest in to bless the place and clean the air.

After carefully inspecting the perimeter of the house, Adrian saw Russ's silver Ford Focus tucked away under a lean-to. Was Finn meeting Russ here?

Adrian walked until he found another door. This time, it was wide open – clearly the way Finn had entered the house. There was obviously no longer any fear of being discovered. The kitchen was huge; the moonlight poured in through the French windows that led onto the lawned back garden. The floor was black-and-white chequered tile, and there was a large wooden island in the centre of the kitchen with a knife block built into it. One of the knives was missing.

Adrian ventured further into the house, his feeling

of unease increasing as he realised there was only one way for him to go, only one more open door. He could hear whispering and a soft murmuring. The sound of a match striking followed by a soft light came from the room he was walking towards. As he leaned against the wall to look in without putting his head inside the room, he saw the arm of someone sitting in a chair, his back to him. He couldn't tell if it was Finn or Russ. He edged forward a little more and tried to get a better look. The man was sitting in a black leather Wassily chair, but the light was too dim to make out who it was.

Carefully, Adrian put his foot on the floorboard in front of him, holding his breath as he pressed down, hoping it wouldn't make a sound. It didn't, but it didn't matter; in that same moment, something hit the back of Adrian's head and he fell to the ground.

Chapter Forty-Six

After getting the address of the disused sixth-form college building from Gary, Imogen and Matt Walsh headed straight over there. It was midnight and so it had been a complete nightmare getting hold of the estate agent with the keys. Eventually they got in contact with someone and he agreed to meet. When they got there, he hadn't arrived. So, now they were just sitting in the car outside, waiting.

The building itself was quite small, but it had factory-style windows. A couple of the windows had been smashed and were covered in chipboard to stop any undesirables from getting in. There was a small unruly hedge in the front yard. It had been empty for over a year now, so inevitably some people had found their way inside.

'I saw the interview with Blackwell,' Walsh said. 'He was evasive, but that's not unusual with younger people, especially stoners, they can be quite paranoid.'

'I don't really want to presume too much at this point, but I think the water just got a lot muddier. His fear of Russ Beacham seemed disproportionate; from what we have heard about the boy so far from everyone else, he was quiet and reserved. But then if he was a part of this game then maybe he is good at pretending to be something he is not to his family and friends.'

'Not to mention those sick videos Gary uncovered. If that is Beacham, then Blackwell's fear seems entirely reasonable. Don't forget we haven't got full access to those psych reports yet,' Matt reminded her.

Just then a car pulled up and a tired, angry-looking man in a tracksuit got out. He pulled out a bunch of keys from his pocket and went straight to the padlock chain on the door without saying a word. Four locks later, the door was open and they were going inside.

Although there had definitely been people inside since the building had shut down, it wasn't inhabited now. Kids probably went there to drink these days, Imogen thought. As they progressed through the corridor, Imogen could smell that unforgettable smell. The sweet rotting odour of a dead body that had been left to its own devices for several days. The last time they had been confronted with something like this, Imogen had thrown her clothes away afterwards. Not even detergent could get rid of that smell. It got inside you. Was this another victim? Whose body were they about to find? Had Parker already found the person he was looking for?

'Have you had a problem with squatters at this building at all?' Imogen asked the estate agent.

'One or two. Nothing significant. They are usually gone after a day or so,' the man said, covering his mouth and squinting. 'What is that smell?'

'You can wait here if you want. I have a feeling you're not going to want to see what we find in that room over there,' Imogen said, looking at Matt Walsh knowingly.

'There's definitely a dead body in this building somewhere,' Matt said rather less subtly.

'Could be a fox? We've had a couple of those getting through the back,' the estate agent said hopefully.

'Best to stay here, be on the safe side,' Matt suggested.

The man's face had softened from anger into obedience. Thankfully he wasn't one of those curious types who were fascinated with the idea of a dead body. Whenever they got one of those, Imogen made a mental note to remember their face, because there was something very disturbing about a person who could take delight in the dead.

Imogen proceeded with caution. There was one closed door at the end of the hallway and they both knew that there was someone inside. Who it was, was another matter. Knowing how this case had gone so far, they couldn't be sure of anything. And they certainly hadn't been ahead of the game at any point in time. The estate agent was a way behind them now, still hovering by the door. Imogen had learned to brace herself whenever the possibility of a body left by Parker was on the cards. She put her hand on the doorknob and glanced at Matt.

'Ready?'

'As I'll ever be,' he said.

Imogen turned the doorknob and pushed the door a little. The smell intensified and she coughed as it hit the back of her throat. She found herself wanting to close her eyes, but she didn't. The room was dark and the blinds were drawn shut. Matt shone his torch into the room. There were some chairs and a couple of tall dark wooden cupboards. That's when they saw the body slumped against the wall in the corner next to one of the cupboards. It was settled like a sack of flour settles into its creases and folds. There was a pulsating buzz around it – the heat of the room had brought in the insects and they had started to feast on whoever it was. There was the unmistakeable sound of rats – hard to explain if you have never heard it, but it was a sinister clicking shuffle with the occasional squeak.

As they got closer, the smell got worse. Imogen could see the fabric was writhing with movement as her eyes pulled into focus. The face was directed at the wall, away from them, so they had to get close and lean over the body in order to see who it was. DI Walsh shone his flashlight into the corner and Imogen leaned over the body, holding onto Matt's arm for support. There was no way to know at first glance how the boy had died, but another piece of the puzzle had been solved. Russ Beacham was dead.

Imogen felt a twinge of dread as she thought about having to tell the mother that her son was gone. In the whole of her job, that was the worst possible part. And whenever she had broken the news to a parent, she'd felt her insides twist up and knot with grief for them. Saying sorry and offering condolences was utterly pointless. The best thing Imogen could do when they found a dead son or daughter was to find the killer and bring them to justice.

'Are you OK?' Matt said.

'He's just a kid. He shouldn't be here.'

'Let's get the techs up here to examine the scene. I can't see any obvious cause of death.'

'This poses another problem. If Russ is here, dead, then he didn't kill Caitlin at the very least. He's been here a few days. Judging by all the activity, a week or more.'

'We need to contact the station and tell them to keep hold of Blackwell.'

They left the room and walked back to the estate agent, who was standing exactly where they had left him, a tired grimace on his face.

'Well?'

'We found a body in one of the back rooms. This site needs to stay closed to the public for the foreseeable, which doesn't look like it's going to be an issue. We do need to call some crime scene technicians in, and some constables will come and mind the scene. I'm sure you don't want to hang around for that.'

'You can keep the keys for now. We have a spare set at the office.' He thrust the keys at Imogen. 'I will let the owner of the building know what's been going on here.'

'OK. Thank you for coming down here. You've been a great help. It's important that we are able to control this information with the press, so if you could see your way to not telling anyone other than the owner that would also be great,' Matt said.

The estate agent was backing away almost imperceptibly; he just wanted to get out of there.

'Could you also send us over any details you know of the building, the owner's contact details and anyone else involved in the sale? If you know of anyone else with access that could also be useful to us.' Imogen handed him her card.

He snatched it and smiled nervously before stuffing it in his pocket.

The estate agent hurried outside; Imogen and Matt followed him just in time to see him slam his car door and pull away noisily, and then they were alone again on the street. It was still dark. Imogen looked at her watch. The way the night was progressing, she wasn't sure she'd even get a chance to go home and have a shower, let alone sleep.

She pulled out her phone and called Adrian. No answer. She called Gary instead.

'Hi, we found Russ Beacham's body in Scarborough Street. DI Walsh is securing the scene and calling techs in. Is Adrian still there?'

'No, he left just before Finn Blackwell was released.'

'Blackwell's gone? Bugger,' Imogen said.

'Only just, last half hour. Don't know where Adrian went though.'

'I have tried his phone, but it went straight to answerphone. I don't suppose you can find out where he is?'

'I'm just checking now. That's funny . . .' Gary said.

'What's funny?' Imogen said.

'His phone is off. He is either out of range or asleep already, I guess.'

'He doesn't switch his phone off to sleep,' Imogen said.

'Oh yeah – how would you know?' Gary jibed, unaware that he had made her blush.

'Because we sometimes get calls in the middle of the night,' she answered quickly.

'I'll see if I can find out where he went. He's not answering his house phone either.'

'We're just waiting for the uniforms then we'll be back at the station. Keep trying.'

Imogen hung up the phone. Something was definitely not right. She didn't even need to think about it for too long to know that Adrian was doing something stupid. Knowing how susceptible he was to guilt, she expected he'd taken it upon himself to try to fix things. Now she just had to figure out where he had gone and what exactly he was trying to do.

Chapter Forty-Seven

The room came into focus and Adrian tried to reach up to his head, but he couldn't move his hands. He was taped to a chair at his wrists, elbows, knees and ankles. He could taste blood on his lips; he'd been punched in the face. The room was dark, with only one candle lit on top of a piano that was nestled in one of the alcoves. Adrian couldn't make much else out about the room; the curtains were drawn and there was a dusty smell in the air. As he adjusted to his surroundings, he could hear gentle breathing. He scoured the room for a sign of his attackers.

'Hello, Detective Miles,' Parker said.

For the briefest of moments, a surge of dread ran through Adrian's body as he thought that Parker had strapped him to the chair. He didn't want to turn but he did. Parker was in a chair not three feet away from him, also strapped in. His face was covered in blood; he looked like he had taken a couple of punches. All in all, this was a better situation than the one Adrian had assumed he was in less than five seconds ago.

'Are you OK?' Adrian asked.

Parker ignored the question.

'Where are we?' Adrian added.

'This is my house, I grew up here,' Parker said.

Adrian felt a chill as Parker said the words, the coldness of the house suddenly making sense. Adrian had seen some of the horrors that Parkers had experienced in his youth and he imagined life wasn't much better at home. He had to shake off the thoughts that were starting to creep up on him and focus on the task at hand. He didn't know why he empathised with this man so much, but he really struggled to look at who he was now without remembering the photographs of the torture Parker had endured as a child. He couldn't think about that now, but he heard Gary's words in his head. Adrian didn't know if he would ever be able to bring Parker in. The fact that Finn had found Parker in his own house made Adrian think he had underestimated Finn Blackwell.

'Where is he? Where is Finn?'

'The boy? He left a few moments ago, he got a phone call. He probably won't be long,' Parker said calmly.

This situation was not upsetting him in the slightest – to look at him he could have been sitting on a sunlounger by a pool.

'Have you been strapped to this chair the whole time he was in custody?' Adrian said; although he had no doubt this was something Parker could easily cope with, after knowing the things he had endured before.

'Is that where he was? Glad you were on to him, because I really wasn't until the last minute.'

'How did he overpower you? You're bigger than him.'

'I needed to know what he knew, so as soon as I realised he had found me here, I allowed him to get the upper hand so that I can find out more about him, find out who the other player is.'

'Do you have a plan to get out of here?' Adrian said, knowing he should be the one with the plan but acknowledging that he was completely unprepared for this.

'Not yet, but something will come to me.'

'Does he know who you are?'

'Someone knows who I am, but he doesn't seem to have a clue. He seems quite paranoid and disturbed.'

'Did you find out anything about who is involved? Do you know who the final professor is?'

'No. But he does take phone calls occasionally. I assume he is working with whoever is on the other end of the phone. They sent him here.'

The chairs were particularly suited to this kind of thing, with the metal bars and leather straps in the exact places where it would be handy to wrap duct tape around and around, but Adrian couldn't imagine that Parker wouldn't have been able to break free in the twenty-four hours Finn Blackwell had been in custody and that made him nervous. What kind of person deliberately stays strapped to a chair for over a day, waiting for their captor to come back?

'We need to get out of here,' Adrian said.

'He doesn't know what he's doing,' Parker said. 'I

think if we hang on, the main player will show their face. This boy isn't making any decisions for himself; he checks every step of the way what he is and is not allowed to do. Whoever the person is, they have covered themselves absolutely. The others were pretty smart, but he or she is like a ghost.'

'You think it could be a woman?'

'I have no idea who it is. I've looked through everything I found. I need more time. You go if you need to,' Parker said as though that were a possibility.

They heard a noise and the sound of Finn's voice getting closer again. He was agitated and muttering to himself, unhappy with what he had heard on the other end of the phone no doubt. The kingpin of this operation was going to hang Finn out to dry, there was no question about that. How could Adrian convince Finn that was the case though?

Adrian couldn't help but wonder what Parker was thinking. Was he planning a way to escape or was his plan literally just to wait and see what happened next, then judge whether he needed to make a move or not? Maybe he was thinking about a way to kill Finn. Was that how simple it was for him? To just decide that someone needed to die and then do it. That was crazy. But then Adrian couldn't deny how horrifying those crime scenes he had attended had been and even worse were the videos that Gary had showed him. The abstract idea of Parker was far more comfortable than being in close proximity to him.

Finn came back into the room, rubbing his hair and scratching at his forehead, distressed and confused, clearly unsure how to handle the situation and conflicted by whatever he had just heard on the phone. He paced and occasionally side-eyed Adrian as though he were an inconvenience he would rather not deal with.

'Talk to me, Finn,' Adrian said, making sure to use his name.

'I can't,' Finn said.

'Where's Russ? Is he coming here?'

'No.'

'Were you just talking to him on the phone?'

'No. Stop talking to me, I know what you're doing.' Finn smacked the side of his own head.

'What is it you think I'm doing?'

'You're going to try and confuse me. He said you would.'

'Who did? Russ?'

'No! Shut up!' Finn was getting more and more distressed.

Adrian noted that Finn had said 'he', so that narrowed the field down a little; of course, this information was useless if Adrian couldn't get out of there before Finn killed him.

'How do you know whoever it is you spoke to hasn't called the police already? Maybe they are on their way here. If you get caught with us like this then you will go to prison for a very long time.'

'I told you to be quiet!'

'Look, just tell me the name of the person who has been telling you what to do.'

'I can't. He can protect me, you can't.'

'I very much doubt he can protect you from the law,

he is protecting himself. We found you, Finn, if he was protecting you then we wouldn't have been able to.'

'Stop talking!' Finn cuffed Adrian hard across the face.

As his head snapped to the side, he saw Parker watching Finn, eyes glassy and wide like marbles, measuring every single thing Finn did. Parker was like a cat watching a mouse, knowing exactly how this encounter was going to end.

Adrian could taste blood inside his mouth where his cheek mashed into his teeth.

'Was he protecting Caitlin, too? Because she didn't come out of this too well,' Adrian said.

'She was going to tell on us, she had to be stopped,' Finn said. It was almost a confession.

'So, it wasn't suicide then?'

Finn punched Adrian again, his fist connecting with his ear. Adrian had braced for it and so he recovered quickly.

'Stop confusing me! Caitlin was talking to the cops. She promised she would never go against me and then she did that. She lied to me. She lied to me just like she lied to everyone else.'

'Is that why you killed Hugh Norris? Did someone tell you to do that? Was it Caitlin? Were you sleeping with her, Finn? How about Doctor Norris, was Caitlin the student he was having the affair with?'

Finn was rubbing his temples, his eyes clamped shut as though he were trying to push the image of Hugh Norris and Caitlin out of his mind.

'I'm trying to think.'

300

'What about the man who tells you what to do? Did he have a thing with Caitlin as well? She was a beautiful girl, maybe he was jealous of your relationship with her and so he lied to you about what she was telling us. Aside from clearing my name, she didn't tell us anything.'

'You're lying! How else would you know all the stuff you know about what we were doing?'

'He might be telling the police you did it all. Caitlin wouldn't tell us anything.'

'She must have!'

'Is that why you killed her? Did the professor tell you that she was talking to us?' Adrian said, assuming he was talking about another professor: all the evidence seemed to point that way.

'I don't have a choice! I have to do what he says!'

'Why is that?' Adrian said.

'Because I've done too many bad things; he knows everything.'

'If you were coerced into doing the things you did then there is a possibility you won't spend the rest of your life in prison.'

'I've killed people, and that's not all I've done,' Finn said.

'Which people did you kill?' Adrian said.

'Owen. Doctor Norris, Russ . . . and Caitlin.'

So, Russ wasn't behind any of it. Finn was a good liar, Adrian would give him that. He had been quite convinced that Finn's account of Russ's involvement was at least partially true.

'In UK law we have a thing called diminished responsibility, there's every chance you could get a reduced sentence because of that.' Adrian had no idea if Finn's case qualified, but he had to keep talking to him. He was opening up and if Adrian could gain his trust then he might give up the name of the person in charge. The cracks were beginning to show.

The sound of something dropping in the kitchen startled them all, their heads snapping around in unison. Was there someone else in the house?

'Who's there?' Adrian shouted, but less than a second later, Finn hit him across the face.

'Shut up.' He darted out of the room to investigate.

Adrian looked back over to Parker, who had just been observing their interaction; Adrian wondered if Finn had any idea what Parker could do to him. While Finn may know who Parker was in terms of this particular case, he had no idea what he was really capable of, not the magnitude of it. How could he? It was entirely likely that Finn hadn't seen the video of what Parker had done to Robert Coley. It didn't seem as though Gillian Mitchell or the other teachers had particularly shared any information with their acolytes. Adrian was sure if Finn had seen the video he might have used significantly more duct tape to secure him. Clattering noises came from the kitchen, followed by the sound of Finn shouting. It became apparent soon after that he was on the phone again, demanding some instructions on how to deal with his prisoners.

'You're very calm, given the situation,' Adrian said to Parker.

'I've been in worse.'

'We could die here. That doesn't bother you?'

'Detective Miles, I know that you have been in other predicaments where you feared you might die, correct?'

'Yes, I have.'

'Growing up, I was forced to face my own mortality on a daily basis. I would wake up and know for certain that today was going to be the day I was going to die. I have woken up strapped to chairs before, more terrifying chairs than this. Even after I was no longer in imminent danger, that feeling does not leave you. So far, I have never been right, but this? This is not even in my top ten list of life-threatening situations.'

'I can't even imagine what it must have been like for you,' Adrian said. Coming from an abusive background himself, he probably felt too much empathy for what Parker had been through. It didn't seem to matter what Parker did, Adrian would never forget the images he had seen of what had happened to him as a child. Maybe Adrian identified with Parker and maybe that's why he couldn't give him up.

'It's all behind me now. Can I ask you something, Detective?'

'I guess.'

'As you know, I am about to become a father. That is more terrifying to me than any experience I have had so far. You have a child. Does it get any easier?'

'Are you worried that your child will be bad, because you think you are?' Adrian said, familiar with those feelings himself. The idea that he had been passed any of his father's genes plagued him throughout his teens and then when Andrea had fallen pregnant, he'd been convinced his genetic make-up would ruin the life of his child.

'How could you know that?'

'Congratulations, you're human, that's a normal way to feel. Can I ask you something? How the hell are we getting out of here?'

After another round of crashing noises in the kitchen, Finn came back with a canister of petrol and started to throw it over the covered furniture.

'What are you doing, Finn?'

'Getting rid of the problem. They can't prosecute me if there is no evidence.'

It looked like Adrian's words had only succeeded in upsetting Finn Blackwell further. He may just have sped up the process. At least if Finn wasn't taking orders any more they had a chance of talking him round. Didn't they?

Chapter Forty-Eight

Imogen felt sick. Where the hell was Adrian? It wasn't like him to turn his phone off. It was like him to do something rash though. She rushed from the car into the station to find Gary; he was the only person she could rely on right now. He had all the facts at least.

'Gary!' was all Imogen could think of to say as she swung the door to his office open to see him hunched over the workstation, furiously tapping away.

'I'm trying, Imogen,' Gary said.

'Do we have any idea where he went?'

'His phone's last location seemed to be on his way home, which is where he said he was going.'

'Has anyone checked there?' Imogen said.

'There's a car on its way there now.'

'What about Finn Blackwell?'

'Adrian left just before he was fully released. Said he was tired and needed to grab a shower, seeing as the Blackwell arrest was a bust and you were off out with

DI Walsh. I found some footage of him leaving the station, but he was hanging back and waiting for something when he got outside.'

'OK, so he's obviously followed Finn Blackwell . . . somewhere. Any idea where?' Imogen said.

'How can you know that?'

'It's probably something we would have done together if I had been here . . .' A thought had just dawned on her. 'Which of course he knew and so he made me go with Matt to the building. Idiot.'

'Well let's find him before we start calling him names, shall we?' Gary said.

Imogen realised her hands were balled into tight fists. Adrian had tried to protect her by making sure she couldn't follow him into his bad decision. Again.

'He didn't say anything at all to you before he left?' she asked Gary.

'We've kind of fallen out, nothing major, but I don't think he would have come to me.'

'Well shit. There must be some clue here,' Imogen said.

'I'm looking. Would help if I knew what I was looking for.'

'Let's start with addresses. Can you pull up any addresses throughout the documents for the computers? Is that possible?'

'You would think, but no. It doesn't work like that. I have, however, kept a file on any addresses or partial addresses I have come across so far. I'll send it to you.'

'Any of them stand out?'

'There are loads that are easily explainable, some

belonging to the people we know about so far. Things like Finn's halls, Lassiter's house, the Beacham flat and of course Caitlin's grandfather's place. A couple of public places turned up as well. There are a few that I couldn't get any information on – three to be exact – which is unusual; even online there is often a trail of information about addresses.'

'Is there?' Imogen said, it wasn't something she had ever thought about before.

'There are sites you can go on to check and see the last sale prices or any planning permissions that pertain to the properties. There are also ancestry-type sites where you can check the historical significance of certain addresses. There are various things that usually pop up.'

'What about Google Street View? If we pull up images of the properties in question, we might be able to rule a couple out. Or at least pick a place to start. If there's nothing else on them then it's worth a shot.'

Imogen was annoyed at having to do this part, but just randomly visiting addresses was a massive time-waster. Sometimes they might turn up to a property only to find out it had been levelled and converted into a nursery school or off-licence. Forewarned was forearmed. Ten extra minutes investigating could save them a good few hours roaming the streets.

'Smart. I'll do that now.'

The first image Gary pulled up was of a small unit in Matford Business Park. On Street View there were no markings on the outside, but they couldn't know how old the photo was.

Gary moved on to the next address.

'What's that one?' Imogen asked, looking at the house on the screen. She wasn't one to judge a book by its cover usually, but she couldn't help but notice how sinister the house was.

'I'll check with the Land Registry who owns this one; I couldn't see anything at all about it. It certainly hasn't been bought or sold in over a hundred years.'

The third one was a building site – a block conversion into flats.

'I'll get on to the developers about it.'

'I'll take DI Walsh and check out this unit at Matford first, but let me know if you find anything else out about that house before we get there.'

The unit seemed like the most likely culprit, the leasing arrangements on places like that could be very loose. There was an unmistakeable eeriness about the house, but Imogen couldn't imagine what possible connection Finn Blackwell might have to the place. She left Gary's office and went to find Matt Walsh.

Chapter Forty-Nine

Adrian's eyes stung from the overwhelming smell of the petrol. He watched the candle on the piano as it burned down. Finn had run out of petrol before he had had a chance to douse either Adrian or Parker with it, which gave Adrian a little hope. Parker still seemed entirely unfazed by the experience. Maybe he had no desire to get out of the situation; Adrian couldn't begin to guess how that man's mind worked.

Finn was still pacing and muttering to himself, on the brink of losing control altogether. He rushed over to the two men and Adrian realised he had a knife in his hand. He focused on the blade, watching the boy's fingers nervously clasping the handle.

'I didn't want it to happen like this. You seem all right. I wish you hadn't followed me,' Finn said.

'You know if you do this that he will control you forever,' Adrian said carefully. 'Killing a police officer is serious business. Even if the authorities don't figure it out, he will know, and he will make you do more bad things. Where does it end?'

'Do you think you are worth any more than any of the other people I killed? Are you worth more than Caitlin?' Finn asked, his voice cracking.

Adrian noted how hard it was for Finn to say Caitlin's name. Maybe Russ wasn't the only one who was in love with her. A love that made him do irrational things.

'You liked Caitlin.'

'Everyone liked Caitlin. Russ was obsessed with her and I just had to pretend I was OK with it. She just had something, you know? Have you ever met anyone like that?'

'I met her. She seemed like a special girl,' Adrian said, unsure what was likely to push Finn over the edge. He wasn't lying; there had been something special about Caitlin. Something that pulled you in and made you want to protect her.

'She was mine first. I loved her.'

'So, what happened?'

'They wanted Russ, so I had to get her to pretend to be into him. I didn't want to, but I told her to sleep with him. He didn't know about us – about me and her. He couldn't believe his luck. Russ wasn't very confident around girls, so when she showed an interest in him, what else was he going to do? She hated me for that, for making her do that. That's when things changed between us and I just wanted to go back to how it was.'

'Then you had to watch them be together?'

'Not just them. She told me they made her sleep with Norris, that dirty old man; he was old enough to be her grandad. He wanted out, they were using her to keep him in.'

'So, you killed him?'

'I smashed his head in, dirty fucker.' Finn smiled to himself. 'And then I had to watch her go after you. You are the first person who ever turned her down. I knew you liked her though; I saw you that night, dropping her off at home. After she went inside, I saw you thinking about it, thinking about ringing her doorbell and going inside. I really enjoyed fucking up your face that night.'

'Killing her must have been hard.' Adrian was trying to buy time. Buy time for what, he didn't know, but he knew that when Finn finally stopped talking there was only one thing left for him to do. He could hear the faintest movement next to him. Parker, who Finn seemed to have forgotten about, was working his way out of his restraints. Adrian wasn't sure if that was a good thing or not.

'I had no choice. I didn't want to do it. She was angry with me for Russ, for Norris . . . she called me, said she wanted out. I thought she was going to tell.' His eyes glazed over a little. The tears started to come. Time was running out for them; Adrian had pushed him too far.

'How did you get into it? How did they get you?' Adrian needed to find a way to calm him down.

'My dad is in prison, they told me they could make things difficult for him.' Finn dragged his sleeve across his nose.

'That never came up when we processed you, that your dad was in prison.'

'Mother's name – Blackwell. She left him off the birth

311

certificate because he's such a liability. He's been in and out of prison since before I was born. He knew though, the guy in charge, he knew exactly who he was and he told me he could get someone to fuck him up.'

'How would they do that?' Adrian asked.

'He said he knew someone on the inside and that they could hurt my dad.'

'I can make sure that doesn't happen. I can keep your father safe,' Adrian said.

'Why would you bother for someone like me?' Finn said.

He was spiralling into that place people go when they think they have run out of options. Given that Finn was holding a large steel knife, Adrian needed to pull him back, fast.

'I don't know what that means, Finn. Someone like you?'

'I worked damn hard to get on that course. No one in my family ever got into university before. I wish I hadn't now. I didn't think it would be like this.'

'It shouldn't have been like this. What they made you do is wrong.'

'I just couldn't stand up to them. You know? I didn't want anyone to know about my dad and I didn't want him to get hurt.'

'What else did they make you do? What was your first mission for them?'

'The first one was silly, but they offered me a grand do to it, that was when it was fun. I just had to duct tape that kid Owen to the wall in the library, high up.'

'Owen Sager? You knew him?'

'Yeah. It was too bad when he hung himself,' Finn said.

Adrian wasn't sure if he heard sarcasm in his voice. There was no reason to lie about killing Sager after having confessed to killing Norris and Caitlin, but Finn Blackwell had already established himself as a liar. Maybe it was Adrian projecting when he was trying to give kids like Finn and Caitlin the benefit of the doubt. He saw them as victims, but at what point does someone become responsible for their own actions? Maybe Finn liked killing people, maybe that's why he was chosen. It was possible that that's what the professors saw in him, what they saw in all of them. Adrian always remembered his own teen years when faced with kids like this on the wrong side of the law. He remembered choosing not to let his life and his past affect him. Adrian was lucky that he'd found a mentor that helped him to make the right decisions when his parents let him down. These kids had been found by a different kind of teacher.

'Did you kill Owen?' Adrian asked.

'What difference does it make whether I did it or not? He's dead either way.'

'I think it would mean something to his mother. She thinks she could have stopped it somehow if she had noticed he was depressed.'

'Well, she couldn't have. He wasn't depressed, and he didn't hang himself. I did it.'

'This is not your fault, Finn. They made you do it. I can protect you. I wish I could have protected Caitlin.'

The mention of her name snapped Finn out of it.

'I bet you do. I bet you wish you could have fucked her, too,' Finn said, his face flushed with anger again. He held up the knife and stepped closer.

Chapter Fifty

Matford Business Park was two miles south of the city centre, located next to Marsh Barton Trading Estate. It was predominantly in use by car showrooms, industrial units and warehouses, meaning it all looked very similar until you got close. Thankfully the satnav was able to pinpoint the location with relative ease, not something that was a given.

Imogen jumped out of the car and peered into the unit through the small glass window on the door. It seemed to be completely deserted. At this time in the morning the chances of getting hold of anyone to open it were even smaller than at the derelict college building. How inconsiderate of Adrian to go missing and not tell anyone where he was going outside of office hours.

'This is ridiculous,' she said as she paced, staring at her phone, waiting for either news that they had found the owner of the unit or for Adrian to call. Wishful thinking in both cases.

'It'll be fine, DS Grey,' DI Matt Walsh said, arms folded, resting against the bonnet of the car.

'With all due respect, sir, you can't possibly know that.'

'Adrian seems like a resilient sort. If he is in trouble, I think he can handle himself.'

'Well, we can ask him when we find him. I am not in the habit of hoping for the best.'

'I know you've both been through a lot together.'

'Yes, we have. What's your point?'

'The DCI told me that he is a little unorthodox sometimes when it comes to what he does outside of work.'

'How would she know?' Imogen tried not to sound as irritated as she was.

'The investigation after the rape allegation threw up a few things about Adrian's behaviour outside of work.'

'And you had access to that, how?'

'As someone unconnected to both of you, DCI Kapoor wanted my opinion on how to handle the situation. She thought I might be able to offer a different perspective.'

'But you are connected to both of us now. Have you had access to my files as well?'

'My point is, irrational behaviour after work is not entirely unusual for DS Miles, is it?'

Admittedly DI Matt Walsh had arrived at an unfortunate time; he probably hadn't seen them in the best light. Not to mention the fact that all the while Imogen defended Adrian's behaviour and professionalism, there was the small chance DI Walsh was right. Adrian did go off and get smashed sometimes when the investigation got on top of him. But it was still unlike him to switch his phone off. No, this didn't feel right. Then,

315

of course, there was the issue of Parker, which she couldn't talk about with DI Walsh, but she suspected if he knew about Parker he wouldn't be so relaxed about Adrian's absence. But whether Adrian liked to admit it or not, Parker was as much Imogen's responsibility as it was his. Still, none of that mattered right now. Nothing mattered until they located Adrian.

'I appreciate your point of view, DI Walsh, but you don't really know DS Miles. This isn't after work, this is the middle of an investigation. He is very unlikely to just switch his phone off and go clubbing. Not answer his phone, yeah, that could happen. But to not be able to locate him? No way. Something's off.'

'Maybe he's out of range,' Matt said.

'If this was a bid to calm me down it has failed miserably,' Imogen snapped.

'I didn't mean to upset you,' Matt offered.

'You're wrong about him. He's a good police officer,' she said, composing herself, knowing full well none of this was Matt's fault.

At that moment the phone rang, and Imogen looked at the screen. It was DCI Kapoor.

'Saved by the bell,' DI Walsh muttered; he did look somewhat apologetic. Maybe Imogen had been a bit hard on him. She couldn't tell if her feelings for Adrian had magnified any reaction she might have normally had. This was exactly why it was a bad idea to get involved with someone from work. *Well done, Imogen, you have gone from one impossible relationship to another.*

'DS Grey, there is a signed warrant for you to enter the property as we have reason to believe DS Miles is in imminent danger. Some officers will arrive on the scene shortly to break the door down.'

'Thank you, Ma'am,' Imogen said, still slightly annoyed that the DCI had been talking to Matt Walsh about either one of them. She made a mental note to investigate the connection between Walsh and Kapoor further as there was obviously a lot of trust between them. So far, as decent as DI Walsh seemed, he was a bit of a mystery. Imogen knew better than to blindly trust someone just because they were nice.

'We'll find him, DS Grey, I promise you that,' DCI Kapoor said before hanging up.

Imogen heard sirens getting closer, which did nothing to make her feel any calmer.

Where the fuck are you, Adrian?

Within moments of the backup arriving, the door to the unit was open. The lock smashed and the handle fell on the floor. Imogen stepped inside, immediately feeling that it was empty. She went through the motions with her torch, shining into every corner, disappointment hitting her like a hammer with every step. They were in the wrong place.

'There's no one here!' Imogen said, alarmed by the panic in her own voice.

Was she losing it? An idea was forming in her mind, an idea she was trying to ignore. She couldn't think about what would happen if they didn't find Adrian. Her feelings of concern for his safety and anger at him for wandering off alone were multiplying. She couldn't not find him, that just wasn't an option.

Chapter Fifty-One

Adrian felt the blade against his cheek. He could see it resting there from the corner of his eye. It wasn't a particularly sharp knife, so it hadn't broken the skin yet. Adrian imagined that wouldn't be the case for long. Had anyone even noticed he was missing? Imogen probably thought he was in a huff about something; she generally left him to his own devices and vices in his free time. She would text once and then it was his turn. If anything, Adrian felt as though he was the needy one. It wasn't that he felt neglected, or that she was disinterested, more that she was protecting herself from getting too close. Adrian understood that and he appreciated it. Thinking about Imogen was taking his mind off the increasing pressure of the knife against his skin. His immediate concern was Imogen wandering into this mess.

Finn whipped his head round as though he'd heard something. Whatever it was, Adrian hadn't noticed, but then he was feeling a little foggy. Finn had hit him several times now.

'Stay there!' Finn laughed as he stood up and disappeared to investigate the noise.

Adrian turned to Parker. 'What are you doing?'

'Trying to get free.'

'And what happens then?'

'We escape,' Parker said.

'Both of us?' Adrian said.

'I'm not going to hurt you, Detective Miles. I have no reason to.'

'You might if you wanted to stay out of prison,' Adrian said.

'I'm not afraid of prison.'

Adrian believed him.

Finn came barrelling back in. 'Where is it?' He thrust the knife in Adrian's direction, the tip of the blade narrowly missing his nose.

'Where is what?' Adrian said, genuinely confused about what Finn was talking about.

'The knife! There's another one missing from the block. Where is it?'

There was someone else here.

'You must have checked me over. Check again, I don't have it. Even if I did, I couldn't use it.'

'It was definitely there before. You're fucking with me!'

Adrian had an idea. It was a long shot, but it had to be worth a try at this point.

'Maybe it's him, your handler. Maybe he's come to clean up the mess. You told him where you are? If you aren't around to grass on him then he gets away with it.'

As he said the words, it occurred to him that he might be right. Maybe it was *him*. Whoever he was.

'No. He wouldn't,' Finn said, contemplating Adrian's words. The boy was unstable; that much was evident. He was already paranoid, it wouldn't take much to push him over the edge.

'How do you know for sure he doesn't have someone else already? You're a liability, Finn, maybe he's sent someone for you, just like he sent you for Caitlin and Russ. You know too much. He's cleaning house.'

'Shut up!' Finn clasped his ears.

'If you turn all the lights on, then he will have nowhere to hide.'

'Stop talking!'

Adrian saw a shadow move from the corner of his eye. He had no idea who it was, but he had to assume whoever it was was on their side. If the person was with Finn, they would have made themselves known. Unless they were here to kill all of them and get rid of the evidence.

Adrian tried to look over to Parker to see if he had noticed; he didn't want Finn to know that he and Parker were acquainted. Parker who hadn't even broken a sweat throughout this whole encounter. He waited until Finn was looking away from him before turning his head. Parker didn't seem to be aware, but Adrian was assuming that he could read Parker on some level, which of course was not true.

Adrian heard someone inhale sharply and the faintest whooshing sound. He heard a shriek and knew that it was Finn. Had they come for him? There was a gurgle and the familiar smell of blood. Then a thud and Finn's muffled gurgles, which now came from the floor. He was clutching at his face, blood dribbling through his fingers.

'Who's there?' Adrian called out, unsure if he wanted the answer. If Finn was on the ground and Parker was strapped to the chair next to him, then who the hell could it be? It certainly wasn't police, they would have announced themselves by now. He hoped he wasn't right about it being the final professor come to finish Finn off.

Adrian squinted as a flurry of light appeared; the candle had fallen and ignited the curtains. It got very warm very quickly. His eyes took a moment to adjust to the sudden brightness before he spotted the figure once more. It was Abbey. Her yellow maternity dress was soaked in blood and she stood over Finn Blackwell with the knife in her hand. He wasn't dead and Adrian watched him reach for his knife with his free hand, stretching his fingers out across the carpet, his other hand clutching at his face. It was possible she had been aiming for his throat, but she had sliced him across the cheek. Half a Chelsea smile. Blood gushed from his face. He moved his hand and the skin gaped open, revealing his teeth and gums, the part you never see. The contrast of Finn's bright blue eyes next to the blood was all Adrian could focus on. His stomach turned at the flaps of skin hanging from Finn's face.

Abbey stamped on his wrist as he made a move for the knife. He tried to grab at her ankle with his other hand, but she kicked it away.

'Cut my restraints, Abbey. I'll take care of him,' Parker said. There was a softness in his voice, a tenderness.

'No time,' she replied.

With one deft move she swiped the knife across Finn's throat and the blood sprayed across all three of them. Finn stopped moving, his face frozen into a startled grimace. Parker seemed as shocked as Adrian for one brief moment. Abbey rushed over and cut the last bit of tape that was holding Parker's arm down. He took the bloody knife from her hand and cut the other hand free, then bent down and cut his legs free. Parker wrapped his arms around Abbey, oblivious to the man bleeding out on the floor, a black slick pooling beneath him.

'Cut me loose,' Adrian said.

'I can't,' Parker replied.

'What do you mean you can't?' Adrian said, aware that they were running out of time as the flames licked at the walls of the living room.

'Not now. There's only one person in the world I care about, Detective Miles, and given what you just saw there is no way I can release you. I can't let you arrest my wife.'

'You said you wouldn't hurt me. Burning alive seems pretty painful to me.'

Parker considered for a moment. 'I need to get Abbey to safety. I'll hand myself in, but we need to let Abbey go.'

'No! You can't! I need you,' Abbey cried.

'It's time, Abbey. After everything I've done. I never wanted to change you. Maybe it's better if I stay away,

I don't want our child to turn out bad. Look what I turned you into.'

'What are you talking about? Him?' She pointed at Finn Blackwell's body. 'Do you think I care about him? I don't. You didn't make me do anything.' She cupped Parker's face with her bloody hand.

'This is very moving, but if we leave it much longer then none of us are getting out of here,' Adrian reminded them.

'He's right, Abbey, you need to go.'

'Detective, isn't there any way you can keep Parker out of prison?' Abbey pleaded. 'You saw what he's been through, you know he isn't a bad person. He never killed anyone who didn't deserve it.'

'That's not up to him to decide though; we have the law for that,' Adrian said, aware that he should probably say anything they wanted to hear if he wanted to get out of there alive.

'The law is impotent when it comes to some people, or worse, apathetic,' Abbey said.

'It's OK, Abbey. We'll be OK. I'll confess. You and the baby will be looked after. We have money, you'll never need anything.'

'You can't take the blame for something I have done,' Abbey said.

'I will if it means you are both safe. That's all that matters.'

'I need you though,' she pleaded with Parker before turning to Adrian. 'Can't he say it was self-defence? This is his home.'

'What about all the other murders? Even if he

promised never to do it again, I couldn't agree to lying in court for him,' Adrian said.

'There's enough blame to go around here. There is no evidence linking Parker to any of those crime scenes, I know because if there was they would be looking for him, you would have been looking for him – and you weren't.'

'Abbey, go now while I cut the detective free. Get away from the house, please!' Parker kissed her on the lips, blood on both of their faces.

'Please, hurry,' she said before rushing from the room.

The flames were reaching the ceiling now. Parker dropped to Adrian's feet and started to cut the tape.

'I wish I could let you go again,' Adrian said. He did, but he knew he couldn't, regardless of the consequences to himself.

'I know, Detective.'

'I'm sorry it turned out this way for you. If only you had never started again. I have no idea how to explain all of this away. I have to take you in.'

'I'm sorry I put you in this position.'

Adrian watched him as he sliced through his restraints. Knowing that a neighbour might call the fire brigade, knowing that the police might turn up – Parker still stayed to let him go. Adrian couldn't help feeling that in another life, where Parker wasn't a brutal murderer, that Adrian would like him. He was a good guy. Except he wasn't.

'How do we get out of here?' Adrian asked, rubbing the parts of his wrists that had been restrained.

He noted that the door he had come in by was engulfed

in flames. His clothes clung to him with sweat as the heat intensified. The thick heavy drape of the curtains were lighting up a treat, also ensuring that it was impossible to jump through one of the windows.

'We have no choice, we have to go through that door. We need to hurry before it gets any worse!' Parker shouted above the noise of the rising flames.

It hadn't occurred to Adrian that it would be so noisy inside a fire.

'We won't make it!' Adrian shouted.

Parker grabbed him by the hand and pulled him towards the door. They both shielded their eyes, and as much as Adrian couldn't quite brave the flames himself, he didn't have time to think about it as Parker pulled him through the doorway.

Finn had poured petrol throughout the house, the stairs were alight, as were the other doorframes. They stood in the central hall. The fire wasn't quite as severe here, although they didn't have long. Adrian knew as soon as they went outside he would have no choice but to arrest Parker and deal with the shitstorm that went with that. He trusted that Parker wouldn't drop him in it, but he couldn't be so sure about Abbey. She would tell the police about his involvement if it meant a lesser sentence for Parker.

Finn had obviously doused the stairwell well, because it was almost entirely obscured by the flames that got closer to the ceiling with every passing second. Parker looked over nervously. It was the first time Adrian had seen anything resembling emotion on his face as he stared up at the landing.

'Head through the kitchen and the conservatory.' Parker pointed the way.

'Where are you going?' Adrian shouted. He knew he shouldn't let him go.

'I have to get something,' he replied over the sound of timber splitting wood. With that, Parker disappeared up the stairs through the flames.

Adrian watched for as long as he could, which wasn't very long at all as it turned out. His eyeballs were burning. He had to get out of there; the staircase was collapsing, so he couldn't go upstairs and get Parker. It felt wrong to leave him, but Adrian had no choice: if he didn't leave now, then he wouldn't get out at all.

Adrian charged for the kitchen, the door igniting fully almost immediately after he had passed through, as though it had permission somehow. It was only a matter of time before the flames reached the stove. His skin was sore; it felt like a bad case of sunburn and it wasn't letting up. Adrian knew had to get out of there, the oxygen was disappearing faster than he could breathe it in. He took a gulp of the disappearing air and pulled his jacket over his head, making a break for the back door, which opened easily. Running to the back of the garden before he could look back, he collapsed onto his knees and gulped in as much fresh air as he could.

After coughing uncontrollably for a few moments as the clean air fought its way inside his body, he turned to look at the house. The trailing ivy on the outside of the building had caught fire and was spreading quickly. The windows were already surrounded by sheets of flickering orange. Adrian couldn't see how Parker would be able to get out.

Over the sound of the house burning, Adrian could hear a siren approaching. It was a fire engine. His phone was still inside the house and so he couldn't call this in and he was still too out of breath to move. He fell back on the grass and tried to focus on breathing enough to get himself moving again. The lack of oxygen was making him dizzy. He just had to calm down and try to breathe slowly. They had had training for this, although he couldn't remember it, all he could think of was Parker trapped inside the house. There was no way in or out now; the most they could hope for was to be able to extinguish the fire before all the evidence completely disappeared and that hope was disappearing quickly.

Dizziness was taking over and Adrian could feel himself slipping. He needed to get further away from the house; as the flames grew, it was getting harder to breathe as the fire stole the oxygen. He heard his name, distant and desperate.

'Adrian!'

'Imogen,' he said, his voice raspy and low. He needed to get someone's attention.

'I'm here!' Imogen said and he could feel her hands on his face, but his eyes were hurting too much and he felt foggy.

The next thing he knew he was being lifted onto a stretcher and then carried into a vehicle. The paramedics were there and when they put the oxygen mask on his face, he started to feel immediately more lucid. He opened his eyes and felt a squeeze on his fingers. Imogen was sitting next to him, holding his hand.

'Just nod yes or no. Was Finn Blackwell in that house?'

Adrian nodded.

He grabbed at his mask to pull it away, so he could speak.

'He's dead. Did you find anyone else?' he managed to whisper.

'No, just you. Don't talk right now, just rest. The firefighters are doing everything they can to stop the fire and if there is anyone else there they will find them.'

'Parker . . .' he said, coughing, the pain in his chest immense.

'Adrian, none of that matters right now, just put the bloody oxygen mask back on will you. You can tell me everything later. We found Russ Beacham's body. He's been dead several days; we don't have a definite TOD yet. We know he couldn't have killed Caitlin though.'

As much as Adrian wanted to talk, he was just so damn tired; he needed to close his eyes for a moment, it was getting too hard to stay awake. He decided just to accept defeat and get the sleeping over with. He was useless until he had regained at least a little energy. Finn was dead and so no one was in any imminent danger. He could explain everything when he woke up. Well, maybe not everything.

Chapter Fifty-Two

Imogen watched Adrian in the hospital bed. She had been here for several hours now and had offered to stay until Adrian woke up, under the guise of being there to question him when he finally re-emerged. She didn't want anyone else to question him, particularly not DI Walsh. As much as she liked Matt, knowing that he had seen through all their personnel files was more than annoying, it was upsetting.

Adrian hadn't moved much since they put him in the bed, but Imogen had spoken to the doctor, who had assured her that he was fine. Any injuries he had sustained were purely superficial. Now that they were in a relationship and she had accepted that, she found herself worrying more. Not that she didn't care before, but now it had been dialled up to eleven. It was a strange thing – when she thought about it, it must be a selfish thing: if Adrian got hurt then it cost her emotionally and so she didn't want him to get hurt.

Was his safety even about him any more? Or was it about how inconvenient it would be to her if anything happened to him? She put her thoughts down to the recent loss of her mother and how annoyed she still was with her for selfishly dying, without even a consideration as to how it would affect Imogen. She was also annoyed with Adrian for putting himself in danger without considering how she would feel if something happened to him, especially after what he had been through. Maybe deflecting her feelings onto Adrian was a way of ignoring how vulnerable she felt now that she cared more deeply about him.

'What are you thinking about?' Adrian said.

She hadn't even noticed him waking up.

'I thought that was supposed to be my line?' She stood up and leaned over the bed.

'How long have I been asleep?' Adrian asked.

'It's only been a few hours, don't worry. How are you feeling?'

'Good. What happened to the house? Did they manage to put it out?' Adrian said.

'Yes, although it was burned to a shell before that happened. They found one body in the downstairs and are still sifting through the rest of the debris for evidence. I would be surprised if we find anything though. We still don't know who lived there or why Finn was there. There were traces of accelerant, so the fire was no accident.'

'Finn Blackwell. He covered the place in petrol,' Adrian said.

'How did you get away?'

'I just kept him talking. I was secured with duct tape, but I worked my way through it while he babbled on. He confessed to the murders.'

'What happened?'

'I followed him to that place, he caught me and then he just lost it. I overheard him talking to someone on the phone, but I don't know who it was. I'm not sure if they instructed him to start the fire or not, but he covered the place in accelerant and then when I got free there was a struggle. He had a knife on me, we wrestled for it, I grabbed it and defended myself. The only light in there was a candle and that got knocked over while we were fighting over the knife.'

'Did you kill him?' Imogen asked.

'Yes,' Adrian said, turning away as he spoke. 'I had no choice, it was him or me.'

'I'm glad it was him, then.' She stroked his forehead; he had a few cuts and bruises, but nothing that wouldn't heal over time. 'Do you know why he was there, whose house it was?'

'I have no idea. My head hurts,' Adrian said, closing his eyes.

'Should I get the doctor?'

'I need to get out of here.' He pulled the breathing tube off of his nose, pushed himself to a sitting position and swung his legs over the side of the bed.

'Not until you've seen someone and they say you can go.'

'I'm not hurt, I just need to get out of here. I hate hospitals.'

'Just wait there,' Imogen said.

331

She understood what it was like to be in the middle of an investigation that was running full pelt and then suddenly to be sitting on the sidelines for whatever reason: you just wanted to get back to work.

'I'm fine, Imogen, help me get out of here.' He pulled the drip out of his arm.

She had no choice but to help him, it was that or watching him do it and hurt himself. He was still shaken by what had happened with Finn Blackwell in that house. He was unusually cagey about it all. Not that they had had much of a chance to speak, but she could tell that he was holding something back. Imogen guessed that he would talk when he was ready.

'I'll tell the nurse we are leaving then,' Imogen said.

'Where's the car?'

'Where is it you think you're going? You need to go home and get some rest.'

'We need to get back to the station. I'm sure the DCI will want to ask me some questions about what happened. I can't relax until I've been debriefed.'

'Suit yourself,' she said, rolling her eyes at the nurse who came rushing over as soon as she realised Adrian was trying to leave.

'Sir, if you wait a few minutes, Dr Hadley will be here soon. She asked me to call when you woke up because she wanted to check on you.'

Imogen felt the unfamiliar pang of jealousy. Knowing that Adrian and this Dr Hadley had been out for a drink together made her feel strange. She had no idea why. Maybe it was because the woman was a doctor and Imogen was intimidated by that. She couldn't worry about any of that now though. She had Adrian back and that was all that mattered. He was safe, and she could stop thinking the worst.

Chapter Fifty-Three

Adrian had crossed a line. Again. Maybe Gary had been right about him. The effects of the fire had worn off and Adrian's cough was nothing but a tickle now. They had only recovered the one body in the fire, which meant that somehow Parker had got out. Adrian was glad of that. There was too much fire damage to find any evidence that didn't corroborate Adrian's story. The worst thing about it all was that he had lied to Imogen. He couldn't tell her the truth, not after the last few weeks – that feeling of guilt he had was not for letting Parker go but for pulling Imogen into his mess. What was even worse was that she trusted him implicitly, she had told him as much on many occasions. In a way, he could justify it to himself by pretending he was doing it for her own good so that the investigation could be wrapped up into a neat little bow and no one would ask any questions.

They were still looking for the final player in the

game. Adrian felt a weight on him as DCI Kapoor, DI Walsh, Gary and Imogen all pored over the incident boards looking for more clues. If he told them what he knew that might help, but it could also throw them off a significant development. He told himself he was keeping quiet for the good of the investigation. So far, no further leads had been discovered and the urgency seemed to be disappearing out of the case, with the knowledge that both Finn Blackwell and Russ Beacham were dead.

'Please, someone tell me we have some idea who was behind all of this. We have got four dead students and four dead teachers. How is it possible that the person who connects all of these murders has completely evaded capture? Go through all of the witness statements, crime scene reports, any photos. Everything. We must have crossed paths with this person at some point, and if not, why not?' DCI Kapoor said.

'I've had an idea,' Adrian said. 'We asked Gary to find any students that had either been in trouble with the law or in the news for any reason going back fifteen years.'

'That doesn't really help us though. It could be dozens. We need to make the list of suspects smaller not bigger,' DCI Kapoor said.

'Well, we found out that Robert Coley worked at the uni thirteen years ago, so it's possible that this game has been going on at least that long. It never made sense to me that they would have a professor from another university involved. So we need to cross-reference those students with their courses and lecturers

335

and see if anyone new pops up in connection with these names Gary has found.'

'Fine. DS Grey, go back to the university and speak to any faculty in the humanities department that you haven't already. If that turns nothing up then speak to the ones you have. Adrian, are you OK to go with her?'

'Of course,' Adrian said, surprised.

He hadn't officially been let off the leash since Caitlin Watts had made the accusations against him. He was a little nervous, if he was honest, but he didn't want to voice those concerns in case he was forced to take some mandatory therapy.

They left immediately. In the car on the way to the university neither one of them spoke. Adrian wanted to ask Imogen what she was thinking about but thought better of it. Fortunately there was no traffic, so they got there in less than five minutes. Adrian couldn't stop himself from cracking first, he always cracked first.

'Is there something wrong?' he asked.

'No.'

'So yes, then.'

Imogen got out of the car. Adrian watched her, deciding whether to say anything or not.

'You knew what you were doing. You deliberately went on your own to that place. You could have been killed.'

'Oh.' Adrian hadn't even considered that she might be upset with him about that. 'I'm sorry.'

'I care about you. I thought I could trust you.'

'You can,' he lied.

'You lost someone recently, you know how much

336

that hurts. Did you even think for a second about how unsafe you were? You're not immortal, Adrian. Bad things can happen to you just like they can to anyone else.'

'I know, I just thought I could get ahead of the curve with it. I didn't want to get you in trouble with the DCI. Besides, it wasn't premeditated, I just thought of it on the spot.'

'Whether that's true or not, you put yourself in danger.'

'I know.'

'Look. Whatever's past is past. I want you to promise me from this moment on that you will be honest with me. And you can't do stupid reckless things unless I'm there with you! You can't just throw your life around like it doesn't matter, OK? It matters to me.'

Adrian smiled while simultaneously feeling like a total bastard. 'OK, I completely understand, I won't do it again.'

'I was terrified something had happened to you. I can't take it at the moment, Adrian. Promise me. No more looking for trouble.'

'I promise.'

'Is there anything else you remember from when Finn had you in the house? Did he say anything about who he was working with?'

'Nothing. I know it's a male, but that's all. Finn kept referring to him as a he.'

'Brilliant.'

They walked into the humanities block and up to the reception desk. There was no one there. Adrian leaned on the counter and peered inside, then knocked on the glass. A woman jumped at the sound and looked over. Adrian pulled his warrant card out of his pocket and pressed it against the glass.

'I wonder if you could help us.'

The woman walked over and examined the warrant card before sliding the glass open.

'Is this about those terrible murders? I heard it was a couple of students, is that right?'

Adrian ignored the question. 'I have a list of students here, who all studied with this department in the uni over the last few years. Do you have a record of which classes they attended?'

'I should do. Can I see the list?'

Imogen pulled the sheets of paper from her pocket and handed them over to the receptionist.

'I'll just put them through the system for you. What is it exactly you are looking for?'

'We just need to speak to any of the teachers that taught these students. So just the names of the professors, please.'

She sat down and started to type from the list into the system.

'Gillian Mitchell, Gillian Mitchell, Hugh Norris, Helen Lassiter, Mitchell, Lassiter, Mitchell, Norris.' She scribbled an initial next to each student's name and stopped speaking aloud, instead just jotting the information on the sheet of paper.

'Who is MP?' Adrian said, noticing the different initials she had written next to a couple of names.

'Dr Pike? He's the head of the department. He doesn't

teach any more. He only works part-time, but you are in luck, he is in today. I'll give him a call if you like and get him to come to the desk.' She picked up the phone.

'So, Dr Pike doesn't teach at all?' Imogen asked.

'He doesn't actually take many classes himself; he might fill in once or twice. His role this academic year is more administrative,' The receptionist smiled, a small look of confusion hidden beneath the surface. She seemed disturbed that no one was answering the phone.

'Everything all right?' Imogen said.

The receptionist smiled and continued to listen to the phone ring. They could hear the distant ring of the unanswered phone reverberating through the hallway.

'I'll go and check his office,' the receptionist offered when she put the phone down. She wandered out through the back door of the admin area.

'Did we talk to a Dr Pike?' Adrian asked.

'Name's familiar,' Imogen said, pulling out her notebook and flipping through it. 'Yes, briefly, although I don't think we questioned him; he was the one who told us Lassiter was away.'

'I've got a bad feeling about this.'

'You think it's Pike?'

'I don't know,' Adrian said.

'Do you think Parker got him already?' Imogen asked.

'No. That's not what I think,' Adrian said; Parker had promised he wouldn't kill whoever the final person was and Adrian believed him. He didn't seem to lie. Even if telling the truth hurt him, he still did it.

'That's strange.' The woman returned. 'His office is empty.'

'What do you mean by empty?' Adrian asked.

'Come and have a look for yourself,' she said.

They followed her through the corridor to a room at the end. She pushed the door open and, sure enough, bar the furniture and a few small stacks of clearly discarded books, the room was empty. It had been cleaned out.

'Do you have any idea why Dr Pike's stuff has gone?' Adrian asked.

'None,' she said, her forehead knotted in confusion.

'Is this unusual behaviour for him?' Adrian pushed as they made their way back to the front desk.

'Well, last year a student of his fell off the cathedral. You probably saw it on the news at the time. It was awful; filmed it for some stupid internet thing. Dr Pike was quite affected by that and I am not sure he ever got over it. He's definitely been different the last couple of months. I do hope he's all right.'

'Toby Hoare? Is that the kid you mean? He was one of Dr Pike's students?' Imogen asked.

'Yes, lovely boy. He was here on a full scholarship. I remember doing his paperwork. No parents or anything to speak of. Very sad.'

'Could you give us a home address for Dr Pike?' Imogen said, pre-empting Adrian's next request.

'Of course. I'll see if there's any reason on the system for his absence. We have been going through some renovations, so maybe his office is being done up; although this block isn't due for refurbishment until the summer.'

The timing of this was beyond suspicious. The lady

340

handed Adrian a printout that contained Pike's home address, along with the list of the previous students with the initials next to their names, and he nodded her a thank you. Adrian rushed out of the building back towards the car park, Imogen following close behind him.

'What are you thinking?' Imogen said.

'The same thing you are, I expect. It has to be him. Call Gary and see if he can find anything; there is still loads on those computers he hasn't been through and he says it's much easier when he knows what he's looking for.'

Adrian got in the car and waited for Imogen to finish on the phone to Gary. She got in and nodded for him to start driving towards the Countess Weir roundabout. He didn't feel much urgency, even though every fibre of his being was telling him that Pike was the one. The state of his office wasn't a recent thing, the dust had well and truly settled.

'Pike's the one who gave me Lassiter's address. I remember him, I didn't get a creepy vibe from him at all,' Imogen said.

'Why would you?'

'You just kind of hope you would know, don't you?' Imogen said.

'Imagine how easy our job would be then.'

'I suppose.'

Adrian turned off the roundabout and headed out towards Woodbury Salterton, the location of Marcus Pike's house. He wondered what he would find when he got there. Part of him hoped that they would walk in to discover Marcus Pike's mutilated corpse, not because he wanted that to happen but because he wanted to know that Parker had made it out of the fire. The fire department had only found partial remains of Finn Blackwell among the bones, but it was possible they had made a mistake, wasn't it? The house was so old it had gone up like kindling, and by the time the fire fighters had hooked their hoses up, the house was a roaring flame. The downside of finding Pike's body was, of course, that Parker being at large would trigger another investigation and who knew what information would come out. Adrian's primary concern was Imogen in all this; he couldn't tell her he had seen Parker in the house, he couldn't make her lie for him any more. From now on he wouldn't put her career in jeopardy just because of his own skewed morality. Even if it meant lying to her.

'This is it,' Imogen said as they approached a white thatched cottage precariously nestled in the centre of the fork in the road.

There was a For Sale sign knocked down in the shrubs in front of the house that opened directly onto the B road. Adrian turned into the driveway and stopped the car.

'Wait here, I'll go and check it out,' he said.

'Not a chance.'

She knew what he was thinking, he could see it on her face. She was right behind him as he walked to the front door. He rang the bell and there was no answer.

'They're gone,' a voice shouted from across the road.

Adrian turned to see the door to the house opposite open and an elderly gentleman standing in the doorway.

'Lorry came this morning, a big 'un. Left about an hour ago.'

'Did Dr Pike say where they were going?' Adrian pulled out his warrant card and walked across the road to speak to the man, Imogen following.

'His wife's Japanese; he said they were moving back to Japan because her mother was seriously ill.'

'Thank you. When was this exactly? Do you remember?'

'I think it was around nine in the morning. It was weird, though, because I used to talk to Kimiko a lot and I'm sure her mother died a few years ago.'

Imogen turned to Adrian. 'Japan? We don't have an extradition agreement with them; if he's gone, he's gone.'

Adrian handed a business card over to the man. 'Thank you for your help, sir. Could I ask your name?'

'My name is Graham Parsi.'

'Thank you, Mr Parsi. I don't suppose you remember the name of the lorry company?' Adrian said, pulling his notebook out and scribbling the time, name and other information on the page.

'I think it was Chadwycks.'

'Thanks.'

They walked back over to Pike's house and looked into the windows. Everything was gone. No pictures on the walls, no rugs or chairs or bric-a-brac, nothing. In terms of timing, this solidified his guilt in Adrian's eyes. It took some time to organise shipping to another country and so Pike had been planning on leaving for a while, probably from the moment Hugh Norris was murdered. The other murders were just to get his affairs in order before he left. Maybe he hoped that he would get away with it. Effectively he *had* got away with it, though.

They got back in the car and Adrian started the engine.

'What do we do now?' Imogen said.

'Japan? It's Heathrow or Gatwick, he's got maybe an hour head start on us. We call it in and then we have to get in touch with the Met police at both Gatwick and Heathrow, so they can be waiting for him. He can't be there yet. We need to get Gary to check and see if Pike has tickets for anywhere and to find out where the Chadwycks lorry was taking all his stuff. Maybe we can intercept his belongings, as well. All the main players are dead apart from Pike; we can't let him get away.'

'Do we just follow him without any evidence?' Imogen asked.

'It's our best lead right now; we need to speak to him at least. If we wait for confirmation before we start driving then he just gets further away from us.'

'How do we keep Parker out of this? *Do* we keep Parker out of this?'

'He's gone. If he wasn't, then Marcus Pike would be dead. He won't be back. He's got no reason to return. We just have to concentrate on bringing Pike in for now. Let's get in the car and start driving. I reckon he would go A303, then via the M3 onto the M4 rather than go to Bristol and around. There's some major delays on the M4, they announced it earlier, so he would want to join that as late as possible if he is going to

Heathrow. Gatwick makes more sense to go M3 anyway. You can call the DCI and we can get in touch with Somerset, Dorset and Wiltshire police on the way; they can be on the lookout for his car.'

If Adrian had to then he would take the blame, lose his job or go to prison for this. For now, the murders would be attributed to Finn Blackwell; he had confessed to two of them in front of Adrian, it wouldn't be that difficult for Adrian to say he remembered more from the night of the fire, to cover for Parker. If he did this though, everything Gary said was right.

Adrian had been disappointed when they didn't find Marcus' dead body in that house. Who had he become? More lies. Adrian couldn't help but feel that he was stacking karma up against himself. He had to stop making decisions outside the law. He knew the difference between what was just and what was legal, but he had no right to make those decisions. Adrian was becoming someone he didn't recognise.

Imogen squeezed his fingers and he knew he had to change. He had to get back to the simplicity of the law, to stop imposing his own morality on others. He was putting Imogen in danger. Was there any way back for him now?

Chapter Fifty-Four

Adrian had just driven past Yeovil when Imogen finally finished speaking to DCI Kapoor on the phone.

'She's going to call us back, but for now we keep going. Gary is suspicious about the lack of mention of Marcus Pike in all the documentation they have,' Imogen said.

'What if we don't get to him in time? What if this is a double bluff?'

'He doesn't have that much of a head start on us. If they can find out where he is flying from then we can get to him.'

'What if it's neither of those airports?' Adrian said, trying not to think the worst.

'The DCI checked and neither Exeter nor Bristol have flights to Japan today. Chadwycks have confirmed the containers are off to the city of Sapporo on the island of Hokkaido, which is where his mother-in-law lived. The neighbour was right; she was already dead.

The DCI is getting someone onto the Road Policing Unit with Pike's reg number. The ANPR will pick it up hopefully and confirm we are going the right way if they get no luck with finding out where he's flying from. Don't forget, at this point he has no idea we are onto him. He thinks he's got away with it. Now that Finn is dead as well there is no way to link him to the murders. He doesn't know that we figured the game out, or that we linked him to previous students.'

'I hope you're right.'

Imogen turned to Adrian. 'What's going on with you? You're not yourself. Are you sure you should be back at work? Being held captive in a burning building can't have been much fun. Maybe you need to see the station shrink? There's no shame in it; I had to.'

'No. I'm fine. Just tired and worried this scumbag is going to get away. How could they get away with this shit for so long without anyone noticing?' He couldn't tell her what was really bothering him.

'Because kids do stupid stuff, kids commit suicide and have accidents. We all just write them off as kids doing irresponsible and dangerous kid things. Who would think of a scenario like this?'

'I guess. I just find it hard to swallow that this has been happening under our noses for so long.'

The phone rang; it was Gary. Imogen put it on loudspeaker.

'Shoot.'

'The Automatic Numberplate Recognition has picked him up going past Stonehenge. It's a bottleneck there at the moment, so the traffic isn't moving anywhere.

347

You should be able to make up some miles. Where are you now?' Gary said.

'Just coming up to Wincanton, so just over half an hour. I'll put the woo-woos on and we can get there in twenty minutes. Are there any local police in the vicinity?' Adrian asked, putting his foot on the accelerator as Imogen reached into the glovebox for the siren.

'The DCI is worried about the jam sandwiches spooking Pike and so they are setting up a roadblock near Andover before the road splits off. There should be enough time to do that before he gets there the way the traffic is at Stonehenge.'

'What's a jam sandwich?' Imogen asked unhelpfully.

'Police car. They used to have a red stripe through them, completely doesn't apply any more,' Gary explained.

'The road is pretty clear here, so we should be able to make some headway,' Adrian confirmed.

'I'll call again with any developments.' Gary rang off.

Imogen put the phone away and gripped the dashboard as Adrian moved as fast as he could. If she was talking, he couldn't hear her. He was so focused on getting to the target that everything disappeared except the road ahead of him.

'We can do this. We can get him,' Adrian said eventually.

Maybe if they got Pike he would feel less guilty about letting Parker go – again. He knew he couldn't let two killers go in as many days. What would be the point of him then? He found himself slowly pressing down harder on the accelerator. He wasn't going to let Pike get away. He couldn't.

'Careful, Miley. There's a roadblock up ahead. We're

going to get him no matter what. We know where he is; he isn't getting away with it,' Imogen said, her voice low and soothing but also slightly panicked.

He couldn't slow down though; he had to keep going.

'We're making good headway, only eighteen miles to go. Any updates from Gary?'

'He says Pike's still on the A303, but he's coming to the end of the bottleneck and he will be out the other side soon enough.'

Adrian had to get there before he got away. He watched the speedo climb until it was almost at the 100 mph mark. He had to make sure he paid attention to the roundabouts dotted along the road. He could do this though. The steering became lighter and he had to concentrate on not moving even a little or he might hurl the car into a country pub. He could get to where Pike was in ten minutes at this speed. Ten minutes, that was all that separated them. Did Pike even have a clue they were onto him? Was he watching over his shoulder? Or did he think he still had the luxury of today and tomorrow, maybe the weekend? After all, he had eluded them thus far.

They approached the bottleneck and Adrian was forced to slow the car down. The cars in front all started to pull away from the centre of the road as the siren approached. He drove the car through the centre and continued to gain ground on Pike, wherever he was. The traffic after the Amesbury bypass was steady and moving at a decent pace; they were gaining ground.

'We're only a few miles from the roadblock now. He is somewhere between there and here,' Imogen said.

Adrian put his foot down again. The stretch of road in front of them was long and tilted upwards and to the right. He could see a long way ahead. His eyes narrowed on the cars up in the distance. At some point, their flashing lights would come into view of Pike's car and he would make a move for it. Natural instinct when you are being chased. As Adrian weaved in and out of the traffic, he realised he had been almost completely ignoring Imogen. He had to admit to himself that he was feeling guilty for lying to her; he didn't need a police-mandated shrink to tell him that. He didn't see that he had any choice though. The selfish thing would be to tell her the truth, so they could share the burden, but he wasn't going to be selfish, he was going to take this on himself.

'Look!' Imogen said, pointing at a car a mile or so ahead of them; it was speeding up.

It was entirely possible, of course, that it was some other shady character on the run from the law, but it was much more likely that it was Marcus Pike, finally feeling the noose closing around his throat.

'Where do you think you're going?' Adrian muttered under his breath to no one but himself.

Pike's car disappeared around the bend up ahead and Adrian accelerated to catch it, his heartbeat thrumming in his chest. He was almost there, he had almost got him. They were closing in on Pike and it wasn't far until the roadblock. They were coming up to Andover. As Adrian pushed forward, he saw smoke up ahead. A car – Pike's no doubt – had tried to swing round on the slip road onto Weyhill and slammed into another car coming the other way, the right way. Adrian pulled up to the car and they both saw the driver's side was open. On the passenger side, a woman who must be Kimiko Pike was groaning, bloodied head against the window, the airbag deployed in front of her.

'I'll see to her. You see if you can find Pike; he must be on foot somewhere. He's clearly not up this slip road.' Imogen got out of the car and slammed the door. Was she annoyed with him?

'He went that way!' a man in a car further back called out. He pointed back towards the A303.

Marcus Pike was running, to where Adrian didn't know. Starting the car again, Adrian drove forward the two hundred feet Pike had travelled and stopped the car. He jumped out. Pike was an old man and so he was never going to outrun a car. As Adrian rushed forward, Pike climbed a brick wall. Adrian realised that they were on top of a railway bridge that ran over the London-bound train tracks.

'Stop!' Adrian called out.

'I'll jump! Just let me go,' Pike shouted.

'I can't do that,' Adrian said. 'Get down and we can talk.'

'There's nothing to talk about! Did Finn talk, is that how you knew about me? I didn't think he would.'

'Finn told me lots of things. Please get down off that wall.'

Pike looked over his shoulder at the train tracks below, clearly trying to gauge whether he could make the jump or not. There was no way he could land that fall and then be able to get up and run afterwards. Still, Adrian watched as he considered it.

'I knew this lot would be the ones. You know? There was something about them. I should have kept Caitlin Watts around, but she was about to crack and I couldn't risk it; she would have kept Finn under control though. She kept all the boys under control. She was a great find.'

'How long had it being going on?' Adrian tried to ignore his personal feelings about what Pike was saying, that Caitlin was coerced into sleeping around as part of their sick little game. It was tantamount to prostituting her.

'It was just me and Coley to begin with. A gentleman's bet twenty-three years ago. But then the others joined in over time. Lassiter was the most recent addition.'

Pike was confessing, this was not a good sign. He was going to jump. There was a distant sound of sirens, coming; Imogen had obviously called for back up.

'Do you have a list of the students you brought into the game?' Adrian said, stalling. As soon as the other police officers arrived on the scene of the crash, Imogen would make her way to him and she could help persuade Pike to hand himself in. The fact that Adrian hadn't been able to talk Finn down had knocked any confidence he had in his own negotiation skills.

'No. I have destroyed everything, you won't find a shred of evidence against me.' Pike turned and looked down onto the tracks again.

'You won't make it; it's too high! Get down.'

'I think we both know it's too late for that,' Pike

said before turning his palms face out and closing his eyes. Adrian lunged forward as Pike tipped backwards, his fingers just centimetres away from his jacket that whipped up as he fell. He couldn't make it in time. Adrian's hands gripped at the wall and he looked over the side. The train was passing through. Pike's arm lay by the side of the track and Adrian heard the screech of the train's brakes. He was dead.

A myriad of mental images, combined with what Adrian had seen, forced his breakfast to the surface as he turned and threw up on the pavement next to the brick wall. Imogen's hand rested on the small of his back; he had not seen her run over to him. Overcome with emotion, he turned and put his arms around her. It had been a long week and an even longer case. He could only hope that it was over now. He made a promise to himself as he felt her arms around him. He would never lie to her again. If he did it would destroy them and she was too important to let go.

'What happened?' Imogen said.

'He jumped,' he said, pulling away, embarrassed by his momentary emotional weakness.

'Are you OK?' she said.

'I will be. What about you?'

'Oh, I'm just dandy. Looking forward to putting this case behind us finally.'

'Maybe we could get away together for a few days,' Adrian said.

He desperately needed a holiday, but he didn't want to be away from Imogen right now. He wanted to move forward and he wanted it to be with her.

'I'd like that. Have you anywhere in mind?'

'As long as you're there, I really don't care where we go.'

'I know exactly what you mean,' Imogen said. He could tell she was thinking about kissing him and what was left of his professionality fought hard not to oblige.

More police cars arrived on the scene and Adrian composed himself. He had to lie one last time to put this all behind them. No one could ever know that Parker had been in the house with him when Finn Blackwell died.

He turned to Imogen. 'Let's hope this is the end of it.'

They would work through the names of the students they had gathered and speak to the very few who had come through the game unscathed. Coley, Lassiter and Mitchell's murders would get lumped in with the rest, and Adrian would go back to praying that Parker stayed away. Even if his gut told him that was unlikely, he was allowed to hope, wasn't he?

Acknowledgements

Firstly, I would like to say a huge thank you to the people who read this series. I love hearing from you through my Facebook page or on twitter. I'm also extremely grateful to those people who leave Amazon reviews, because I love seeing what you guys think.

Thank you also to my family for putting up with me leaving half empty notebooks and scraps of paper everywhere.

Thanks to everyone at Avon Books, my wonderful publisher, for my great covers and all the hard work you put in. Thank you as well to Phoebe Morgan, my editor, who does an excellent job of turning my messy first drafts into something people want to read.

Thanks to Diane Banks and Kate Burke at Northbank Talent, for working so hard on my behalf. I absolutely couldn't do this without you. Thanks as well to Ciara and James.

Thanks to Jeremy Fewster, for advice on the scenes I hate writing.

Thanks to all the book bloggers who support me and take part in the blog tours on my novels, as well as writing kickass reviews. You do a fab job and I really appreciate it. Also thanks to the Book Clubs on Facebook, including TBC and The Fiction Café – keep reading books!

Thanks as well to my fellow moderators in Crime Time Book Club on Facebook.

To my crime writing friends, thank you for being the most brilliant bunch. After years of feeling like the weird freak who says wildly inappropriate stuff in social situations, I met you lot. You are all wildly inappropriate and I love hanging out with you. I finally found my tribe.

Go back to where it all began . . .

The first smash-hit crime novel from Katerina Diamond.
NOT for the faint-hearted . . .

Everything you *think* you know is a lie . . .

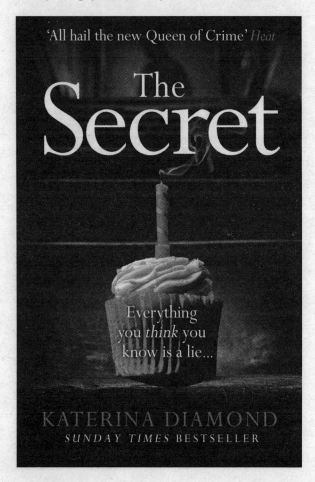

'All hail the new Queen of Crime' *Heat*

The Secret

Everything
you *think* you
know is a lie...

KATERINA DIAMOND

SUNDAY TIMES BESTSELLER

The second Miles and Grey novel

Some things can't be forgiven . . .

'All hail the new Queen of Crime' *Heat*

The Angel

Some things can't be forgiven...

THE *SUNDAY TIMES* BESTSELLER
KATERINA DIAMOND

The third bestselling Miles and Grey novel

No one can protect you from your past . . .

You make it. You break it.

The Promise

KATERINA DIAMOND

THE *SUNDAY TIMES* BESTSELLER

The *Sunday Times* bestseller